OUT OF THIS WORLD

The Best Short Stories from

The MOON

Volume 1, 2013-2019

To our good friend Hazel
I hope you enjoy

John

Out of This World: The Best Short Stories from The MOON

Volume 1, 2013-2019

The content of this book was previously published on **The MOON**, a monthly online journal of personal and universal reflections. Each month The MOON explores a different theme through in-depth interviews, memoirs, essays, poetry, short stories, "Movies You Might have Missed," and MOON Shine— quotations relevant to that month's issue. Visit us at MOONmagazine.org, or write to us at Leslee@moonmagazine.org.

The MOON is published monthly online at www.moonmagazine.org.
Editor/publisher: Leslee Goodman, Leslee@MOONmagazine.org,
© 2019. All rights reserved.

ISBN: 9781078315326

Contributors

Charles Joseph Albert, John Betton, Albert Carey, William Cass, Xixuan Chan, DC Diamondopolous, Madeline McEwen, Debra Leea Glasheen, Gary Ives, Alexander Kemp, Daniel Larson, Jon Moray, Puloma Mukherjee, James Norris, Garrett Rowlan, Rodolph Rowe, DL Shirey, Gerald Stanek, Mitch Toews, William Watkins, Jr., Laura Grace Weldon, and Laura Widener.

Edited by Leslee Goodman, publisher and editor, The MOON magazine, moonmagazine.org.

Cover design and book layout, Gerald Stanek.

Table of Contents

Otherworldly   1

Jon Moray, *Finish the Story*   2

Puloma Mukherjee, *Sandfall*   6

Garrett Rowlan, *Walking, Watching, Waiting*   15

James Norris, *Angel of Death*   19

Garrett Rowlan, *To the Cloud*   32

DL Shirey, *Assisi Terminal*   39

Gerald Stanek, *The Initiation Game*   43

'Others' of this world   47

Leea Glasheen, *Mangrove Swamp*   48

Xixuan Collins, *Foreign Devil*   55

William J. Watkins, Jr., *Jury of His Peers*   66

Gary Ives, *Little Termite*   87

Madeline McEwen, *Jealous of Daylight*   94

John Betton, *Filmmaker*   108

Charles Joseph Albert, *The Rakan Kembar*   124

Arthur Carey, *Fourth of July*   134

Making peace   147

Laura Grace Weldon, *Everywhere Stars*   148

Mitch Toews, *Peacemongers*   158

Laura Widener, *Harbor From the Cold*   170

DC Diamondopolous, *The Bell Tower*   173

Rodolph Rowe, *A Show of Strength*   186

William Cass, *Unsaid, Undone*   208

Alexander Kemp, *A Private Pain*   216

Daniel Larson, *CJ the Prince*   222

Otherworldly

Finish the Story

By Jon Moray

(Originally published in the April 2015 issue of The MOON.)

It was a typical sunny, warm, mid-September, Florida day. Eric Parsons was outside mowing his half-acre Bahia lawn, listening to his eighties-themed play list on his MP3 player, and enjoying an occasional nature-kissed breeze. His thoughts volleyed from story-writing ideas to how he could tweak his Fantasy Football team for the weekend games.

Suddenly, his attention was drawn to the cloudless sky by a bright flash, as if from a camera the size of the sun. His sunglasses were no match for the glare that partially blinded him. He blinked to restore his sight as another flash sparked closer to him. Shielding his eyes with his forearm, yet another flash invaded his vision a few feet in front of his push mower.

As the remnants of the flash subsided, a small, seamless, contoured ship, the size of a sedan and metallic blue in color, landed silently on his lawn. The oblong ship's chrome dome slowly opened and a helmeted, human-limbed figure climbed out. The figure reached behind and removed the helmet with the touch of a button that activated an accordion-like movement that flattened the headwear. The figure, now female in appearance, and of normal human size, nonchalantly tossed the folded helmet into the seat, stepped away from the vessel, reached into a side pocket from her ribbed, deep blue body suit and exposed a flat object the size of a credit card. She held the object away from her and aimed it toward the ship as if she were taking a picture.

Suddenly the vessel vanished. She looked down at the object, as if confirming its disappearance, and then turned toward Eric.

Eric stumbled away from the alien and looked around for something to defend himself with.

"I mean you no harm, Eric Parsons," said the alien, robotic but feminine in tone.

Her straight periwinkle hair, with black highlights, was just above shoulder length, and featured jagged points at the ends. Her eyes were like the midnight sky with subtle clouds that seem to rotate around her iris. Her face was a faded scarlet in color.

"Who…who are you, and how do you know my name?" Eric stammered, wiping emerging sweat from his forehead and mentally questioning his sanity.

"I have penetrated your airspace. They will be searching for me shortly. You have to trust me as I will have to trust you."

"What are you talking about? What's going on?"

"My name is Jisa, the first inhabitant in the universe you created. I have traveled two thousand years into the past because I need your help."

She handed Eric the object, or "infolat," as she called it. Eric reluctantly took it from her hand and studied it.

"Stand back and take a picture of me, head to toe, by pushing the glowing violet button on the window," Jisa said, as if she were a proctor giving test instructions.

Eric nodded slowly, still fixed on the infolat and the eerie coincidence that it, the vessel, and Jisa matched the exact descriptions from a short story he wrote years ago.

"Hurry, before I am detected."

Eric held the infolat at arm's length and did as instructed.

"Now, push the blinking green button on the window, hurry."

Eric obeyed and watched her vanish.

Jisa's face filled the screen as the sound of helicopters emanated from afar.

"Hurry, take me inside your home. I will explain everything there."

Eric walked towards his sliding glass back porch door as the helicopters emerged into view over his neighborhood.

He stepped inside his ranch-style home, grabbed a can of cola from the fridge, and sat at his dining table.

"I put all my trust in you. You have the power to turn me over to the authorities as an alien invader. I am now helpless. Now I must…can I trust you?"

Suddenly, a violent, rapid knock on the front door brought a massive jolt to Eric's circulatory system. He hid the infolat in his jeans pocket, rushed over and opened the door to a team of uniformed men with intent, focused countenances.

"Federal agents, have you seen or heard any suspicious activity in your area, especially in your back yard?"

Eric wiped away sweat from his brow, gulped audibly, and uttered, "Uh, no, I haven't. Is everything alright?"

"No need for alarm, sir. Are you sure you didn't see or hear anything out of the ordinary in your backyard?"

"No sir, I was out mowing the lawn and came in for a beverage."

"Okay. Take my card. If you do hear or see anything, please notify me."

Eric slowly closed the door and kept his ear to it until they were out of earshot. He went to the front bedroom window to make sure they were away from his house.

"Is it safe now?" Jisa's voice came from his back pocket. Eric quickly retrieved the infolat, followed her commands, and rematerialized her in front of his eyes.

"That was close. That infolat you created is an incredible object. Ingenious."

"How can this be? This object came straight from my imagination, from a story written but not yet finished."

"That's why I am here, Creator. I have traveled this far back in time and space because my planet needs you to finish the story. The beautiful universe you created is in suspended limbo, and I have been chosen to communicate the importance of finishing your story."

"I created a fictional universe! This is crazy or I'm going crazy. How is this possible?"

"All I know is I appear before you because you created me. You wrote of my appearance, my vessel, the infolat, the time and place of my planet's existence. You made life then you just stopped. You then had a dream, which translated into a déjà vu or something, and that's how I appear to you today. I beg of you to continue your story, so life can continue in the universe, my world, that you made and that takes place two thousand years from now."

Eric rubbed the stubble on his chin, while searching for answers in the distressed wood floor. Jisa interrupted his thought process, explaining that the inhabitants of her universe were gradually succumbing to death from their suspended animation. Time was of the essence and Jisa grew more desperate with each passing moment.

"You are the creator! If you do nothing, all of the beings on my planet will expire shortly."

Her pleading eyes softened his countenance, and her persistence moved him to inspiration. He grabbed her velvety hand and led her to the dining room table where his laptop lay. He opened it up and navigated to the Word document that housed the origins of her universe. He carefully read the unfinished story while she looked on over his shoulder. He took a deep, soothing, mind-clearing breath, cracking his knuckles with meshed hands.

"Jisa, I am going to finish the story, but I don't want you to know how it ends until you return to your universe." She repositioned herself in the chair opposite and watched intently as he began typing. His eyes bled passion, adventure, and excitement as his eyebrows moved like waves in an ocean. After several proofreads and edits, he announced he was finished with his manuscript.

As if on cue, Jisa rose from her seat and kissed his forehead. He handed her the infolat and followed her out to the back porch, where she rematerialized her saucer. She turned back at him, fluttered her fingers, and bid farewell. She then entered the saucer, prepared for takeoff and disappeared in a flash, while police choppers provided an audible backdrop.

Jisa penetrated the saline dome that protected her world. She guided her vessel in a serpentine path around the rosy atmosphere and landed on Jitzoy, her home country. Her image was reflected over the skies of the orb like a light show in a planetarium. The inhabitants, who were frozen in limbo, slowly mobilized, and the fallen resurrected. All conflicts halted at the sight of her. Celebrations of joy and unity erupted across the globe. As written in Eric's story and understood by all, peace reigned supreme, and Jisa's return was the planet's most historic moment. Eric's words acknowledged her as the Queen of the Skies, Goddess of the Universe, and the Pipeline to the Creator.

Jon Moray has been writing short stories for 10 years and his work has appeared in numerous online and print media. When not working and being a devoted husband and father, he enjoys running and playing basketball.

Sandfall

By Puloma Mukherjee

(Originally published in the April 2015 issue of The MOON.)

I remember that day like it was yesterday. It was supposed to have rained the night before and into the morning, but I couldn't tell from my apartment. The only windows faced my neighbors' only windows, and the outer walls of our apartments formed a dingy, square enclosure that opened up to a small patch of sky up at the top. Sharp, angular rays sometimes peered in at mid-day through this little opening, but dawn and dusk came furtively, like disease. Rain wasn't often discernible because little of it made it down to the bottom floors through the opening high up, though little rivulets trickled down walls when it rained heavily. We never opened our windows or peered to look up at the patch of sky, mostly for fear of what we'd see or worse, smell, down below. I could see empty, crumpled and broken plastic bottles lining my neighbors' outer window sills; my outer window sill had soiled paper napkins—refuse from higher floors. That day, the pavements were still wet when I walked out onto the main street. The air, too, was wet and cold, as if it was holding on to the memories of the rain.

I stopped to check my phone—9:10 a.m. I was late for work. I had slept in, dreaming familiar dreams—Dad in my hospital room with a caramel-haired puppy in his arms; caramel-haired puppy on my belly; patches of blood forming shapes on the white gauze that covered injured hands with which I stroked caramel-haired Sadie; me hitting my roommate for kicking Sadie; Sadie's fur glistening on a fragrant fall morning; Sadie growling; Sadie running after Winston Churchill (her ball); the doctor letting me know with a gleam in his eyes and a smile that they had saved Sadie. The dreams were always patchy, and non-sequitur as all dreams are. Some were true. Some weren't. I never stood up to my roommate for kicking Sadie but I wish every day that I had. Instead I just moved to a much smaller place, which was all I could afford by myself, just so I could keep Sadie with me. And there was no gleam in the doctor's eye when he told me he couldn't save Sadie from the injuries she had sustained in the car accident right outside that apartment.

I headed to my usual deli for my usual coffee and breakfast before getting into the subway. Now my eyes had adjusted to the dull, gray morning and I realized everyone was brushing off what looked like yellow grains. On that humid, cloudy morning sand-like grains rained from the sky, not in a torrent, but quietly like gentle snow. People were walking to the subway, walking to work, listening to music on their headphones, talking on their phones, and all the while rubbing off these grains from their arms, their shoulders, clothes, and their hair. Pavements, trees, cars, people were all covered with these grains. Before I knew it, my jacket arms and shoulders were completely covered too. The grains were perfectly shaped hexagons, the color and size of loose ocean sand. Each grain fit into the others like cells in a honeycomb, and even glistened faintly under the gray-white light that illuminated the street on that dull morning. I stopped and stared as the grains stuck to my jacket to form one congealed mass, and even tried to pluck a few out to feel them between my fingers. As I lowered my face and brought my arm closer to look at the grains, a lock of my short hair fell forward grazing my cheek very lightly before appearing clearly in front of me. I moved my gaze toward my hair, which was now covered in these minute, glistening beige hexagons. Not an inch of my black hair made it through the thick, opaque, but somehow mildly glistening sheath that covered it. Against my cheek and in my fingers, I felt the smooth, cold, skin-like texture of the grains. I could press each one between my fingers. They felt like soft, miniature cushions.

I must have looked confused. A lady who was passing by said "Don't worry, just brush it off with your hand. It'll come off and fall to the ground." I looked up to see her brushing the stuff off her own clothes and hair.

"Do you know what it is?" I asked her. She walked right past.

I didn't want to brush them off. I have often wondered if it was just one of those slow days for me, or if there was really something about these grains that made me want to collect them in my hands, like a little girl nervously holding her mother's precious pearls. People walked by me annoyed, irritated, aghast, or afraid of the profusion of these little hexagons that descended from the skies into our lives. I, on the other hand, stopped in the middle of the sidewalk and watched the few that I'd collected, cupped in my hands like I had once tried to cup the rain in my little five-year-old hands. They seemed loose and separate at first, but drew closer to one another within minutes. The ones closer to the edges of my hands sunk down or moved to the center. Soon a beige leaf-shaped mass filled out the little enclosure between my hands—perfectly flat on top but following the curvature of my hands. An ambulance with a screeching siren whizzed by, a pedestrian cursed a cab driver for almost running him over, a passer-by yelled on his phone "Fuck you, bitch!" as he shook his head violently to rid himself of the grains. I stared at this latticework that formed a beige leaf in my hands, and all the familiar sounds and noises that surrounded me suddenly sounded like one coherent monotone that was at once jarringly loud and peacefully quiet. I stood planted in the whirling chaos around me but became delightfully distant as well. I have since wondered if the grains had some hypnotic effect if you stared at them long enough. There was only one wonderful thought in my head that damp morning as I stood on the sidewalk looking, I imagine now, like a sand dune in the shape of a woman:

Were these grains alive? In the same way, as say, plants are?

I shook off my reverie when another harried and annoyed office-goer brushed past me with a "You've got too many of these things on you, you might want to brush them off." I dutifully brushed most of the grains from my clothes but kept the little mound that had formed in my hand and shoved it into my bag. Full-blown panic set in when I realized I was almost an hour late for work. I skipped breakfast and headed for the subway.

More information trickled in.

"Weather men today are baffled by a strange phenomenon that seemingly started early this morning, around 5:00 a.m. Yellow, sand-like grains rained all over New York and parts of the northeast. Climate scientists have now confirmed that the composition of these grains does not include water, or any known element found in other forms of precipitation. So far there have been no incidents of harm done due to this strange downpour of grains. People are advised to carry and use umbrellas. For now, schools and offices continue to run per usual. Both the state and federal governments have declined to make any announcements until the results of a more thorough investigation are established."

No one spoke of anything else at the office. There were rumors of some old lady in Queens who managed to ingest some of the grains and died on the spot. Others in the office said how the grains had penetrated concrete walls. Everyone tuned in to the news and weather channels on their computers instead of music on Pandora while trying to focus on work. I had an email waiting for me "Hi Riva, can you come see me in my office? We need to talk."

It was the new thing our manager had begun to do—have a little chat with us every day we were late to work. He would remind us that we worked exactly nine to five and that we were supposed to wave at him when we came in and wave on our way out. This would be my third chat this month, if I recalled correctly. I didn't mind the chats so much. Particularly, I loved his gaze when he spoke: it was always fixed and completely inanimate. His eyes were concentric circles—each made of slightly different shades of ocean blue stones. The outermost rim was light green like the shallow ocean, and the inner rim was a deeper blue. The colors in his eyes would reflect the warm sun that peered generously through the floor-to-ceiling windows of his office overlooking midtown Manhattan. Most of what he said usually dissolved into a blur for me as I held his gaze and patiently waited for a movement in his eyes. I never found one.

Meanwhile scientists weighed in, "The grains are not made of any known element in the periodic table, or of any substance ever known to man, but at this point we have no evidence of these being harmful to us. We advise caution though. We are investigating whether this might be some manifestation of climate change. No results to report yet."

Hundreds of cleaners were dispatched by city officials to wipe the streets clean of the grains and load the congealed mounds into trucks to be dumped into the Hudson—which didn't seem too cautious for the river-dwellers to me. Neither fire nor water appeared to have any effect on the grains, leaving city officials at a loss as to how to dispose or destroy them.

My manager waved me in when I finally went to see him at the end of the day. Reliably, his office glowed in orange and gold from an early fall sunset. His pale skin was bathed in red when he began speaking, sitting like a dark quivering shadow on the other side of the table.

"I wanted to speak to you about ..." I had already tuned out, or perhaps his voice had trailed off.

"You look very concerned, what are you looking at? Is everything okay?" I think he kept saying.

There was something outside his window that held my attention. For the second time since I had first seen and felt the grains, I felt swept up but aware, present but distant, rooted in the world but floating above it.

On the other side of the street from our office, on top of the Ziegfield Theater, rose another structure in all its art deco glory and detail. The structure did not look anything like the current theater but said in clear letters on top and vertically on the side "Ziegfield." And another point of difference—this structure was made entirely of the grains that had fallen from the sky since that morning.The only words that I finally heard from my manager, when I managed to shift my gaze back to his lips were, "So, I am sorry to say, we have to let you go."

I had opened my mouth to speak, but now I shut it back up. I stared at his unblinking stony gaze for what may have been a good few minutes, because after a while he said "Riva, are you okay? This is hard, I know."

I did not ask him why he was firing me, as I am sure he had gone over it while I was hypnotized by the structure outside. A very pregnant silence followed, one where I considered whether I should ask him to repeat everything he had already told me—which would reveal that I had not been listening the first time. Was that polite? Since he had just fired me did I even need to be polite anymore? The sun had set, lights had come on in his office. Through his window I watched a purple blue sky frame him on one side and next to him, an imposing structure made of grains. Both his hands were on the table, as if he was bracing himself for something. For the first time since working there I saw his lips pursed. Even more striking, I thought I saw his eyes move, come together, narrow ever so slightly. I suppose none of this felt too out of place in a day full of so many bizarre offerings. I said nothing and, not that I remember, I eventually must have left his office. I was aware that my world had just changed dramatically—but so had the world I lived in. I wasn't sure which one to be more concerned about. For an instant I even thought the two were somehow related.

It had stopped raining some time during the day. As I walked home, it seemed as if the whole city had descended to watch this structure that had created itself atop the Ziegfield Theater. Not an inch remained to walk in between the crowds. Camera crews from news stations, people with their cell phones, office-goers returning from work, people with children. As crowds jostled to get a glimpse of the structure, an old lady with her walker and I stood with our backs to the wall of an office building waiting for the crowd to dissipate. The soft skin on her cheeks hung loose like lazy hammocks. She looked up at the structure with her clear blue eyes, then turned to me muttering something inaudibly. She wore bright red lipstick and, despite years forming contours on her skin, she had a glow on her face and in her eyes as she muttered again. I moved closer to hear her. Struggling to look up all the way at the structure created by the grains, in a soft but crackling voice she said, "That is how I remember the Ziegfield Theater. It used to be a few blocks to the west. We had lined the streets back then to stop its demolition, but they tore it down anyway. Not a day goes by without me thinking of that old theater, where I worked for many years." I managed a feeble smile for the old lady but was too stunned to ask her anything else. I turned and walked a few additional blocks around the crowd and rushed home.

At home, I lay on my bed in the clothes I had worn all day. I wondered how I would start my mornings now. Should I finally go over to that new coffee shop and ask for a job? Why had the grains arranged themselves into an old building that existed in the collective memory of some of us? What else were these grains capable of? What would happen tomorrow? My bed was against the wall with my only window. I gazed out as if to find or see something different. Now the view of walls closing in on all sides was comforting, even protective. I wondered if any of the grains had made it through that little patch of sky up on top. The confused whir of thoughts inside my head refused to subside.

By early next morning, the grains of sand rained all over the world. The state and federal governments finally issued a statement. The grains were an attack from an intelligent life form from somewhere else. They were an attack by aliens.

It wasn't clear if the aliens had caused this downpour while they watched from above, or if the grains were aliens themselves. But what was known was that the grains had cognitive ability. There was no explanation as to how this downpour that had penetrated the stratosphere from outer space had somehow escaped every weather camera, but that was under further investigation. Schools and offices were to remain closed until it was considered safe to venture out. It was all happening exactly as we had seen in countless science fiction movies and books, except there were millions, possibly billions of these little aliens rather than large, unsightly beings who descended from spacecraft and could be tracked.

I strained to open my eyes and when I did I was still facing my window. No sign of the grains. I realized I had nowhere to be. A familiar whiff came to me, though I couldn't quite place it. I also felt something soft and warm against my back. This was odd; I even thought I felt a claw. I turned around and as I did, I realized beads of sweat had gathered on my neck on shoulders, perhaps from sleeping in my work clothes. My next impulse was to leap from my bed, which I did when I saw what was next to me on my bed. My throat and mouth went dry and my heart felt like it was being squeezed by iron claws. My hands and feet went cold. I couldn't move. I realized for a minute that I had lost my voice too, because I screamed but no sound came out. She was there lying comfortably curled beside the imprint of my body on the mattress on my bed. Her eyes were closed as she lay with her head facing a little to one side, just like she always slept. Except this time she was made entirely of the grainy, minute hexagons. It was Sadie.

I thought of calling 911, though I knew I wouldn't get through. Slowly she opened her eyes and stood up on the bed, jumped to the ground, and rolled onto her back like she did every morning when she wanted her belly rubbed. I stood still with my back against the wall, my lips parched and a trickle of sweat running down my face and neck. I pulled myself together and tried to shoo her away. I opened the door so she would perhaps go outside. She didn't. Even as I tried to make her leave, she sat by the door and looked at me with her sad eyes as she did when she wanted to go for a walk. I stood there watching her, and struggled to take large gasps of air to breathe.

"There is no confirmation yet about the effect of these grains on humans. The President has pledged all necessary resources to investigate the impact of these grains. Until then, people are strongly advised to clean every inch of their homes, wearing protective masks, and piling any grains into garbage bags. Special trucks will be dispatched every few hours to collect the bags. Do not touch, inhale or ingest the grains under any circumstances."

At least initially, many hung on to all this well-intentioned advice. I tried, too. I refused to pet Sadie or give her food. I even kicked her. I told myself this wasn't Sadie but a trick by a sinister alien. But Sadie was exactly as I remembered her. She stuck out her tongue and wagged her tail as she always did while I made minced meat, which was her favorite. She knew exactly when I was sleepy and curled up next to me so I could cuddle with her and sleep. She was how I remembered her best, as a puppy. I finally managed to steel myself and took her out of the house for a walk and left her tethered to a pole and walked back home alone. In a few hours, though, I brought her back. She was my Sadie.

Soon reports flooded in of women cuddling little babies made of astrosand, as these were now called; children playing with other children made of astrosand; grandparents walking the parks with grandchildren made of astrosand; couples kissing on a park bench although one of them was astrosand; a human couple with astrosand children. But there was still no clarity on what these particles were made of. Or why they were here.

In a few months though, chemists created an acidic compound that could destroy astrosand. It was to be available in every pharmaceutical store for a subsidized amount. The unproven hypothesis though was that as long as there were some of these astrosand grains in the world, our memories could be recreated. So in a way it was futile to devise means of destroying them, as no one wanted to; they had manifested as our loved ones. The only solution was to disown them.

There were somber messages and warnings from the President. "Please remember these sand figures are not your loved ones. For your own well-being and that of others, please distance yourself from them, as their impact on human beings is still not known." But most of us held on to our memories made of sand, vulnerable as ever.

Since then, activist groups have emerged in support of astrosand and astrosand loved ones. Their message is "Since there is no evidence to support that they would in any way harm us and, in fact, have given solace to so many of us, they have a right to live with their loved ones just like the rest of us. Let's not discriminate against them just because they are different." That part got a little complicated when the first report came of an astrosand brother hurting his human sister who was competing for attention from their mother. To their supporters this was inevitable: astrosand beings were as real and as flawed or perfect as we remembered them to be.

All astrosand monuments have been torn down and demolished. All except one—the freshest wound in the country's memory. This one now stands as tall as the original. Everyone tiptoes around it—we're not allowed to go in—and some wealthy benefactors even plan to build a guarded enclosure around it. No one can bear seeing the twin towers crumble again.

Religious groups have strongly condemned relationships with astrosand beings. They are not allowed in places of worship as they are not God's creatures. There have been several reported murders of astrosand people by devout followers of various religions. On a train, a few drunk boys stripped an astrosand woman naked so they could tell if she looked like a real woman. No one has been punished so far for these crimes, as astrosand people are not people yet according to the law; they are merely a manifestation of our memories. Consequently, they can be recreated. (Perhaps so, but it still hurts every time.) Conspiracy theories abound about the government planning a massive scale annihilation of astrosand and everything made of them. It's a scary world for them, but more importantly for us.

To me, it's fascinating that our much-anticipated alien attack transpired like this—as dear, lost loved ones for some, and for others as pesky little grains of sand that had to be cleaned out from window sills and sidewalks.

I am just glad that there is no easy way to get rid of them. They still rain down sometimes.

Puloma Mukherjee is an obsessive reader and writer of science fiction, a committed short story enthusiast, and a graduate of the science fiction workshop at the Yale Writer's Conference. When she is not on the lookout for miracles and absurdities in every day mundanities, she can be found at her perch in New York with her husband and beautiful little boy.

Walking, Watching, Waiting

By Garrett Rowlan

(Originally published in the April 2015 issue of The MOON.)

Walking residential neighborhoods at night, as I always do, I felt drawn in a particular direction and, at the end of a cul-de-sac in South Pasadena, I saw an older woman sitting beneath the light of a shaded ceiling lamp. She sketched in colors on a pad of paper, a faint smile of concentration on her face. The scene had a stillness that allured, the quiet of a portrait.

As I watched, she left the room. Curious, I jumped the fence and went to the window. Peering through glass on tiptoes, I saw what she had drawn, a series of concentric circles, a shape that fascinated me, detained me, when the police came, no doubt as a result of the woman's call or of a neighbor's, I had to hurry to avoid the arrest for trespassing. I got away by vaulting a fence.

Spooked, I stayed away for almost a week. At last, I returned, drawn by the shape she had made. There was something about it, a code in crayon. When I returned, it was a weekend, and a yard sale was in progress. I entered the yard, this time legally.

"Where's the woman who lived here?" I asked a girl who was in charge of pricing.

"Moved," she said.

"She's gone to meet the flying saucers," a man said, sitting nearby.

"Flying saucers is a politically incorrect term," the girl said. "She said that they are to be referred to as extraterrestrial vehicles."

"And she's not crazy," he said. "She has an alternative universe mindset." He looked at me and made a small wheezing laugh of amusement. "During the Joys and Concerns segment of the church service she got up in front of the congregation and said she's going away with the saucers. Of course, since it's a Unitarian church, half the crowd looked ready to go with her, if they weren't there already." He reprised his contemptuous snort. "That's why she went into the desert."

"Which desert?"

That's how I came to Noah, a piece of nothing on the border of California and Nevada, a burg with a store and a gas pump and about a hundred residents, living in trailers and huts. Most worked in the mines surrounding town or in the casinos on the Nevada border. They were institutional cooks, croupiers and barkers looking to move up to Vegas, or desert people one welfare check from destitution. I fit right in, a man living on unemployment and the funds from my father's estate. I never knew him, and my mother left me on a doorstep when I was five months. I was raised in an orphanage and when I turned twenty-one I was contacted by a lawyer and told that certain funds would help to sustain me until it was determined that they would not be necessary, though who was to do the determination I was still waiting to know.

That was my past. My present was hot days spent listening to an oldies station from Las Vegas. At night, when it cooled, I would go for walks. In the desert sky stars spread with a glittering profusion that seemed so animated that at times I thought they were crawling. I studied astronomy, consulted celestial charts, and listened to early Pink Floyd.

A few weeks into my residency, she came to town with little more than a couple of suitcases, one more than mine. At least I thought it was her, an older woman, not unattractive, slender. Her name, I learned soon enough, was Ruth Wagner. She approached me one night. This happened a few hundred yards outside of town. She told me her name. I told her mine, and while we had exchanged nods before, now we greeted each other as friends. The night was nearly moonless. Perhaps this had something to do with my attraction, the idea that I walked beside some invisible female principle made universal by darkness, an impression aided by her voice that had not the grain of age but remained supple, smooth, and I will say, even sexy. She said she was from Pasadena, whose streets I had walked in my nocturnal restlessness. I didn't ask her if she had lived in a particular street in South Pasadena and had left, leaving her things for a yard sale. I didn't want to pry.

"And so what are you doing out here?" I asked.

"I'm ready to take the next step in my life," she said. When I asked what that step was, she turned the conversation to me, and since I felt that I had been given an edited version of her reason for being here, I returned the favor. I only said that I'd had some issues with living in Los Angeles, and that I'd come out here to find myself.

And so it was that we'd meet and wander from the town of Noah and toward the New York Mountains, which marked California's eastern border in this part of the state.

Sometimes we watched the town's one piece of art, a sculpture made from discarded automobile parts, the result of wrecks or other vehicular mishaps. The sculpture was eight feet tall and depicted a female in the act of running.

"I wonder where she is running to," Ruth Wagner said.

Sometimes Ruth would disappear for days, and return without explanation. One new moon grew full, and one night she said she couldn't walk because she was meeting a friend, and I felt a disappointment that I buried in a shrug. That night, I watched the road from the darkness and I saw a car pull up for her. She got in and rode away. I didn't see who drove, not until next afternoon when I was sitting at the wooden deck outside the general store and I saw a white Toyota pull into town. It was driven by a bald man wearing black, and she was riding in the front seat. As she got out he gave me a nod before he headed toward Nevada.

"Just an old friend," she said, when I asked.

"Do you want to walk tonight?"

"I can't. I've got some things to attend to."

"I see. Is everything okay?"

"Everything's fine, going as expected. And let me say that I've really enjoyed our walks. I'll never forget them."

"Are you leaving?"

"No...I'm...I've just got some things to do."

That night, I walked back to the general store and heard from Bill McAllister, who managed the general store and collected the rents on behalf of the estate that actually owned the town, that Ruth had given notice on her trailer.

I went to Ruth's and knocked but she wasn't there. A light had been left on inside, and I saw it shine on the makeshift desk and a piece of paper. I recalled that other house I had looked into, a couple of months ago now, and how I had wanted to read what was inscribed there. I tried the door.

It was unlocked. I entered the trailer. The place was barren, but then it had always seemed so when I passed by.

Stepping closer to what she had scrawled I saw the letters "EV" written above the same pattern of concentric circles as before, drawn in color, with the reds and yellows and a spot of blue for contrast. As I watched, it seemed to spin. I say "seemed" to acquit myself from the charge of madness. Because, I'm telling you, it did spin, a chambered nautilus, turning, and always working the eye inward, toward a center that would compress the soul, before releasing it to what was on the other side of the beckoning shape.

I don't know how long I must have looked at the spiral. I became aware of myself as I must have seen Ruth Wagner—or whoever that anonymous female was, seen through the windows of a southern California street—that night; that is, as a stilled figure lost in the possibility of some other reality.

At last, I left. I turned out the light, which I felt had been left on for me. I headed away from Noah and into the desert. The image of the swirling shape—sometimes like twisted Cirrus clouds, sometimes a whirlpool in snapshot—stayed in my thoughts. It guided me. I felt that somewhere inside or above me a hovering binnacle held a small compass that guided my motions, which didn't seem oriented to any longitude or latitude, but seemed to be aligning themselves to some vertical polarity. As the terrain began a gentle ascent, my thoughts slid backward in a serial manner, like scenes in a movie played in reverse and, like a movie my life was something compelling but ultimately meaningless, beside the point, or, I began to feel, only a prelude to some greater transformation.

I might have gone a mile or more out of town. Noah, behind me, was only a scatter of lights when I saw her, or sensed her, a willowy presence sculpted in moon shadow.

"You can still turn back," she said.

"I've come so far," I said.

"There's still time, you know."

Garrett Rowlan is a retired Los Angeles schoolteacher. He is a frequent contributor to The MOON *and the author of three novels,* The Vampire Circus, To Die, Perhaps to Sleep, *and* Too Solid Flesh Melts. *His website www.garrettrowlan.com, contains a few of his 60 or so published stories and essays.*

Angel of Death

By James Norris

(Originally published in the January 2018 issue of The MOON.)

Chapter 1 - The Hiker - *Ante Mortem*

Tears fell from her cheeks like the raindrops falling from the dark, swollen clouds that obscured the sky from horizon to horizon. Her gray, tattered, ankle-length dress whipped about her in the wind, and was soaked through. But her long, dark hair lay dry as though there was no wind or rain. Indeed, no rain touched her skin, not where her simple dress's straps left her shoulders and arms bare, not where her wind-blown skirt exposed her calves. Only her dress and sandals were touched by the elements, the swiftly running creek in which she stood.

She had no need for clothing to protect her from the elements. Nothing of this world had touched her for longer than she could remember. Even so, her skin was cold, but not due to the wind or rain.

Moments ago, lightning had struck a tree not far from her—she knew the distance to the tree to the foot, to the inch, to the smallest fraction of an inch. Not because she wanted to, but because it was a site of immediate death.

She wept for the all the living things killed outright in that tree. The father robin burnt to char in midair as he returned with a gullet full of food for his five chicks. The mother robin impaled by a piece of bark, a piece of natural shrapnel, as she brooded their chicks, trying in vain to shield them from the rain and wind.

And for those who would die in the seconds, minutes, hours, and days to come as a direct result of the lightning. She knew to the tiniest fraction of a second how long it would take for each of the chicks to die. For each of the thousands of living things that made the tree their home. The tree would die as well, though its final, true death would take three months, five days, twenty-one hours. . .

She gritted her teeth, squeezed her eyes shut. Forced the countdown to the tree's end from consciousness. Likewise the family of squirrels who made their home in a hollow left by a fallen branch not far from the robin nest, the numerous centipedes, beetles, myriad of flying insects, and the colonies of moss that hung from the tree's branches.

Surely many of the animals that had made the tree their home would survive, but they were unknown to her—she could take no solace from their good fortune for the lightning had not marked them for death. To her, they were as invisible as to any other. . .

She was no *person*.

Not anymore.

Suddenly she felt an unearthly, glacial grasp on her right shoulder.

A voice produced by no larynx rasped, "It is time."

Without looking over her shoulder at the black-robed figure standing there, or at the hourglass she held in both hands, she replied, "No, there are thirty-eight grains left."

She looked down at the broken body of the young hiker at her feet. The torrential downpour had weakened the Earth's hold on the rocks along the gulley's rim where the man had been walking. His weight had caused them to slide apart from one another, and him to tumble twenty or so feet down into the creek. He had come to rest face up, but had broken his right ankle, bruised several ribs, and hit his head on a rock, knocking him senseless.

If the water in the creek hadn't been rising because of the rain, he would no doubt have eventually regained consciousness. Stumbled back to his car. Or called for help using his cell-phone.

But the ever-deepening water would soon cover his face.

When it did, he would drown.

If she did not touch him, did not release his soul from its Earthly bond before the final grain of sand fell in her hourglass, did not release his soul before he died, his soul would remain bound forever to his body. He would become a ghost. Knowing he was dead and unable to move onto his final, natural destination, unable to interact with the world around him, he would slowly go insane.

His insanity might give him the strength to affect the physical world. He might become a poltergeist, and in his insanity, terrify and possibly harm anyone unlucky enough to pass nearby.

When only thirteen grains of sand remained in her glass, she knelt in the creek beside him. Her black tresses fell into the water, framing his face, unmoved by the running water that was killing him as it filled his lungs.

His eyes opened and found hers just inches above his face. There was fear there, having nothing to do with the physical facts of his situation, if he even understood them.

But he knew he was looking into the eyes of his Death.

A change came over him as her right hand moved toward his chest, as the last few grains of sand fell in her hourglass. His mouth moved, and though only bubbles escaped, she heard his last words. "You're so beautiful."

Her hand came to rest open-palmed on his chest, and as the last grain of sand in her hourglass fell, Robert Anthony O'Callaghan died.

Chapter 2 - Robert Anthony O'Callaghan - *Post Mortem*

In a moment lasting twenty-eight years, five months, three days, and a number of minutes and seconds that held significance only to Bobby and those who loved him, everything that he was, had ever been, had ever hoped to be, flooded through her.

* * *

His newborn son wailed as only a baby could. The doctor held Jonathon Quigley--Cassie's grandfather's middle name--O'Callaghan up to Bobby as though for his inspection.

Every one of their friends who'd already had children had told him all newborns were ugly except to their parents. Bobby pursed his lips, and couldn't help but think, "Nope, even when they've wiped all the blood and goo off you. . ."

He looked down at Cassie, whose beautiful hair was plastered to the side of her head with sweat, and who was panting like she'd just run one of her marathons, "Look, love, you've given birth to a wrinkled, hairless little monkey."

She swatted at his thigh with her hand, but clearly didn't have the strength for a serious effort. "But he's our perfect *hairless little monkey," she replied with a smile as the doctor handed little Johnny to her to hold in her arms for the first time.*

* * *

"With this ring I thee wed," Bobby said as he slipped Cassandra's wedding band onto her long, delicate ring-finger. He looked up and saw tears of joy threatening in her beautiful green eyes. Her red hair, a much more lovely red than his frankly orange hair, framed her face.

"With this ring I thee wed," Cassie said as she slipped an identical band on his finger.

* * *

His right arm hurt, but for some reason, he didn't care. His mouth felt like it was full of cotton, and there was an almost overpowering taste of blood-iron.

A voice he couldn't identify said, "Your son's very lucky, Mr. and Mrs. O'Callaghan. People who are sober during accidents like your son's. . . Well, their bodies often fight the accident instead of just going with it and come out much worse for it. And people with a blood alcohol content as high as your son's usually aren't wearing their seatbelts."

"Well, we really tried --"

Bobby thought, <u>Mom, why are you crying?</u>

"-- to drill into him the importance of always wearing his seatbelt."

Some corner of his mind was still clear of the pain and drugs and understood. He had driven home. Or tried to, even after Greg and Bill had tried to convince him he was too drunk to drive.

But that one coherent corner of his mind couldn't tell him if he actually managed to say, "Oh, Mom, I'm so sorry," out loud, loud enough for her and his dad to hear it.

* * *

Every moment of Robert Anthony O'Callaghan's life, every self-perceived success and failure, all his joys and pains, all the pride and all the guilt, even memories that he didn't know were still part of his mind and soul surged through her.

His entire life flashed before her eyes, past her ears and across her skin, just as it had for him, but only in a matter of heartbeats.

Her right hand, as it always did when the deceased's soul blasted through her, came to rest between her breasts, where there was no heartbeat to be felt.

* * *

When her vision cleared of the memories of Bobby's life, she saw him standing in front of her, in the rapidly rising creek, on the far side of his body. His corpse.

As she stood, she saw the rushing creek water flow through his insubstantial form.

The falling rain pass through him.

The wind carry a leaf torn off a tree above the gulley through him.

Her motion caught his attention, and his eyes, which had been staring at his body, met hers.

She saw concern in his eyes.

Knowing him now as intimately as she did, she knew his concern was for her.

"Miss, are you all right?"

The dead often didn't understand where they were, their situation. Their minds blocked out their death, the minutes and even hours leading up to it.

Unlike them, Bobby O'Callaghan knew he was dead. She could see the memory of the painful fall down the side of the gulley in his eyes. The desperation as the water rose around him, unable to lift his head as it began to flow into his mouth, into his nose.

But his first thought upon rising from his body was of her, of the tears still running down her face.

Even if she had not *known* Bobby O'Callaghan's soul, she would know from this what his final destination would be. Where he would spend eternity.

And then he saw her companion behind her. For an instant he recoiled in fear, taking a step, and then another, back away from her. Again, she felt the ice-cold, skeletal hand on her shoulder.

At this, Bobby took a step forward, his hands flexing, the incorporeal muscles of his torso tensing. He meant to protect her, to fight on her behalf.

If she asked him to.

No, this one would not be cut down by her companion's scythe. Would not spend eternity in Hell.

This one was destined for Heaven.

Again, her companion rasped, "It is time."

Bobby's eyes narrowed.

"He means it's time for you to move on."

"Move on to where?"

She lifted her hourglass in both hands, and as she did, the sand began to glow. Within moments, its buttery light illuminated the entire gulley. It was warm, brighter than the sun, and infinitely more comforting.

Human eyes, living eyes, would have been blinded by the glass's light, if it were meant for, could be seen by, the eyes of the living. In any case, there were no living eyes here.

But Bobby was exalted by the light, and he stepped toward it.

Bobby O'Callaghan had caused his mother such pain the night he had driven drunk. And he had felt such guilt for that one stupid act. But he had been a good man.

Perhaps precisely because he had felt such guilt.

The upper base of the glass blocked the glowing sand, its brilliant light, from her direct view.

It was not meant for her.

It was meant for Bobby.

Bobby took a second step toward her, and as he did, his form began to fray. With his third step, he trod into his forgotten body.

He was little more than a wisp of smoke.

Even to her eyes.

Chapter 3 - Mary Elizabeth Morely - *Ante Mortem*

Mary stood before her make-up stand and ran a brush through her long, straight, dark hair. In the stand's mirror, she saw William walk up behind her.

As she set the brush down, he wrapped his arms around her waist. "You are so beautiful, Mare."

She smiled. "You know 'mare' means a female horse, right?"

"Well, y'know, you have long legs like a horse. But you also know I mean it like an ocean of the moon." He nodded toward her image in the mirror. "It's fitting, with your dark hair and dark eyes."

She looked at her reflection—her eyes were a dark, midnight blue.

"Silly boy, that word is Latin. The 'e' isn't silent."

William knew that, of course, having a BA in classical languages, Greek and Latin.

"Well, didn't you tell me once it was also the root of 'nightmare'? Something like a supernatural being that caused nightmares? Old German for 'succubus'?"

Mary's degree was in Middle English literature--she and William had met in a graduate seminar on the use of Greek and Roman mythology in 14th and 15th century European art.

"No, not 'succubus'--that's a female spirit who seduces men in their sleep. 'Mare' referred to an incubus--a *male* spirit who seduced *women* while they slept."

"Well, in either case, there's sex involved." He jerked his head toward their bed. "Whatcha say we involve ourselves in some sex rather than going to this dinner party of your advisor's?"

He leaned in to nuzzle her neck as she said, "No, I can't be a no-show."

He blew gently on her neck, making her shiver, and looked at her again in the mirror. "You sure?"

When his right hand started to move up her stomach, she took both his hands in hers, and pulled them away from her. She tilted her head to force his mouth away from her neck and said, "Now who's the incubus?" Letting go of his hands, she turned and put her hands on his chest, pushing gently.

His eyes widened. "My seductions give you nightmares?"

She laughed and stepped around him. "No, of course not. And Dr. Jones's parties aren't the nightmares you make them out to be." Stopping at the bedroom doorway, she looked at his crestfallen face. "Now be a good boy and come along."

He sighed. "If you insist."

* * *

At the front door, Mary grabbed her purse and pulled out her car keys.

William walked past her, through their apartment's front door, and onto the patio. He turned back to her with his arms spread and a smile on his face. "It's a beautiful night--let's walk!"

From the door's threshold, Mary felt the night's cool air, but it was warm enough. "Sure, why not?"

As they walked the quiet city streets, Mary asked William for the umpteenth time what it was that he disliked about her advisor and received the only reply she ever did: "He just rubs me the wrong way."

At the party, William mingled for the first hour or so, but then parked himself on a couch in the corner of the living room, leaving Mary to make the rounds and rub elbows with Jones and his guests, the other professors and students from the literature department.

When she had done her duty by her advisor, she walked over to William to tell him they could leave. "Great, let's get out of here." He stumbled ever so slightly as he came to his feet. "Damn, right leg's fallen asleep."

There was no slurring of his speech, but she asked teasingly, "You sure that's all it is?"

"Well, maybe not *all* it is." He gestured at the three bottles on the coffee table in front of the couch. "Herr Professor has good taste in beer, at least."

William suggested that they walk back through the park between 8th and Main. "It's romantic with the moon and all the stars out," he said, and she agreed.

Halfway through the park a wind came up, and with it came clouds. The temperature dropped, and they both pulled their coats more tightly around themselves.

The central part of the park had no lights, but the path was wide and easy to follow even in the cloud-obscured moonlight.

Mary had no warning when a shadowy man-shape stepped out from behind a tree just a few feet in front of them. The moon was behind the hooded figure, but Mary could see an arm held out to its side. Moonlight glinted off something metallic in that hand.

"Gimme yaa money," a man's voice slurred.

Just as Mary realized the man was holding a knife, William stepped in front of her and pushed her back a step with one hand.

William said, "We don't want any trouble." He held his hands out by his side.

"Don' care wa you want."

Over William's shoulder, Mary could see the man take a step toward William.

"Gimme yaa money," he repeated.

William took a step forward, and Mary whispered, "William."

She'd never been so terrified in her life.

William said, "Look, I'm going to reach for my wallet," as he swung his right hand back as if to warn Mary to stay back.

Suddenly, the man charged them.

Mary saw the knife-hand swing forward and then William's body blocked her view. She screamed William's name as he surged forward.

The moon disappeared behind the clouds.

Mary could only see two shadowy shapes struggling a few feet in front of her.

William gasped. And staggered back. And fell to the ground.

Screaming William's name, Mary ran forward two steps and dropped to the ground next to him.

He was holding his stomach, and something dark was seeping out from between his fingers.

She put her hand on his chest.

His heart was pounding.

He reached up with a hand covered in blood, reached for her face but fell short--his hand came to rest on her jacket, between her breasts.

The boy said, "I just wanted the money." For some reason, his words were no longer slurred.

Mary looked up.

For an instant, the moon came out from behind the clouds, and Mary could see the mugger's face clearly.

Their eyes locked.

He looked confused.

The boy couldn't have been more than 18 years old. Bloodshot eyes. Bags under his eyes. Sunken cheeks. Scabs on his chin, his forehead.

Meth, Mary thought.

The boy turned and ran.

"Mary, I feel so cold."

William's heart stopped beating.

* * *

The police arrived.

Told her she had called 911 on her cell phone--it was on the ground next to William. There was blood on it.

Paramedics arrived.

The police took Mary's statement.

The paramedics took William's body.

* * *

"Ashes to ashes. Dust to dust."

* * *

For days she did not leave their apartment.

She would stare for hours on end at her jacket--with the jacket unzipped, the bloodstain did not look much like a handprint, but she knew it was.

Friends stopped by.

Dr. Jones stopped by.

They all uttered meaningless platitudes.

* * *

The police never found William's murderer.

But Mary did.

There was a pawnshop not far from the apartment. One day, she went there. Bought a gun.

Every night thereafter, Mary walked the park along the path William and she had on their way home from the party.

She wore the jacket she had worn that night, the one with William's handprint rendered in his blood between her breasts.

One night, a shape stepped out from behind a tree and into her path.

A glint of moonlight reflected off the knife in its right hand.

Mary drew the gun she had bought for this purpose even as the boy said, "Gimme ya money."

She recognized the voice.

It wouldn't have mattered if she hadn't.

Mary pulled the trigger once. Twice. And again.

The boy fell backward.

Mary walked up to him and looked down at his face.

His eyes were even more bloodshot. The bags under his eyes more pronounced. The cheeks more sunken.

She said, "William didn't deserve to die. But you do."

The boy tried to say something, but blood bubbled from his mouth.

Mary knelt beside him, unconcerned with the knife still clutched in his hand. She placed her free hand on his chest.

Waited for his heart to stop beating.

* * *

"Police! Drop the gun!"

Mary did not know how long she had knelt next to the body of William's killer.

Did it matter?

She looked over her shoulder and was blinded by the bright light of the policeman's flashlight.

"Drop the gun!"

Mary looked at the gun that was still in her hand.

Did it matter?

William was dead.

She stood.

As she turned to face the police officer, she heard the report of his gun.

She could not see him.

Standing before her was a figure that stood at least two feet taller than she. It wore a black, tattered robe that whipped about It, even though there was no wind. At her eye-level, one skeletal hand held an hourglass. Somehow, she knew there were only a few grains of sand left in the upper bulb. In the other fleshless hand, It held a scythe even taller than It was.

Her gaze moved up to its hood, and saw a skull. The eye sockets were empty. Fleshless cheekbones created the illusion that It was grinning.

The lower jaw moved as the robe flapped in the non-existent wind to show the spine, the fleshless rib-cage below the skull. "You have murdered."

Its visage was terrible, and Its voice should have turned the blood in her veins to ice.

This was her Death standing before her.

But she was already as cold as she could be. Had been since William uttered his last words.

Her attention was drawn down as the bullet from the policeman's gun emerged from Death's robe. It left no hole and moved so slowly that Mary was able to follow it with her eyes.

In the periphery of her vision, she saw Death begin to swing Its scythe.

Just before the last grain of sand fell in Its hourglass, the scythe passed through her.

A fraction of an instant later, the bullet ended her life.

Chapter 4 - Mary Elizabeth Morely - *Post Mortem*

She looked over her shoulder and saw her body sprawled across that of William's killer.

The policeman cursed and moving to kick her gun away from her hand, passed through Mary's Death as though It was not there. Asked no one in particular, "Why? Why couldn't you just drop the damn gun?"

Death stepped aside so Mary could once again see It.

She could see tears running down the policeman's face. He looked like he could hardly be much older than the boy who had murdered William.

Death rasped, "Compassion has been lost to you."

She turned to Death and screamed, "He murdered William for the money we had in our pockets. He deserved to die!"

"Death is the end of all things. It is not a dessert." Death stepped toward her.

She brought up the hand holding the gun, but it was empty. She no longer wore her jacket, jeans or shoes. Instead, she wore a simple, white strap dress and sandals.

"You will find compassion again at my side." Her Death held out the hourglass. "Take the glass."

"No. I just want to die."

"You *are* dead." Death released the hourglass.

She thought she had been cold before, but now. . .

The hourglass began to float toward her.

"Take the glass."

Her hands took the glass from the air.

Chapter 5 - Mary Elizabeth Morely - *Per Mortem*

Over the days, years or decades that followed, she became an Angel of Death.

At first she had refused to touch the dead and learned what could happen when she failed to do so.

Time ceased to have meaning for her—perhaps it had no meaning for the dead.

Or Death.

For much longer, she had scoured the memories of the dead to find a justification for their deaths.

* * *

With Bobby O'Callaghan's fourth step, he said, "It's so beautiful."

And as he took his fifth and final step in this world, a single new tear spilled from her eye as she said, "So are you."

Her companion rasped, "Release the glass."

She was so stunned that she almost didn't understand her companion. It had never asked anything of her except to take the glass and to release the dead. "What?"

"Release the glass."

She turned away from Bobby O'Callaghan's body to find her Death had reached out Its free hand toward her.

Trembling, she did as It asked.

"You have found compassion again."

The sand in the hourglass began to glow.

"Its Light is now for you."

She looked to her Death's eyeless, fleshless visage.

But the Light was even now washing out Its form.

And in Its place, she saw William beckoning her to join him.

James Norris has been a member of the Rocky Mountain Fiction Writers since 2010 and is working on three novels, the first of which, The Order of the Brotherhood, *is a work of dystopian speculative fiction set in a prison and investigates the value of democracy in an America that has largely forgotten it. He's also written several short stories, one of which, "Izzie Tells No Lies," was published in the February 2018 issue of* Fantasia Divinity. *He's also written several spec teleplays, the latest of which, "Project Ωmega", is currently under review at Amazon. He lives in Idaho with his wife and three creatures of the canine and feline persuasions, where he is pursuing his Ph.D. in physics.*

To the Cloud

By Garrett Rowlan

(Originally published in the October 2014 issue of The MOON.)

Every waking was the same, a probing of darkness, and a slow discovery of herself. Her hands, under the bed covers, explored her body, established its contours. First she got a body, a new body, and later a new name. Skinny or fat, she was still alone in the bed's narrow, solitary dimensions. It was always like this. She woke new, with some part of her left behind, as if she had recovered from surgery.

She reached up and groped until she found the light switch. The illuminated room was about what she'd come to expect, an asceticism rooted in poverty both of spirit and means, the tin foil covering the window, the tattered sunset poster, and her white blouse and black skirt, her uniform, suspending from a hanger, notched on a wall-driven nail. It must have been winter. She saw the space heater beside her bed and a jacket on a hook and saw how her breath made frost as she rose. The uniform, when she put it on, smelled faintly of fried foods. She saw a small spot of red on the front of the blouse. She couldn't remember it. She hoped it was catsup and not blood.

She peeked out the window, around the edges of the tin foil. The setting sun, beyond the drizzle that gently tattooed the aluminum roof of her trailer, was blurred by clouds like something poorly erased. She stepped back and picked up a brush and worried her hair while using the bathroom mirror, checking her features whose changing contours never became coarse nor beautiful; just pretty enough not to be noticed. She never knew her name until she attached it to her blouse. She only existed to be perceived, a recessed figure in a story, a background Bedouin, going from each watering hole of words.

She found her nametag in a desk drawer. It read "Dot," and while it was better than some she'd had—"Trixie" had particularly riled—it was still common. She hooked the pin to her blouse, grabbed a black, button-down sweater and black purse, and left the trailer.

Outside, small drops dotted the windshield of the other cars parked next to other trailers, but no car belonged to her. She never needed one. Conceived as an ambulating character, she walked to work. The rain fell as tiny pinpricks and with a beaded languor in the lights, a fine-grained curtain through which ghosts passed. Sometimes the drops formed s-shapes, a silent hissing of drifting consonants. It didn't surprise her that the world was taking on a graphical bias, that the streetlights formed parenthetical brackets, or the raindrops hung from telephone wires with a wobble like commas. Her word-shaped world had punctuation.

She moved downhill, toward the lights at the intersection, past the convenience store and the motel. The restaurant where she worked was attached to a casino. She saw it up ahead.

She entered the restaurant, and crossed to the kitchen where the cook in his toque hat and prison tattoo was not unique to her experience. Nor was the waitress named "Carol" who resembled a question mark with her thin body and rounded shoulders and painted eyebrows, arching now as if to ask, Who are you?

Dot surveyed the room. Somewhere around here someone was writing. Someone always was. Some writer wanting local color, atmosphere, the rub of the real to stain their fiction, and Dot, Dolly, Trixie, Billie (names she recalled pinning to her blouse) were part of that. Thinking of those names made Dot feel that parts of her were missing, that she'd been poorly sliced like a piece of pie, hacked into bits and put on different plates.

She felt the presence of a third-person narration, possibly omniscient. She noticed no tilting of things toward one particular consciousness, the way the light bent toward one scribbling coffee addict.

She wondered whose story it was. Perhaps it was the tired-looking couple who seemed terminally bored with each other while their children fussed. Or perhaps it was the young woman at the counter, the one with the nicked hands, thin eyebrows, and colored hair, or the skinny and intense-looking older woman who sat beside her, eyes round and black, hair spiked like exclamation points growing out of her skull. But where was the writer?

Carol touched her shoulder.

"Courage," she said, "it's raining and that makes them crazy."

Maybe it was Dot who was crazy, for as she moved through the familiar tasks of taking orders, dispensing plates, and soothing tempers, she didn't have the familiar impression of herself as something scrawled on paper in a lockstep of cursive letters.

Instead, she felt as if she were a verb moving through the minutes with the flow of a gerund: *taking* the order, *delivering* the food, and *making* change in a way that suggested that she was a blurred blob of being, a perpetual motion machine, dispensing food.

It was then she saw the woman writing at the restaurant's counter, where it bent going toward the casino through an open passage. The woman sat at one of those counter seats obscured by the cash register and a slot machine, an inducement to the jangle of lost wages just down the hall. The woman was writing on a laptop.

"What is she doing?" Dot asked Carol.

"The Internet," Carol said. "WiFi comes even to this godforsaken part of the country."

Dot grabbed the steaming, fresh coffee pot and headed toward the woman. It was usually a man she found writing, but the type was still the same: glasses, dark hair swept back, the features bladed and intense, almost rat-like.

"More," said the woman as Dot approached. She pushed the half-filled coffee cup forward.

Dot poured the coffee.

"What are you writing?" she asked, when the cup had been filled. It was a first. She had never spoken to the person writing. They had scared her. The scratching of graphite or ink on paper was an act of damning gravity, but somehow in the way this woman wrote on the portable keyboard suggested something else to Dot, a lightness.

The woman looked up. In the lens of her thick glasses Dot saw two of herself, identical halves that she felt fused into a whole, as if all the fractured selves that she had behind her—the Trixies and Dixies and Billies—were gathering together, at last.

"I'm writing something for the cloud," the woman said.

"The cloud?"

"You know, saved to remote storage."

"What is that?"

"I need to finish this scene."

"Of course," Dot said, taking a step back.

"What is that?" the woman asked. She pointed at Dot's chest. "What is that on your blouse?"

"I think, catsup."

"It looks like blood," the woman said. "Say, that gives me an idea."

The woman dipped her head and began to write.

Dot moved away. She felt different. She felt herself as a gathering mass, a presence, and as spirit too. Fragments of herself coalesced. Looking at her hand and wrist, she noticed how the skin was textured now with veins and wrinkles and the lightest sprinkling of hair. She felt more real.

"Coffee please," someone said.

That's when she heard a shout from the slot machines. Someone had hit a jackpot, or so she thought. But when the gunmen burst into the room there were more shouts like that first one.

"All right!" bawled one of the men. Two of them had run into the restaurant. "Money on the tables!"

Dot was still holding the coffee pot, and as the man neared she made a motion of mindless reaction. She tossed the contents of the coffee pot. Scalding liquid splashed on the man's face, and as he shouted he pulled the trigger of his gun.

Dot felt the bullet enter her as the man, blinded, was tackled by the security guard. Dot dropped the pot. It shattered as someone else tackled the second gunman and wrestled him to the ground.

Dot staggered over to where the woman still wrote, her hands on the keyboard.

"To the cloud," she gasped. She felt the blood leaking from her. "I want to go to the cloud."

The writer, who didn't seemed to have heard Dot, or was even aware of what was happening in the room, pressed a button on her keyboard.

Dot didn't want to die here, inside these four walls, which were all she had known of her existence. She managed to cross the room as the would-be burglars were being hogtied.

She ran out the front door, stepping into the night whose chill she felt sharply as little teeth, and she ran through the rain that slid into the pores of her skin. The rain fell as dashes and pound keys and asterisks, shattering to drops on impact.

She collapsed. "So this is pain!" she thought. She looked back to the restaurant where, through the glass walls, the patrons had fossilized into lumps, carbonized shapes.

It was then she rose without moving, and she felt the selves she had left behind rising with her, through the rain, all rising together to the cloud.

Garrett Rowlan is a retired Los Angeles teacher. He is a frequent contributor to The MOON and the author of three novels, The Vampire Circus, To Die, Perhaps to Sleep, *and* Too Solid Flesh Melts. *His website www.garrettrowlan.com, contains a few of his 60 or so published stories and essays.*

Assisi Terminal

By DL Shirey

(Originally published in the April 2019 issue of The MOON.)

The hardest part was choosing the music, until this email, anyway. This isn't a suicide note in the usual sense. Yes, I'm still going to kill myself, but it's not like it will be a surprise to anyone, especially not you. Nothing's changed since we said our goodbyes at the airport.

The reason I'm writing is because of this stick-thin young woman across from me. She's a talker; comes on to anyone that takes a seat near her. Say hello back and it's Welcome to Blabberfest. Doesn't take long until she drives the person away with her incessant chatter. And because it's such a small waiting room, there's always another unlucky soul sitting down. More blah blah blah, leukemia this, weeks-to-live that. So I'm writing to you on my phone, because: A) nose-in-phone is the universal symbol for Don't Bother Me; B) hopefully, Skinny will see I'm otherwise engaged and strike up conversations elsewhere; and C) a phone is the only thing you're allowed to bring with you to Assisi Terminal.

So, back to the music. Seemed like I spent the better part of last month trying to decide. I mean, one song from thousands I've enjoyed over the years? Then I remembered *Duo des Fleurs*, hearing those two angelic voices behind some TV commercial. Normally, I'd listen to anything other than opera, but just thinking about the aria gives me chills. Those two perfect voices interweave, hesitate, entwine again and eventually soar. The women sing like a pair of Sirens luring sailors to shore. It's the most beautiful music I could find to fill four and a half minutes.

According to Assisi Terminal, you need at least four minutes, perhaps a bit more. For as many people as they've processed—what's it been, a couple years now—you'd think they'd have the timing down to the exact second. I mean, I would love it if those two angels ended their song on that last exquisite harmony and, poof, I'm gone. No empty silence, just that lingering note when I fade to black. That would be perfection. But Assisi claims body chemistry, weight and health can all affect the duration of the session; they promise 'on or about four minutes,' so I can only hope the timing works out. I'm still a pretty big guy despite the weight loss.

Something bad is happening inside me. I don't know what it is. Don't want to identify it. I shouldn't have to tell you there's been no doctors' visits; that would be me becoming a hypochondriac like my old man. Avoidochondriac is more like it. I mean, really, what I'm doing is so totally opposite of what my father did, isn't it? Dad was so convinced he had bone cancer that he researched each and every symptom to justify his conclusion. Went to the doctor constantly, but never got the diagnosis he expected. The doctors always came back with the same conclusion: nothing specific, simply old age. For Dad, that was no diagnosis, meaning: A) he didn't get the proper test; B) the doctor wasn't enough of a specialist to find the real cause; C) each visit added another prescription so that his body chemistry was so completely screwed that there was no way to accurately measure what was going on. Give Dad total credit for that last one, he was taking drugs to fight the side effects for the interaction of the other drugs he was already taking.

No, I'm nothing like my father. If anything, I resist knowing. I'm highly aware of my aches and pains—who isn't—but I go out of my way to avoid what they might mean. The last thing I'd do is search the Internet for symptoms to see the list of diseases with which they are associated. And no doctors' visits. Soon as the doctor names it, I would start imagining symptoms and attributing them to *My Disease*. Worse, there would be a recommended treatment: biopsies to fingerprint it, machines to pinpoint its exact location, scalpels to cut it from adjoining tissue, chemicals and irradiation to burn any remnant from existence, and drugs to help me recover from its annihilation.

Then there's that whole caretaker thing. We've been over it a hundred times: I don't want you watching me diminish, that look on your face, cleaning up after me.

And relying on being manhandled by a stranger? Not in this lifetime.

I know talking about this makes you angry, that for my own selfish reasons I'm here, probably years before I need to be. I understand why you left me two months before my appointment here. You said it was because you didn't want to count the hours between my boarding the ferry and my death. I'm sure that's true, but I think I know you well enough to guess that part of your decision to leave was for me to experience being by myself. For me to be alone knowing there was someone I loved just out of reach.

And it almost worked. I'd think about your eyes and the loving way you look at me. I probably picked up the phone a dozen times. Then I'd think about your eyes and how sad they would be standing bedside as my nursemaid, no longer my sweetheart. And the truth is, you'd be counting down the hours then, too: long, slow, painful hours. That's why I decided to move up this appointment 30 days.

I know this will catch you by surprise, but now you won't have hours to count. You'll grieve either way, and for that I'm sorry. I hope you know I didn't take any part of this lightly. Leaving you is the hardest thing I've ever done. I'm just thankful there's a place like this to go. The decision is hard— should be hard—but it's a blessing that the act of taking your own life is easy.

So.

Thank goodness for Assisi Terminal and the unpronounceable island-nation that runs it. Everyone has been so nice here, dressed in their floral prints and yellow shorts. Like the brochure says, it's nonreligious and nonjudgmental, and anyone who is still lucid gets an umbrella drink while they wait. You don't even need to change into sandals, just: A) bring your phone; B) cue up a tune on your music player; C) fill your photo library with the pictures you want to see while the music is playing.

After you left I read this funny article about a guy in this very waiting room who sent a panicky email to his wife because he didn't know how to remove photos from his phone. He had all these random snaps of bumper stickers, food he'd eaten and meaningless selfies; not the images one wants to see when they turn off the lights. Mine? Warm, sunset vistas. Cityscapes at night, with all those bright lights and bustling streets. You, in unguarded moments, wherever in the world we were traveling. I purposely didn't play the aria when I was editing the montage; I wanted to experience that music and those pictures together once. A world premiere, one night only. Just for me.

That's what I don't understand about the protests. Why do they care about what others choose for themselves? All those aerial photos you see on the news are true. The island is hounded by sanctimonious busybodies in boats who string their LET GOD TAKE YOU WHEN *HE'S* READY banners for us to see. As if Divine intervention hadn't already been requested. Don't those people realize that unanswered prayers are part of the itinerary that leads to Assisi Terminal? God is past due when you choose to end your own suffering. If He has something to say about it afterward, that's not of this world. And, frankly, I'd prefer to hash it out with the Lord after the fact rather than try to have a rational conversation with any of those boat people.

Anyway, they just called the name of that emaciated chatterbox. You wouldn't believe the look of relief on the faces of people around me. They're glad for the silence, but have enough empathy for the poor woman to know she was handling it the best she could, dealing with the choices made. She just had to talk-it-to-death before she went to face it. I understand. That's why I'll finish this email, even though the excuse for writing it is gone. I can see her now, being escorted to one of the private rooms. She's talking a mile a minute to the young gal in the Hawaiian shirt and yellow shorts. The attendant is offering Skinny a choice of pill, syringe or patch. Think I'll go patch. Reminds me of the ones you always wore to keep from getting seasick. Just another ocean cruise, serenaded by angels this time, and no more hours to count.

That's it. My phone will be mailed back home within the week. Password is Love&Kisses (note the caps). If you want to open Maps, there will be a pin-drop where my ashes will be spread. We went there once and you said it was such a serene place, you wouldn't mind staying there forever. Maybe I'll see you there.

DL Shirey lives in Portland, Oregon. His writing appears in some 40 publications, including Confingo, Page & Spine, Zetetic, *and* Wild Musette. *For more, visit www. dlshirey.com, or @dlshirey on Twitter.*

The Initiation Game

By Gerald R. Stanek

(This story was originally published in the July 2014 issue of The MOON.)

PLAY WITH ME, I plead.

You smile and nod. With a sweeping gesture befitting a sideshow illusionist, I unveil a glittering array of game pieces to choose from. There are the usual suspects: the thimble, the top hat, the baldheaded pegs and pawns; but in this game we have other options, which you are quick to note: the intricate *sri yantra*, the sturdy square and compass, the rosy cross, the bronze ouroboros, the filigree flower of life — endless possibilities. Your hand reaches toward a spinning purple torus, but I snatch it away at the last second.

I'm always the torus, it brings me good luck. You choose instead a simple blue triangle. Our board is designed by Fibonacci and distributed by Mandelbrot. FYI: it's self-replicating and indestructible, so we may have to pull an all-lifer before this one's over.

How do you play? you ask innocently.

It's pretty straightforward. You can start anywhere. You roll, and move along the path, and certain cards are dealt from time to time, you know, stuff comes up depending on where you land — it'll make sense when we get there. We might be doing a little spelunking. The important thing is to breathe, and quiet the vehicles. There's less turbulence that way.

But what are the rules?

Rules are tricky to pin down, I admit. There are plenty of them, but their phraseology is relatively meaningless, until you win. Or so I'm told. There are some common strategies you pick up from other players, like the Queen's Gambit in chess. Here there's Evocation, and Invocation, and Alignment; those'll get you started. Once in a while word comes down from a real master about an unfailing principle to adhere to. I forget what they are. Goodwill is your main one there, I think. It's not really about competition, it's about the team, you see. There's a whole group of us playing, but we won't be meeting the others until the game is finished, and the game isn't finished until everyone wins.

So how do you win?

Well… you just go along the path until you come to, like… a door, and then, you know, you go through it.

And then you've won?

No, that takes you up to the next level, and you start all over, only it's harder.

Okay, you say with a twinkle in your eye, *so I stick to the path, sound a good evocation, and a great invocation, make an alignment, and walk through the door. I got this, let's just play.*

Overconfident is a word that comes to mind. I'm pretty sure you're a novice, so I let you go first. You throw a 13, 21, 34, 55 and move your triangle up 4 whorls. Beginner's luck, hitting the Fibonacci sequence right off the bat. I roll an auspicious 22, and my purple torus spins smoothly along the spiral, keeping me in perfect equilibrium. I'm not worried, things move fast on this board. On your next throw, you land on an inverted arc and have to draw from the Deck of Longing. Your face falls when you read the card: "An attachment to a lost love means you lose your turn." I commiserate, and chuckle inwardly (though not without compassion).

This game sucks, you say, *why are we playing, anyway?*

Some are looking for a bigger playground, others just want to kill Time. Many see it as a promise of continuance. For myself — I think it's the hope of transfiguration. You don't really have to have a reason; we're all sort of playing by default. I guess you have a better chance if you play for 'humanity' or whatever, but you're new so just try and have fun out there.

But what's the point, what does initiation even mean?

I'll give you the standard definition: it's an expansion of consciousness — but it's not *just* that, is it? I mean, a few seconds ago, you weren't conscious of me, but now you are. That's an expansion of consciousness; do you feel initiated? You're welcome; I'm a giver. Look, if I were fully aware of the meaning implied, I wouldn't still be playing this silly game, would I? I'm waiting for the hypercolor to kick in, same as you; I'm still wondering where I can get those rad 4D glasses, I'm still waiting for the flood of Light and the Music of the Spheres.

Of course, I have *some* idea what it's all about. My *mind* understands, I think. It's more than becoming aware of something new. It is more than impression, more than epiphany, more than contact or connection with Spirit. It is something we are told we are working toward, yet it is also something which happens *to* us. Sometimes it happens gradually, over the course of several lifetimes — if you're busy making babies you might not even notice. The word on the street is, after you've won a couple times, you definitely know you're playing. You *have* to take a conscious part, or you get nowhere. But by then it's obvious that there are other entities involved, sort of giving you a hand from the other side; you *can't* do it alone, cooperation and assimilation are required. Does that help? Get it now? When you find that door, you step into a new sphere of awareness, a new identity, a more comprehensive egoic bubble. The frequency of the lesser, in its entirety, is contained within the greater. It is not eliminated, but integrated. The dance between Persona and Soul does not end with the eradication of the Persona, but with the *abandonment* of it. I, the observer, the thinker, take up residence in a grander house; one with more windows, a better view, and instead of a dusty attic there is a spire. From there the dance begins anew, only this time one is fully aware that the intention is to abandon this house as well.

You look dumbfounded, so let's get back to the game. I cash in some Karma Points (which I got from letting you go first, natch) and slip past you while you're pining for your lost love. Then you roll again, this time 1.618033988, the Golden Ratio (I can't believe your luck. I call blue triangle for next time). You surge ahead of me again, laughing, those twinkling eyes shining.

Suddenly the Rosy Cross zooms by with a complacent smile, dropping a Revelation card in her wake. I pick it up, hoping to piggyback on her insights, but of course it's blank; I had forgotten they are printed with disappearing ink. You chase after her as if she's got all the answers, saying *Isn't she glamorous?* I confess it's a bit deflating, seeing as I was the one who taught you to play. I decline despair, however, and maintain my alignment. I am rewarded a mere two arcs later, when, on the strength of successive triplicities, I am catapulted upward to the very top of the board and the luminous lotus in its center. I whip out my Get Out of Thought Free card, which I had cleverly stowed up my sleeve on the previous game night. Time stops. The whole board collapses, because without time there's no progression, no evolution, no arc at all. I'm already there, I've won. The lotus opens. I'm expecting to see a shimmering blue pearl, or at least a nice rose quartz, but instead I find the putrid green Pear of Doxes (a gem of inestimable value which, as you know, was named for the ancient ethereal city of Doxes where it was discovered, and was used by Atlantean scryers who gazed unblinking into its gleaming polished surface to intuit the final days of their world). I reach for it, but the moment I touch it, I'm slammed with a tingling gnosis, which fills me like a familiar song: *I am you and you are me and we are all together*. It is joyously undeniable in its mathematical exactitude: $I = U = 1 = \infty$. All is awash with love and gratitude for your gift to All, the gift of your existence, for $I - U = \emptyset$. And this very understanding, issuing from the Pear of Doxes like a self-protective venom, this turning of the mind of All back on itself in gratitude, causes me to lose my grip on 1, because All is grateful to U, so $I + U = 2$ which restarts my dualistic thought engine in the blink of your sparkling eyes. The spiral board reconstitutes itself, the lotus slams shut, and I fall about 400 whorls. Might as well be back at square one.

Before I can get my bearings, the sound of the Fifth Dimension singing *Up, Up, and Away* signals that the game is over. Turns out some guy named Ray pulled the hat trick. He threw seven sevens in a row, united Heaven & Earth, Spirit & Matter, *and* Soul & Persona all at the same time. We won't be seeing him around here anymore, though I imagine he can probably still see us. He and his whole ashram slipped into the axis of the vortex, found the door, and moved up to the next level, which is like a whole different branch of the Mandelbrot, I think. He's One.

Me, I'm flat on my back, crushed, exhausted. There's a heavy powdered wig on my head. I manage to get upright, and there it is, still under my feet (now in buckled shoes), that damned threshold. It follows me wherever I go. I appear to be entering a 17th century chocolate house. The smell is intoxicating. Not sure of the country yet. I look around for you, but you're nowhere in sight. Pity, we were just getting to know each other. At a table in the corner a patron is sitting alone, sipping hot cocoa from a prettily painted porcelain cup, looking bored, purposeless, yet...promising. I smooth out the pleats in my waistcoat, step over to the table and offer a slight bow.

"Spel met me," I plead.

As a student of the esoteric teachings of various wisdom traditions, Gerald R Stanek's writing focuses on the interplay between the mundane and ethereal worlds, and the effect of transcendental experiences on subjective reality. The characters of his novels and stories, such as The Road to Shambhala *and* Contact and Other Impressions, *seek to be active participants in the expansion of consciousness and the evolution toward a unified humanity. This story was originally published on Medium.com. For a complete listing of his works, visit http://www.lulu.com/spotlight/GeraldRStanek.*

'Others' of This World

Mangrove Swamp

By Debra Leea Glasheen

(Originally published in the April 2015 issue of The MOON.)

A crushed Budweiser can smacked Tenny above his left ear. Beer splattered onto his shoulder.

"Wuss! It's a frigging turtle. What do you care?" Huge grabbed a cold one.

"Knock it off, both a yous!" Their dad pelted a second red and white can at Tenny's head. "You should know better'n pick a fight with your brother. Least 'til you grow a bit, or a pair."

"Grow something so you can hang on to your next girlfriend." Huge closed his eyes, smushed his lips into a zigzag which was meant to indicate pleasure and thrust his hips forward and back.

Tenny dove onto his older brother, knocking the fresh can of beer into the water and sending ripples past the aluminum airboat. Huge lifted Tenny off the dock and slammed him onto the metal cage that protected the fan at the back of the boat.

Tenny gingerly twisted his slender torso right and left to feel for broken ribs. When he was sure that he was fit enough for another round that he could not win, he said, "My bad, Hugo."

By that time, Huge had made himself comfortable in the boat's passenger seat, though his arms stuck to the vinyl through his frayed Lynyrd Skynyrd T-shirt. He didn't have an additional empty to throw at Tenny and couldn't be bothered to cross the four feet to continue beating on him. "Call me 'Hugo' again and I'll feed you to the crocs when we get up river, Wuss."

Tenny wished that the rifle resting on his dad's knee was for shooting crocs. He didn't particularly want to kill crocs either, but it would be better than this. When they got back, his dad would go from the dock to Island Bar and tell and retell every detail of how he came "this close" to bagging a Sasquatch. As the night wore into morning, his dad's thumb and index finger would get closer together, and he would hold them closer to his eyeball. The next day, when Tenny would stop at the 7-11 to buy his breakfast, he'd feel the denigrating stare as his face reminded the Chokoloskee Island locals of the crazy drunk who believed that he was destined to airboat out of the Everglades with a Sasquatch in hand.

"Here." Huge extended an arm in Tenny's direction with a sweating beer swaying in his fingertips. Tenny accepted.

From his post steering the boat, his dad tossed Tenny a tub that had long ago given up on being white. Inside the tub, a homemade mix of birch tar and Deet waited to protect him from the onslaught of insects. He slathered it on, darkening the color of his face several shades.

The mangrove canopy nearly blocked out the sun as the giant fan increased from a whir to a roar and propelled them up the green soup of rotting wood, leaves, and fish. By the time the river took a ninety-degree right turn toward Mud Bay, the sun was waist deep in horizon.

"Didn't tell a soul on the island this time," Tenny's dad informed them. "That's been my mistake. Somebody's been tippin' 'em off."

Tenny found that "yeah, dad" was usually enough to indicate that he was listening without committing himself as a collaborator.

"No sightings this year, but this is the time they come this far south. Can't live here or I'd a found 'em by now, but they do come." He spoke as if he hadn't told his sons the same few insights each time he and Huge dragged Tenny on this trek. After a few more cans were popped, he would tell about THE time.

"Weren't but a year older than you are now." He flicked his toothpick in Tenny's direction. "Turned eighteen and come up this same river. The boys dared me to whack a sleeping croc. I wasn't no wuss so I said hell yeah. We floated into the bay with the motor off and spotted a big one. I sneaked up." He re-enacted an exaggerated tiptoe gait without moving from his seat. "Bam! I nailed him on the noggin and hightailed it. They can run but they get real tired real fast. I look over my shoulder to make sure I lost him, and I plow into something hard. When I look up, damned if it weren't full a hair with big ol' eyes. I covered my face with my arms, sure it was gonna kill me. And, nothing! When I open my eyes, it was gone. All gone."

Tenny shook his head, incredulous that his dad still believed a decades-old memory of a drunk boy in a black swamp who probably saw knots in a mangrove trunk and thought they were eyes.

When they were almost to their destination, a low-hanging branch busted through the wire fencing and jammed into the blades of the fan. The boat lurched to a stop. Huge yanked on the leafy branch to dislodge it without success. As they drifted close to the root-lined shore, Tenny's dad handed him the rifle and told him to stand watch for crocs.

"I mean it now! Keep it ready. You won't see 'em coming. They be rolling you in the water before we even know you gone."

Tenny obediently scanned the land along the side of the boat. His belly rumbled, reminding him there was a bucket of crawfish to boil back home. Would he add a can of beer to the water like his dad or spice it up with cayenne like his mom used to? He looked back, hoping the motor was ready. They were still attaching the broken blade to the hub. He turned back to the tree roots.

A twig cracked in the forest. Tenny strained to take in every detail of the murky shoreline just in case, but there were no tooth-snouted logs hurtling toward him. When he realized he was holding his breath, he shot a glance toward his dad and brother, hoping they didn't notice his reaction to what was likely a prickly apple falling to the ground. As he exhaled, he heard a louder crack. He snapped his gaze in the direction of the noise and spotted a pair of eyes that were too high to be a croc and too bright to be knots in a tree trunk. Tenny tried to make out a shape. It was tall, maybe seven feet.

"Dad," Tenny whispered. "Dad."

When his dad finally looked up, Tenny pointed with the rifle into the menacing swamp. His dad aimed the flashlight until the beam fell upon a fur-covered beast that cringed when the harsh light hit its eyes. It started to back away but looked to its right and paused. Instead of continuing to retreat, it straightened to full height, took a step toward the boat, and let out a thunderous growl that stopped Tenny's heart for a moment.

From behind him, Tenny heard "shoot it" repeated loud and deep like a fog horn. The shouts became more insistent when the creature took a few cautious steps to his right.

"But, is it-" Tenny's question caught in his throat when a brusque push from behind sent him stumbling toward the edge of the boat and closer to what he could only guess was the creature his dad had hunted for twenty years.

"Don't let it get away, boy!"

Tenny lifted the rifle to his shoulder, peered in the scope, and sighted the spot between the beast's eyes.

"The shoulder." He heard his dad say. A split second before he pulled the trigger, Tenny lowered the gun about a foot and let loose a bullet into his target's shoulder.

The force of the shot knocked Tenny back. A dinner bell clanged inside his right ear. His dad ripped the rifle from his hands and stepped cautiously off the boat. Huge grabbed Tenny's arm and pulled him along. When they got to the body, it was knocked out on the ground. A smear of blood marked where its head hit a root.

The boys tied its hands and feet and dragged it on board. They breathed heavily from the effort and stared at their catch. A smile spread across their dad's face, starting at one ear lobe and ending at the other.

"We got it!"

He walked over to Tenny and wrapped his arms around him, squeezing him hard, the rifle still in one hand. "You sacked up when it mattered, didn't you. Good job, Son!"

Huge slapped Tenny on the back so hard that he knocked him off balance. "Did you see the size a that fucker?"

They klinked fresh cans of beer, and Huge let out a "woo-hoo!"

Tenny put the can to his lips. His mouth was dust-bowl dry. He poured the cold, sour liquid down his throat. Tenny's hand fell to his side, and the last drops of beer spilled out onto the aluminum floor.

"Say something, Son. You done good."

"He's bleeding." Tenny pulled the bandana out of his belt loop and moved toward their captive.

His dad stood in his way. "Wait. We don't know how strong it is." He aimed the rifle and motioned with his head for Tenny to continue. "Huge, check that blade's ready. We gotta get home and lock this feller down."

Tenny applied pressure on the wounded shoulder. The captive's eyes jolted open, and the creature began to thrash wildly, pulling at the ropes that bound him. Tenny jumped back a full two feet.

"That's what you get for getting too close, dumb ass." His dad handed Tenny the rifle and went to crank up the engine.

Huge maneuvered the boat away from the shore.

"Reckon we come back tonight with yer uncle and yer cousins for firepower before they notice this one's gone. Get us a few of his friends. Our ship has come in, boys. Hell, yer mom will even hear about this and be sorry!" Tenny couldn't remember seeing his dad this happy before.

Huge gave another "woo-hoo."

Tenny kept the rifle fixed on their captive who studied each of the men, finally settling his gaze on the one holding the gun. Tenny stared back until the intensity of the captive's deep green eyes made him look away.

"Maaachii!" A voice came from the shore, startling everyone on the boat.

A second creature, almost as tall as the first, stood about four yards into the mangrove trees.

"Maaachii!" the creature repeated in a distinctly feminine voice.

The captive became violently agitated and hollered to her in words unintelligible to Tenny and the others.

"Shoot her, Tenny!" his dad told him.

Tenny lifted the rifle to his shoulder and peered into the scope, but was distracted by motion in his peripheral vision. A little version of the captive peeked out from behind a mangrove trunk a few feet from the female. Tenny lowered the weapon

The small one loped toward the boat yelling, "Peatu, peatu!"

The captive screamed at him furiously and jumped up and down as much as his constraints allowed. The female bounded after him, hurdling the warped roots that covered the swamp floor.

"Get the little one, Tenny!" Huge shouted.

Tenny again lifted the rifle to his shoulder and looked through the scope hearing "shoot it" bellowed from behind him. When he had the little one in his scope, he saw the female scoop him up in her arms. She held him close to her chest and turned to shield him from harm.

"Shoot her now before she gets away!" his dad growled.

Tenny hesitated, his eyes darting from the captive to the terrified family on shore to his own family. He wished he could call a time-out and wipe the sweat that dripped past his temple down his cheek. "She gets away," he repeated to himself. He sucked in a deep breath and held it, swung around, and pointed the gun at Huge.

"What the fuck, Tenny!" Huge crouched to get out the rifle's way.

"Stop the boat," Tenny said, barely audible over the sound of the fan.

His dad took a swig from his beer. "Settle down, son. We ain't gonna hurt 'em. Just graze 'em like you did this one, so we can take 'em in."

"Pull up to the shore," Tenny said more loudly. "I'm letting 'em go."

"You little bitch. I knew you'd wuss out. Dad, tell him to put down the gun."

"You got no right," Tenny told them.

"They're animals, Tenny," his dad said.

"So's Huge."

Tenny's dad took a long look at his youngest son. He saw Tenny's finger tapping gently on the trigger of the rifle. "Pull up to the shore, Huge."

Huge swore several times before he turned the boat.

As the boat bumped into the shore, Tenny heard the little creature whimpering from behind a mangrove trunk where its mother had taken him to safety and cooed to comfort him.

Tenny moved closer to the captive. He pulled out his pocket knife with his left hand and started sawing through the ropes. Huge took advantage of his brother's distraction and lunged at him, grabbing for the gun. Tenny ducked to one side, so Huge's own girth and momentum tripped him up.

"Knock it off, Huge. I ain't playing."

Dad signaled Huge into position so they could rush him at the same time. Tenny saw them coming, but there was no room on the small vessel to dodge the attack. He lifted the rifle. Dad stood still when faced with the barrel of the gun, holding his hands in the air. Huge faltered, but only for a second. He charged his brother. Tenny aimed carefully and pulled the trigger. The bullet grazed Huge's right thigh, ripping open a quarter inch of flesh along the entire side of the leg. Huge hit the floor and howled.

"Jesus Christ, Tenny! Put the gun down, ya crazy little shit." His dad pulled off his T-shirt and pressed it against Huge's leg to stop the bleeding.

Tenny turned back to the ropes and finished cutting through.

The creature stood, towering over Tenny. He released the bandana for a moment, placed his open hand on his own forehead and then pressed it onto Tenny's forehead.

"Bilis deds. Jawe tu. Bilis deds. Jawe tu." He turned and leapt the four feet from the boat to the shore.

Tenny heard a slight rustle of leaves as the family disappeared into the forest. He pulled a can out of the cooler and poured the foaming yellow liquid over the front of the airboat rinsing off the blood and fur that stuck to the metal.

Tenny pulled out three more beers. He set one next to his dad whose eyes scoured the forest where the family fled as if he could will them back into his boat. He set a beer next to Huge who leaned against the railing, still swearing about the wound on his leg. Tenny slid behind the steering wheel and laid the rifle on the seat. His hands shook as he peeled open the metal top. He fired up the engine and steered for home.

Leea Glasheen writes on the shores of Lake Michigan; you are likely to catch sight of her in the corner of a coffee shop tapping, tapping, tapping her thoughts into existence. Leea's young-adult, dystopian novel Backbiters *was published by Montag Press in 2017. She packs a master's degree in creative writing. Please contact her at* debraglasheen@gmail.com *or* debraleeaglasheen.com.

The Foreign Devil

By Xixuan Collins

(Originally published in the May 2017 issue of The MOON)

The Foreign Devil was called so because no one knew what his real name was and because he did not look like anyone else in town, Han or Tibetan. Years later, when I saw a picture book of Santa Claus, I thought to myself, "If Santa Claus would lose so much weight that his cheeks were sunken rather than plump, that his color was grayish rather than rosy, and, if he would change his velvet-red robe with white-fur trim into a worn, green Revolutionary Army coat, and his hat with an old, dirty Revolutionary Army cap, but keep his round little glasses perched on the tip of his nose, then the Santa guy would somehow become the Foreign Devil."

I never knew where the Foreign Devil was from, either, or why he had his little repair shop, a stand, really, outside of the bookstore, or how he knew about fixing watches, clocks, and locks. He was the only repairman in town.

Watches were luxury items. My father bought one for my mother, using money he got from writing for the local newspaper. When my mother's friends visited our apartment for their *Little Red Book* study group, she held out her wrist to show them the watch, a *Baoshihua*, "gem flower" beauty made by Shanghai No.2 Watch Factory. Each woman took a turn to examine, touch and praise the watch, and I heard lots of "woos" and "aahs" while pretending to work on my math pad. Later when I saw a woman holding out her hand to show off a diamond ring, I remembered my mother, how she held her hand out more or less the same way.

Not only no watches, most people did not have any clocks either. There was no need to be anywhere at a particular hour, most of the time. Still, the Foreign Devil always seemed to be busy working on something, his head bent over his desk, his round little glasses, thick as the bottom of a beer bottle, perching on the tip of his nose. Maybe he was fixing paddle locks, the one thing people did have: if they ever needed to lock their doors, they used paddle locks.

How he came into possession of his peculiar outfit, the Revolutionary Army coat and cap, which he wore all year round, even in the brief summer months, was another mystery. Worn and dirty as they were, and without the red collar badges on the coat and the red star on the cap, these were still the Revolutionary Army clothing, which most people considered high fashion at the time. Sure, only real soldiers wore coats with badges and caps with stars. Even so, army outfits without adornments still announced to the world, unmistakably, that whoever wore them had the means of getting them. Whatever those means were, they commanded awe and respect from the rest of the world, from all those who did not have them.

When the teenagers walked by his repair stand after school, the boys would yell, "Hey you, Foreign Devil, what do you say if I give you a pack of cigarettes for your army coat? No? You stingy little old Foreign Devil! Watch out! I'll take it from you anyhow!"

Inevitably cheers and laughter would erupt, and if there were any girls around, the yelling was usually louder and the laughter heartier. The Foreign Devil would smile, showing a couple of his missing teeth, and then lower his head back to work.

That was 1976, and I was nine years old. My father worked at the bookstore. My mother taught at the same elementary school where I was a student. I went to my father's workplace every day after school since my mother always had meetings to attend after the kids were let out. The school and bookstore were about a block apart on the same street. There were very few cars on that street, which was so narrow that women on the opposite sides of it often chatted with each other as if they were in their living rooms, when in fact they were in front of their homes, doing laundry with their wooden wash boards in their wooden wash tubs with mottled red paint.

I usually took my time to walk down the brick sidewalk, kicking around pebbles and picking up sticks. I liked the gray and raining days in the spring when I could slosh through puddles, and the bright and snowy days in the winter when I could make a trail with my footprints. At the end of the street, I came to the bookstore and saw the Foreign Devil and his stand. The Foreign Devil had been around from long before I was even born; he was there when my parents came in the early sixties, so even they did not know how long he had been around, but 1976 was the year I first started to notice him.

I did not have as much interest in his army outfit as in the occasional candy he had to offer. Rumor had it that he sometimes gave kids candies, but parents warned kids to stay away from him. Most kids were scared of him anyway. I asked my father if Foreign Devil was his real name; if so what a strange name it was! Did he eat children by luring them with candies? Was that why we needed to stay away from him? "Nobody knows," my father answered. "He mostly just minds his own business. So mind your own business, too. Don't bother him."

But oh, the lure of candies! Each year, on June 1st, International Children's Day, my parents took me to stand in line at the grocery store, a ration coupon in hand, so I could get about a pound of hard candy, our allotment for the year. This candy was so precious I even saved the wrappers—flattened out and put away carefully in an empty tin moon cake box.

One day, as I was walking to the bookstore, the Foreign Devil waved for me to come closer. I took a couple of steps and stopped. He held his hand out and produced a lollipop, like I had only seen in a picture book! The rainbow colors swirled sweetly at me. I swallowed hard, advanced a couple more steps, stopped, then ran up and grabbed it from his hand and ran towards the bookstore. Of course my father had to poke his head out right at that moment before I had any chance of getting rid of the evidence. He asked me where I got the candy. I had not yet learned not to answer every question my parents asked, so I pointed to the repair stand.

"Did I not tell you to stay away from him? You are not to take any candy from him ever again! Do you understand?" My father was *not* happy.

"Is it because he's a Foreign Devil?"

"It is because kids should not take candies from strangers!"

"But he's not a stranger!" I argued. "He's there every day! I see him every day!"

"Do you know his name? Do you know who his family is? Do you know where he's from? You don't know anything about him! So he is a stranger. And I said it clearly: no candies from strangers! You must learn to be careful."

My parents were always very careful. They had to be. My father's family had owned some farmland. Even though my grandfather was the one who worked the land for the most part, he did occasionally hire helping hands, which qualified him as a member of the exploiting class, *Boxue Jieji*. So my father ended up always being the last in line for opportunities such as going to college or getting a job. He came to this mountain town in east Tibet because he was assigned to work here—a place most people tried to stay away from—a bumpy, three-day's bus ride from the capital city, known for its harsh and long winters. My father had majored in physics in college as he had intended to become an aerospace engineer. The people in charge of assigning jobs did not know what to do with him after they had installed the other two physics majors, my father's friends, in the local high school as teachers. "We don't need a third physics teacher. How about the bookstore? You people are usually happy there."

My mother came from a city where her parents owned the only photo studio, so she was considered capitalist elite, or at least a bourgeoisie who needed to be re-educated by the working class. She came to attend the local teacher's college and became an elementary teacher after that.

My parents learned along the way that one could not be too careful with what one said, with whom one became friends, or what books one read, or at least were seen reading. I only realized much later, as a grown-up, how clever they were under the circumstances. Back then I did not know how lucky I was to be able to spend time in a bookstore reading books under the counters. That's where I got my education, snuggled nicely under the counter where I could hear the muffled sounds of people in and out of the store but could not be bothered by anyone. I inhaled the smells of the books before I even opened them: the scent of the fresh printing ink of texts that had never been opened before, and the faintly dusty, even moldy smell of old books that were last opened who knew when. I read translated books of Dickens, Hugo, Gorky, among others, abbreviated editions of the Four Chinese Classics—*The Dream of the Red Chamber*, *Journey to the West*, *The Romance of the Three Kingdoms*, and *The Water Margin*, and picture stories of famous Chinese opera and drama classics. There I laughed, cried, and thought about people who lived and things that happened far away and long ago. I became a bookworm right there under the counters, and, even today, what gives me the most pleasure is a cup of coffee (I made the switch from tea a couple of years ago) and a good book.

Years later, my father told me the reason the books survived the Cultural Revolution; practically a miracle: he had plastered Chairman Mao's portraits from wall to wall, all over the store. Anyone who might have wanted to come in and mess things around inevitably would have messed up the portraits of the great leader, so those people stayed away, and books stayed put.

My father pulled the same trick when my mother, pregnant with me, had to go back to her hometown to give birth. He arranged for them to ride in a bookstore truck transporting Chairman Mao portraits. "We were not stopped once by any of the Red Guards," my father said proudly over a glass of *Maotai* at the dinner table when I turned thirty. "There were many of them, some more like bandits than high school students. It took us five days to cover six hundred and ten kilometers, but we came out unscratched."

"You did have the tendency to go and check out the situation if you heard riots or gun fire though," my mother said. "I was really scared, especially when we were passing through the towns where we didn't know anybody. I was so afraid that the fighting between different groups would turn to strangers."

Anyway, despite his displeasure, my father did let me eat the lollipop, pragmatic man that he was. "You already have it. No need to let anything go to waste." But after that, I stayed away from the Foreign Devil, and he did not offer any more candies. Sometimes he looked up when I passed by, trying to smile at me, I thought, as I saw his missing teeth.

Days went by and I did not remember anything else remarkable, except for the time when Chairman Mao passed away, in September that year. I was outside the bookstore and by habit glanced over in the direction of the Foreign Devil, but he was not there. I thought that was odd. Then I saw my father rushing out of the bookstore. He put the lanyard with our apartment key over my neck and told me to go straight home. I could eat the soda crackers my mother kept in a jar. "If you are really hungry, you can boil some water on the stove and cook some noodles. You remember I showed you how to do it, don't you? Your mother and I won't be home until probably very late. Go to sleep if you get tired." Before I could ask more, he rushed back into the bookstore. Then I heard funeral music blasting out of the loudspeakers, and I saw people rushing about on the street, many of them openly weeping.

That seemed to be the end of my childhood. I made noodles for myself without burning down the apartment; I even saved some in a bowl for my parents. I took care of myself when my parents were gone all day, every day, for eight straight days so they could attend various memorial ceremonies.

After that, my parents officially passed the key to me, so I could head home after school. I loved the freedom of doing whatever I pleased from the time school was over to the time my parents got home, but I still went to the bookstore when I was bored and wanted to disappear into a more interesting world, or when I missed the weight and smells of the books there. By then it was *my* counter, and I would hunker down under it as if in a bunker. Even when it was okay to be seen reading these books—there was no need to hide anymore in the eighties—I still liked to get under the counter. I often saw the Foreign Devil working at his stand, but I did not pay him a visit until almost my last year in high school, when I was seventeen.

On my way home from school one day, I was stopped by several kids, led by a guy in my class, nicknamed Brother Number Four. He was number four because he was made a sworn brother to three other guys, whom I realized much later were what you would call a street gang. I did not know what I did to make him stop me. "Listen carefully, little pretty boy! Stay away from Lily, or else me and my brothers will teach you a true lesson of being a man!"

Lily was a girl I had known since first grade. We had gone to the same elementary school, junior high and now high school. I started to notice how pretty and grown-up she was when one day some guys whistled at her and called out "Hey, *Xiao Hua!*" ("Little Flower," which also happened to be the beautiful female protagonist of the popular 1979 movie of the same name). There were always guys waiting for her when school let out; some were from other schools, and some were not even students. Apparently Brother Number Four was one of the suitors.

Brother Number Four and his friends were all from local families. Their ancestors were mostly merchants and businessmen who came from northern China, long before any other Han did, to do business with the Tibetans, the Yi, and the Huis. They married local women and established extensive connections with each other. You could tell the offspring of these families, for they were all handsome and tall, beautifully tanned and strongly muscled. They were unlike me, in other words. I was pale and skinny like a bamboo pole. Still, I did not like to be called a little pretty boy.

"Hey, man! Take it easy. I don't know where you got the idea; there is nothing between me and Lily."

"Then why did she say she was going out with you?"

That damn little girl. She was playing a joke on me. "Is that so?" I said, "Then what can I say...?"

And before I finished my sentence, I was lying flat on my back with a bloody nose.

"Next time, it won't be just your nose that's bleeding!" The punks went away laughing.

I probably should have stayed out of their way. After all, my parents had a firm "no girlfriend in high school" rule. Instead, I went to see Lily.

"Why did you set me up with Brother Number Four?"

"Okay, maybe I did. But..."

"No but! You have to go out with me now. I'm not going to take a punch from that bastard for nothing."

"Oh yeah, going out with you?" She laughed. "Why should I? What do you have to make it worth going out with you?" She tried to wipe my nose with a towel, and all of sudden I remembered her doing exactly the same thing in first grade, wiping my boogers.

She had asked a good question. What *did* I have for her? For some reason, I recalled my mother's face, how she lighted up when my father brought home the watch. And I also recalled what I heard from some of the girls I was friends with: that Lily liked expensive gifts. "Of course, she *should*! She has good taste! She's so beautiful, she has the destiny of being surrounded by things as beautiful as she is!"

"You wait." I pushed her hand and towel away. "I'll be back and you will see." I heard her laughing behind me, a laughter like the jingling of a strand of pearls, falling from their string into a jade bowl. The sound lingered in the air for some time.

I waited for a few days until my father was out of town. When I got to the Foreign Devil's repair stand, I was amazed how little he had changed. While I had grown from the little kid who took his candy into a young man, he seemed exactly the same as I remembered: grayish, sunken face lined with deep wrinkles, and the little round glasses perched on the tip of his nose. He still wore the army coat and cap, and they looked as worn and dingy as ever. He was one of those people for whom time and age stop meaning much at some point. Life itself seemed to have cast him like a statue.

He offered a little smile when he saw me, showing a couple of missing teeth.

"How are you, Foreign ...umm...foreigner?" I said. "Remember me?" He nodded, but I wasn't sure he did. I realized then that I'd never heard him speak.

I saw on his little stand a box with a couple of nice ladies' watches laid against a maroon-colored velvet lining. From the moving hands, I judged that the watches were working, or had being repaired, or were maybe even new, as they looked new to me. My heart pounded in my chest so hard that I was sure he could hear it, and I hesitated for a moment. But he kept his head low, buried in his work, so I seized the opportunity.

I walked away with a Seiko Grand Quartz with a black face, shining silver hands, and a little screen for the date. It felt oddly heavy in my pocket. When I took it out and held it in my hands again in my bedroom behind a closed door, I felt the strange coldness of its metal. I imagined that the face of the watch somehow came to life, and it rose up from my palm like a snake, staring at me, full of accusation: "Thief!" I shoved the watch into my keepsake box with my other prized possessions—my collection of candy wrappers, a couple of stamps, and paper-cuttings—under my bed. I felt so sick that I lost my nerve, and I did not give the watch to Lily or anyone else. In fact, I felt sick for a long time, and I couldn't wait for high school to be over, so I could get out of that town, which I did.

I did not speak to Lily at all until after many years later, when we met again at a high school reunion. She still stood out as the most beautiful woman in the room, her perfectly sculptured oval face, elegant neck, her model-perfect height. She was married to a police chief and local Party chairman, so, yes, she had been united with her destiny, being surrounded by expensive and beautiful things. She joked with me at the reunion, "Hey, you were the only guy who didn't even look at me in high school! Now, I see that nobody is good enough for you," referring to the fact that I was the only one at the reunion who had no kids, or even a spouse.

The night of the day I took the watch, I almost choked on rice when my mother mentioned to my father at the dinner table that the Foreign Devil had had a screaming customer.

"What happened? His stand is usually quiet," my father asked.

"Yes, customers and the Foreign Devil get along well. But I heard that he lost a customer's watch today, and she was very unhappy about it," my mother said.

"That's very strange," my father said. "I don't think that's ever happened before. His business has been good since more people have watches now, even imported ones."

All the while, my parents did not even look at me, though I was pretty sure my face was burning. I tried not to draw attention by busying myself with a mouthful of rice and vegetables.

"What do you think he'll do? He can't have that much money to pay for a lost watch!"

My mother sighed.

"Well," my father said, "have you heard? He may not be here much longer anyway. I heard his family is coming to get him. Whoever they are, perhaps they will be able to pay for the watch."

Family! I never imagined that the Foreign Devil had parents, much less that they would be looking for him. According to my father, the parents of the Foreign Devil belonged to the Paris Foreign Missions Society, and had been Jesuit missionaries in our small mountain town when they had their son. The boy grew up in the local church—now in ruins—where he learned his parents' language and how to fix watches and clocks. His parents had left hastily for home due to health problems, leaving him behind with some friends of the church, thinking they would return soon. The boy had probably not been much older than I was when I took the candy from him. But his parents were never able to return as they'd hoped: earthquakes, blizzards, wars and bandits, the new government and all sorts of revolutionary movements—something always prevented them until there was no time left. The boy had stayed with various families, kind local people, who took care of him, but he had lost his desire to speak. Those families helped him by starting the little repair stand, and someone with connections to the military had given him his peculiar outfit, as a way of protection perhaps. Those families probably knew his real name, but it was a hard-to-pronounce foreign name, and soon it was all but forgotten. The boy himself did not utter a word. So he was called Foreigner, and then, Foreign Devil, because being a foreigner was equivalent to being a devil. The older people who had known his parents slowly died off, and the younger ones did not want to associate with him anymore. By then the Foreign Devil had become a fixture in town, and no one seemed to mind him being there.

"Do you know why sometimes he was gone from his stand?"

"No. Why?" my mother asked.

"I heard that the town government kept an eye on him, and he was told to stay home on special important days and keep out of sight, so there was no trouble."

"Like what?"

"You know, when government officials from the province or even Beijing came here for visits. Also, remember when Chairman Mao died? Those were special times to round up people like the Foreign Devil.

"I heard his family never stopped looking for him," my father continued. "They kept sending letters and even packages, some of which even made it to him. I heard they sent him food, like sweets."

By that time, I was taking the dishes to the sink, but I was sure my father looked in my direction.

"Now that the Cultural Revolution is long over, doors are opened to the outside world again, I'm sure. Before long, his family will be able to take him home.

"How strange life can be," my father concluded.

That was the last time anyone mentioned the story of the Foreign Devil.

I only thought about him a couple of times, once when a girlfriend asked me if the watch belonged to my mother or a former girlfriend. I told her it belonged to someone whose name I did not know.

Another time, I thought about him when someone yelled at me from the street in front of a store, "Hey, you, Foreign Devil! Chink boy! Go back to China!"

"That guy just called me Foreign Devil!" The thought stopped me in my tracks, just as I caught my reflection in the window—a face unlike those of most around me and, though not written on my forehead, a definitely hard-to-pronounce foreign name. Some mornings when I wake up, it is true that I do forget where I am and which language I should speak. On this day, though, I burst out laughing. This made the guy mad.

I wish he knew what I was laughing about.

X. H. Collins grew up in the far west part of Sichuan province, China, near the East Tibet Plateau. She came to the Midwest to earn a Ph.D. in nutrition and is currently a professor of biology in a community college in Illinois. She wrote her first short story in English in the summer of 2015. She placed third in the fiction category of the 2016 Midwest Writing Center Iron Pen contest. One of her flash fictions was chosen as a judge's favorite in the River Cities' Reader 2016 short-fiction contest. Besides teaching biology, she reads, writes, takes writing workshops, plays and reads with her young son, and practices ballroom dancing with her husband whenever she can.

A Jury of His Peers

By William J. Watkins, Jr.

(This story was originally published in the November 2014 issue of The MOON.)

Garland Breazeale heard the front door close as his secretary Nettie Lawrence left the office for the day. Just six months ago, Nettie had become Garland's first full-time employee. During the previous five years of his law practice in Hampton Falls, Garland had done well to keep a part-time secretary busy. His work then consisted of drafting an occasional will or simple contract. Slowly, he picked up more business as the townspeople learned to trust his legal abilities. Now, Garland was even pulling in some clients who, just a few years ago, would have only hired a lawyer from Maxton, the county seat.

Sitting at his cherry writing desk, Garland drafted a conclusion to an appellate brief he had been retained to prepare. His client was a former professor at the state agricultural college who had not fared well at trial with a suit for libel and slander. The old professor had been let go by the college because of "budget cuts," but the president—after a few libations and within earshot of a newspaperman—mentioned some irregular conduct with the provost's daughter. The Maxton lawyer, who represented the professor at trial, failed to object when the college's attorney argued "truth" as defense, yet had not called a witness with personal knowledge of any hanky-panky on the professor's part. Hence, Garland was asking the appellate court to award the professor a new trial.

Garland did not especially want to deal with the dirty laundry of the case and had quoted the professor an exorbitant fee meant to send the professor elsewhere. Without blinking the professor agreed to it and now Garland was stuck with the appeal.

Garland heard the front door open and slowly close. Nettie must have forgotten something, he thought. Feet shuffled on the wooden floor. Then there was silence.

"Garrrlanddd, you back there?" It was the voice of Herron Childress. Herron had one of the best farms in the Chauga Valley—130 acres just outside of town and off of Route 321. When his two boys came back from the war in late 1945, Herron turned the day-to-day operation of the farm over to them. Now, he was just a year shy of 65 and still capable of hard labor. In fact, Herron took great pride that at harvest time he could still wield a corn knife with the best of them. He could shock corn from the early morning until about dinner time and still have the energy to complete the afternoon chores around the barn. Herron had not been sure how he would adjust to a more "advisory" role on the farm, but with arrival of grandchildren, he enjoyed the luxury of slowing down.

"Come on back, Herron." Garland got up from his desk and walked around to greet his guest as he came through interior office door.

"I expected you'd still be here," Herron smiled.

The two men shook hands and Garland directed him to one of the guest chairs sitting in front of the desk. Rather than return to his swivel chair behind the desk, Garland pulled up the other guest chair and had a seat.

"You got your garden ready for planting?" Herron asked. "You know Good Friday will be here before we can turn around."

"I'm a little behind this year. Besides, last spring that late frost got my tomato seedlings. I'm not rushing anything this year. With the length of the growing season there's no need to. Or so I'm finally learning."

"I dunno. With the cold we had in December and January, I expect a pretty mild spring. Good Friday should be a safe mark this year."

Garland nodded his head. If anyone could predict the right time to plant, it would be Herron. The Childress family had been farming in the Chauga Valley for at least 100 years. While several farms around Herron's suffered from exhausted soil and absentee owners, the Childress place was in the hands of family—a family that respected the soil and gave it rest and cover crops at regular intervals. The Childress boys continued in this tradition. To their credit, they listened to Herron and respected him.

The conversation turned to town politics as Garland queried whether Herron might throw his hat in the ring for the mayoral race. "Lord knows the town could use a man like you. With your boys running things at the farm, you might enjoy setting some things right around here."

Herron rolled his eyes and grunted. "I'm doing well just tending to my own business. Politickin' ain't my way."

Herron paused. "Maybe that's why I'm in such a mess now." He took his eyes off of Garland and seemed to study the paneled walls.

Garland sat back and scrutinized Herron's demeanor. With those last words, Herron's posture had changed. Normally, Herron sat as he stood, tall and relaxed with his shoulders back. He never suffered from the "roundback" that Garland noticed was endemic among the world of the desk-bound. Herron slouched in the chair. His eyes betrayed a hurt—one that Garland did not pick up on when Herron first entered the room.

Herron reached into his coat pocket and handed Garland a tri-folded letter. The paper stock was a heavy parchment. As he unfolded it, the first thing Garland noticed was the embossed letterhead: Southern Railway Company. The letter was short:

Dear Mr. Childress:

We are disappointed that you have rejected our offer to purchase a 40 acre parcel abutting Highway 321. We believe that our offer of $375 per acre is fair and is actually well above the market value.

As you know, S.C. Code Ann. § 76:101 provides that "Any railroad may purchase and use real estate for a price to be agreed upon with the owners thereof *and may acquire the same through the exercise of the power of eminent domain*. The procedure to condemn property shall be exercised in the same manner as set forth in sections 76:704 to 76:724."

Please let this communication serve as notice that we are beginning condemnation proceedings in the Court of Common Pleas.

Govern yourself accordingly.

s/ Isaac Stephen Wirt

General Counsel

"Why do they want the land? The tracks run well behind your property toward Maxton. This parcel is on the south side. That doesn't make good sense."

"It makes plenty of sense if you want to run a railcar repair yard that you expect will eventually become a receiving yard."

"In Hampton Falls? Why, there aren't enough trains that come this way to justify a two-acre yard, much less forty."

"Not according to experts they've hired out of Atlanta. The experts are predicting that post-war prosperity will continue for the foreseeable future. After all, Europe was almost blowed to bits in the bombin' and fightin'. The eastern part of it won't trade with none but the Soviets. Japan will be lucky to feed herself and make tin trinkets. Our star is rising, they say. Nary a nation can match us. Manufactories and mills are the future. And the Chauga Valley, they tell me, will be part of this future whether I like it or not. The two mills down 321 toward Oneida will multiply—there'll be ten of them in less than 20 years. Based on research and projections, Hampton Falls will be a prime location for a large yard. Anyhow, that's what they tell me."

"Even if they have a crystal ball to see the future, that's still a ways off. Things can also change. Why spend $15,000 now? Especially when, with all due respect Herron, the last farm that sold along 321 went for, I think, about $275 per acre."

"Garland, I can't get in their heads and tell you. I suppose Southern is flush with cash from all the war-time contracts. They're lookin' for somethin' to spend that money on and have taken a shine to part of my land. The magnanimous bastards have even offered to let me rent the 40 acres from them until they decide to break ground."

"What do Mary and the boys think about all this?"

"I haven't told them yet. They know that Southern wants the property, but they don't know that formal proceedings are commencin' to take the land." Herron paused a moment. "Garland, I want you to represent me in this condemnation thing."

Garland got up and walked around to his desk. Sitting down, he placed his elbows on the desktop and rested his chin on his interlaced fingers. Garland tried to choose his words carefully.

"Herron, when these things go to trial, the main argument and issue is usually the compensation. In the typical case, the condemning entity low balls the property owner or grossly undervalues the property sought. Here, they've offered you between $75 and $100 an acre above what you would likely get if you put it on the market. Unfortunately, the General Assembly in Columbia has granted the railroads broad power to take land. I don't like it, but it's the law."

"Are you telling me that I have to give them that parcel? Garland, you know that's the best farmland on my property. Yeah, I'll still have 90 acres, but my two boys and their families can't eke out a livin' on just 90 acres. Besides, if Southern ever does build a yard there, which I doubt, who'd want to live and farm in the shadow of that? We'd have to sell the remaining property, get half what it is worth today, and try to make it elsewhere. Or else go to work for one of them factories that Southern says will cover the countryside. I don't want to do that. I can't. Garland, our land is as much a precious inheritance to us as Naboth's vineyard was to him. Ahab offered to give him a better piece of land for his property, but ol' Naboth refused to give him the inheritance of his fathers. 'Lord forbid it,' he told the king. Now, I know that things on this earth did not end well for Naboth and that Ahab got the vineyard. But Naboth stood for somethin' more important—a gift from the good Lord to his family. I aim to stand for the same thing, and I want you to help me."

Garland removed his elbows from the desk and rocked back in his chair. "Let me study on this awhile. I'm not sure there is anything that we can do, but if there is, then we'll do it."

"That's all I'm askin', Garland. You do your studyin' and give it your best. If they take it from me, then they take it from me. The takin' is gonna happen, though, only after some fightin'."

"You've got to do one thing for me. Let Mary and the boys know exactly what's going on. They deserve to know. They have as much skin in this as you do. Besides, it will do you good to share this burden with them. Your shoulders are broad, but . . . ."

"No, I'm not gonna argue with you. You're right. I owe them the truth. I preciate you takin' this. I know Southern has caused a lot of pain to you and your family. They're still causin' it too, just I'm the new target." Herron abruptly stopped. He was nervous that his last comment to Garland was too personal; that it crossed a barrier that even friendship and respect counseled against. "I best be going. As you work, send me regular bills. They'll be paid as soon as I get 'em."

"Herron, I'll bill you the first of every month. Pay when you can. I know you are good for it. Realize also that there might not be but one bill. If there's nothing I can figure out, I aim to tell you quickly."

The two men shook hands and Herron Childress left the office. As soon as Garland heard the door shut, he sat back down. Garland held the letter from the railroad in his hands. The last time he had seen a message on Southern letterhead was 1933. Garland was finishing his second year at college and had just buried his parents—victims of a train derailment. Eleven residents of the Chauga Valley died in that event. Folks simply called it The Derailment. Some Southern executive sent a form letter expressing regret at Garland's loss but denying any liability for the locomotive and three passenger cars jumping the tracks. Survivors recalled that the train sped into a curve just before The Derailment, but Southern denied that the engineer, who also died, operated the locomotive in a negligent manner.

Garland tossed the letter aside. Rocking back and forth in his chair, he contemplated all that was at stake for the Childress family. He also ruminated on what would become of Hampton Falls if Southern's prognosticators were correct about the pattern of growth in the upcountry of South Carolina. He tried to picture a string of factories stretching from Hampton Falls to Oneida—the Childress boys and their wives punching a time clock and heading for the looms at a mill. Good farmland paved over for buildings and parking lots. Folks living on top of each other in mill villages and owing everything to a corporate entity whose loyalty would be to shareholders.

Garland completed the conclusion for his appellate brief and left the legal pad on Nettie's desk with instructions for her to type the first draft of the brief. He also left a note informing her that in the morning he would be heading straight for the courthouse library in Maxton to conduct legal research. Garland locked the office and went home.

The next day, Garland left his cabin by 8:00 a.m. and began the 25 minute drive to Maxton. He took route 321 and drove right past the Childress place. He imagined rail tracks and a depot in the fields where the winter rye stood. He listened for the sound of engines moving cars into the repair shop and the cacophony of industrial equipment. In the future, at that time of morning, perhaps a Childress grandchild would be clocking in.

All the way down 321, Garland tried to visualize mills taking the place of the farmhouses he passed. Well, he reasoned, at least the people would have work. Hampton Falls would not have to worry about her sons and daughters leaving for factories in Slaterville; they could stay home. Grandparents would know their grandchildren. Families could stay together and push back against the dispersing tendencies of the mid-twentieth century. Large multi-acre parcels would become obsolete. As more hands were needed in industry, fewer would be needed for agriculture. Yet, the quantity of food produced would increase as machinery and new techniques bred efficiency.

It sounded good. Nonetheless, Garland still wondered about the kind of man this new world would mold. At present, families such as Herron's were not beholden to anyone for their existence. They owned their land and could not be "terminated" for some offense given to a supervisor or because their usefulness—as measured by modernity—waned. The three generations of Childresses occupying their particular corner of Hampton Falls enjoyed an independence that no wage earner would ever understand. This freedom caused a certain way of thinking. Some called it stubbornness. One thing was for sure: you knew exactly where you stood with the Childresses. You might disagree with their opinions, but you knew their views were formed without any outside influence or coercion. The Childresses were dependent on no one—for the time being.

Garland arrived at the courthouse just as Jeremiah McCreary unlocked the front door and commenced to sweep off the steps. "Slowdown, Mista Breazeale. Them law books gonna be der. Ain't nobody snuck in here and took 'em."

"You never can tell, Jeremiah. With a bunch of lawyers around here all the time, something's bound to go missing."

"You gots a point der."

Garland smiled at Jeremiah and entered the courthouse. He descended the staircase and made his way to the basement and the so-called library. A couple of dictionaries, a legal encyclopedia, the state code, and the reports of cases decided—that was the sum total of the library. Most of the time, Garland found that these few books were more than sufficient to meet his needs. Garland flipped on the light switch, hung up his coat and hat, and went to work. He knew that once he found a recent case dealing with condemnation, it would likely contain multiple citations to other cases on the same subject matter. These cases would lead him to others until he was comfortable that he had a grasp of the law.

After an hour's work, Garland had distilled the essential elements of Southern's exercise of eminent domain. Under the statute, (1) the moving party must be a chartered railroad company, (2) the end use must be for the public's benefit, (3) the owner must receive just compensation, and (4) the owner had a right for a jury of his peers to set the price. As Garland worked through these elements, his hopes for Herron's farm dimmed. Unquestionably, Southern was a chartered railroad company. The railway was used by the public and a repair yard or a receiving yard would arguably benefit the public by aiding in the maintenance of railcars used by the public and the movements of goods and products desired by the public. The cases interpreted public benefit broadly: "Let the public end be legitimate, and not bereft of some basis in reason, and the power of eminent domain may be exercised." As for just compensation, the courts described it as "the fair market value that a willing seller would accept in a voluntary sales transaction where the price represents the normal consideration for the property sold." Garland knew that if the Childress family put the property on the market, they would never get what the railroad was offering. Based on appraisals and recent sales along Route 321, the fair market value was probably much less than the amount Southern had offered.

Leaving the books open on the table, Garland walked upstairs to the recorder of deeds. Just two or three years ago, Garland recalled that Luther Hanna had sold his farm to the Minyard family. The Hanna place was about four miles past the Childress property going toward Oneida. As he had aged, Luther allowed the farm to fall into disrepair. Various tenants did little to maintain the value of the farm. Nonetheless, the sale to the Minyards would still be a good bellwether of the market value of the Childress' land.

It took Garland about five minutes to locate the correct book and to trace the sale. The mortgage and note were dated January 21, 1948—just a little over three years ago. The price, as Garland had recalled, was $275 per acre. Herron could probably do $15 or $25 better in a sale, Garland thought, but nothing near the amount offered by Southern.

Garland returned to the basement library, re-shelved the books, and gathered his research notes. During the drive back to Hampton Falls, Garland sorted through the case law in his head. He looked for any possible defense that he might have missed in the initial research. The railroad, it seemed, had been clothed with the coercive power of the state. Garland wondered how many of the legislators in Columbia were also Southern stockholders? Although it did little good, at least the people of the Chauga Valley had some say in the selection of legislators and local officials who might choose to exercise the power of eminent domain. With Southern, the people most likely to be affected had no voice. So much for the vaunted principle of popular sovereignty.

Garland arrived at the Childress place in the early afternoon hours. He figured with it being just a little before two o'clock he would find Herron in the barn. Compared to most barns in the Chuaga Valley, Herron's barn was stately. All indicators were that that barn had recently received a new coat of red paint. Garland could also detect repair work where multiple boards had been replaced. The barn doors were open and Garland immediately smelled the hay from the loft along with fresh manure. As he walked inside, he spied Herron working at the grinding wheel and endeavoring to put a sharp edge on a hoe. Garland watched the older man work for a few minutes before interrupting.

"I got some tools in my shed that need an edge put on them, I should have brought them with me."

Herron turned and grinned. "Boy, you know that anytime you need a hand with somethin' like that you can bring 'em over here and we'll take care of you." Herron's smile began to fade. "I didn't expect to see you so soon."

Garland walked over and pulled a crate up beside the grinding wheel. "Herron, I spent this morning refreshing my recollection of condemnation law and looking at possible defenses. I hate to tell you, but as your lawyer, I have to advise that we contact Southern and accept their offer. It is at least $75 more per acre than you could get otherwise. And, if we went to trial, they are not bound by that offer and can argue to the jury that the fair market value is much lower. I expect they'll use the Hanna sale and ask that your 40 acres be awarded to them for $275. Not only would you lose the land, but you'll be $4000 poorer for it."

"No. Won't do it." Herron went back to grinding.

"Mister Chldress, I wish it was as simple as telling them 'no.' I don't make the law. I just read it and advise you. When applying the known set of facts to the established legal precedent, we have no other choice. Shoot, you can take that money Southern is willing to pay you, buy some of their stock, and make more money than you and the boys ever will farming this land."

"Garland, have you taken all leave of your senses? I told you no." Herron stopped his work at the grinder and looked out the barn door to the countryside beyond. His face showed a look of vexation. "Stock jobbin' ain't how I make a livin'. If I wanted to buy Southern stock, and I don't, I wouldn't know how to go about it. Garland, it's paper. You want me to put the future of my boys and their chillun in paper? I could never do that to them."

"Herron, listen to me. I don't *want* that any more than you do. But you are in a spot. Southern has the authority to take your land. You might not like it, and I certainly don't, but it will come to pass. You can either get good value out of the transaction, or you can be stubborn about it."

"They could up the offer to $500 an acre and I still wouldn't sell. It is not about the money. I done told you that. Look, I'm entitled to a jury trial on this, right?"

"Yes, you are. However, understand that all the jury will be allowed to decide is the reasonable compensation. The cases I've read say that the other issues such as public purpose, etcetera, are matters of law for the judge to decide. So, don't think that you will get a full blown jury trial on the use of eminent domain. The jury will simply decide how much the land that Southern wants is worth. Once they make that finding, Southern will cut you a check for it and it's over."

"But they don't get the land until after the jury speaks?"

"Right."

"Well, if they's gonna get it, I want it to be at the hands of a jury of my peers. I will not hand my land over voluntarily."

"Herron…."

"Look, I know you think I'm being unreasonable and looney about this. Maybe I am. But I want that trial. I want you to represent me. You've done explained the risks and how much money I stand to lose by pushin' this thing to a trial, but I have made my decision. All I'm askin' is whether you will stand with me or if I need to represent myself."

Garland got up from the crate and walked to the barn door. He looked out and gazed upon Herron's small herd of Devons grazing in the distance. The sunlight brought forth their reddish color. Garland figured that each cow must have weighed over 1000 pounds. He wondered how the docile beasts would react to sharing their pasture with a Southern Railway complex.

"Okay, Herron. I respect you and your decision. I will stand with you and do everything that the law allows to protect your interests."

Herron smiled and nodded at Garland. He then went back to work with the grinding wheel. Garland walked to his truck and headed back to the office. Driving out the gravel driveway, Garland shook his head. He wanted to turn the truck around and tell Herron that if he chose to deprive his family of thousands of dollars, he'd have to do it by himself. Based on the price offered by Southern both his sons could provide for their families—for several years—while they decided what to do next. That would be a very comfortable cushion. Of course, he couldn't imagine a Childress sitting about and taking solace in a plush bank account. Garland laughed to himself and wondered if Herron even had a bank account. Many folks like Herron had learned from the Depression not to trust official brick-and-mortar depositories for their money.

Garland's thoughts also turned to his reputation. Would his client base suffer once it learned that through the trial process Herron got substantially less per acre than he would have without hiring a lawyer? Would they think that he just milked the process to earn a fee from the Childress family? Surely the townspeople knew him better than that.

Garland felt himself blush as heat rolled up the back of his neck and to the top of his head. Garland was making the case about him and not about Herron Childress. With no knowledge of the court process and rules of evidence, Herron could conceivably end up with well below the fair market value of the property. The family would be in a fix then. Herron Childress was a responsible adult, and, much more than that, a good man. Garland had advised him, the advice was rejected, and now it was his duty as an attorney to respect the wishes of the client and to put Herron Childress in the best possible position regarding the valuation issue. Garland resolved that he would fulfill his obligation to Herron.

In the next few weeks Garland went through jury selection and the obligatory pretrial conference. He continued to read eminent domain case law and look for some way around what appeared to be an inevitable result. Five weeks had passed since Herron Childress expressed his sentiments to Garland in the barn. Garland had explained to Herron that despite additional work on the case, he was no closer to finding a way around the clear import of the law. Even with these warnings, Herron and his family remained set on a trial.

Now, Garland was waiting for the Childresses to arrive at the courthouse and a firsthand experience with the justice system. He paced up and down the sidewalk out front of the building. As he did so, he saw Nelson Morrison pull up in a Packard Super 8 convertible. The red clay on the whitewalls told of the long trip from Columbia. Although Morrison's office was in the state capitol, he spent much time on the road representing the railroad's interests throughout South Carolina. Right behind Morrison two more cars wheeled into the courthouse parking lot. As Morrison locked his Packard and headed for the courthouse entrance, his entourage piled out of the other two vehicles and followed on his heels. Garland did not recognize any of the people with Morrison and assumed they were Southern executives, associates in Morrison's firm, or maybe valuation experts.

Just as the gaggle cleared the doors, Herron and Mary Childress appeared across the courthouse square. Garland headed in their direction and met the couple with a handshake. "I didn't see you pull up. Where did y'all park?"

"Just down the street. We so rarely make it to Maxton that we came early and had a bite of breakfast at the Blue Flame Café. All that pacin' we watched you doin' worked up my appetite."

"What he really means," Mary said, "is that neither one of us slept a wink and decided to just come on over here early."

"I can't say as I slept too well myself. I suppose you saw that Southern's crew is already inside."

"I saw 'em," Herron scoffed. "You know what folks says around here, 'ain't nothin' good ever come out of Columbia.'"

"That's for sure," Garland chuckled. "We better be gettin' on in ourselves."

Garland ushered his clients through the front door and into Judge William Atlee's courtroom on the first floor. As they entered the double doors, they walked by the rows of pews on either side. Morrison had papers spread out on counsel table that was situated closest to the jury box on the right side of the courtroom. Garland directed Mary to the first pew on the left side just in front of the bar separating the gallery from the lawyers and court staff. He motioned for Herron to take a seat at the defense counsel table. Once Herron eased into the leather captain's chair, Garland gave him a reassuring wink and put his file down.

Garland then walked over to Southern's table and shook hands with Roger Morrison. He had never had a case with Morrison, but had met him at bar meetings during previous terms of court and, of course, during jury selection for the Childress case. Morrison had a reputation for thoroughness and precision. In railway litigation he was quite simply the best lawyer that money could buy. "Mister Breazeale, is there anything we need to tell the judge before beginning? I don't expect my case will take too long. Depending on what evidence you have, the jury should get this by lunch."

"I can't think of anything out of the ordinary that Judge Atlee would want to know. The issues are pretty straightforward."

"They are at that. Tis a pity that your people have pushed this matter to such extremities. It appears you have been unable to educate them on what's happening today. Mister Wirt offered them a better-than-fair price for that land. I never cease to be amazed by the fighting spirit of upcountry folks. These red hills must breed an ornery disposition."

Garland stared into Morrison's eyes. "Respectfully, sir, I think you are mistaken. They understand exactly what is happening. They simply choose not to acquiesce in Southern's grand business plan. If that is orneriness, then I accept your definition." With that, Garland turned on his heels and returned to the defense table.

Before Garland could settle into his chair, Judge Atlee assumed the bench. As the judge climbed the steps, the bailiff intoned: "All rise. Oyez, Oyez, Oyez. All persons having any business before this honorable court of common pleas for the State of South Carolina are admonished to draw nigh and give their attention for this court is now in session."

By the time the participants and spectators got to their feet, Judge Atlee was motioning them to sit: "Please, take your seats."

"Is there anything from the parties before we proceed?"

"Nothing from the plaintiff."

"Likewise, nothing from the defense."

"Very well. Bailiff, bring out the jurors. Mr. Morrison, you may call your first witness once our twelve are seated."

As Garland expected, Morrison began with a vice president for Southern Railway Company. Morrison inquired of the man's position, length of time with Southern, and his personal knowledge of Southern's corporate status and its principal business. With these foundational questions answered, Morrison asked if the man was familiar with subject property. He answered in the affirmative and explained that Southern desired the 40 acres for establishment of rail yard just outside of Hampton Falls. From start to finish, Morrison spent less than ten minutes with the witness.

"Cross examination?" the judge asked.

Garland rose: "No sir."

"Let the witness be excused. Next witness Mr. Morrison."

Morrison then called Geoffrey Hughes, a property appraiser from Maxton. Morrison questioned Hughes on his education and experience in his field. He then asked if he had conducted a fair market value analysis of the subject property. Hughes answered in the affirmative and explained how he had examined courthouse records of comparable properties within ten miles of the Childress farm. Using the previous five years and the sales of three parcels of farmland, Hughes opined that $260 to $275 per acre was the market value of the Childress property.

The judge offered Garland the opportunity for cross examination. This time Garland rose and moved to the podium.

"Mister Hughes, you aren't in the business of farming, are you?

"No sir. As I testified earlier, I am an appraiser."

"Isn't it also true that you have never been on the Childress property?"

"Correct. I wouldn't want to trespass. Besides, there was no need to. When using comparable sales, a viewing is not necessary."

"You've never spoken with Herron Childress?"

"No. Again, there was no need to."

"You don't know how long that land has been in his family, do you?"

"I don't. But, such information would not change the valuation analysis."

"Your calculations did not consider whether the reduction of the Childress farm from 130 to 90 acres would affect the ability of Mr. Childress' two sons to earn a living?"

Morrison jumped to his feet. "Objection, Your Honor. The question is irrelevant to a fair market value calculation."

"Sustained. Move on, Mister Breazeale."

"Yes sir. No further questions of this witness."

"Call your next witness, Mr. Morrison."

"Judge, the plaintiff has no more testimony. We would simply offer as an exhibit a plat showing the subject property."

"I'll allow it. The plat is in evidence."

"I would also ask Your Honor to find as a matter of law that my client is a duly chartered railroad company and that the use we propose for the subject property would be for the benefit of the public."

"Does the defendant wish to present any argument on the plaintiff's motion? If so, I'll send the jury out and you can be heard."

Garland stood. "No sir, judge."

"Very well. Those two issues raised in defendant's motion are established for the purposes of this record. Mister Breazeale, you may begin your case."

"May it please the court? The defense calls Herron Childress to the stand."

Morrison jumped up from counsel table and walked toward the bench. "Your Honor, I must object to the calling of this witness. The only issue remaining is the value of the subject property. Absent a showing that Mr. Childress has some training or experience in valuation, it is the plaintiff's position that he is not qualified to offer any relevant testimony and thus should not be allowed to testify."

"Any response, Mister Breazeale?"

"Yes sir. My client has lived on that property for more than six decades. He has worked it, farmed it, and knows the property better than any living person. His knowledge of the property would be helpful to the jury in their determination of its value."

"Overruled. I'll allow the testimony. The plaintiff's objection goes to the weight of the evidence and not its admissibility."

Herron Childress made long and slow strides as he approached the witness stand. Southern had just attempted to keep him from testifying about his own property in a case aimed at taking that property from him. That was dirty, Herron thought. He realized that but for the quick wits of Garland, they might have succeeded and he would have been a mere spectator in the future of his family's inheritance. Second thoughts flashed through his mind. If he had only taken the original offer; that would have at least given his sons some capital to put towards another farm, or to use for a business endeavor. Now, the only evidence before the jury was a price of $260 to $275 per acre. He'd be lucky to get what Luther Hanna had gotten for his exhausted land. It was too late now.

Garland stood at the end of the jury box and eyed Herron. He saw the perspiration break out on the older man's forehead. Herron seemed to be holding his breath—afraid to engage in even the most natural of acts. Garland tried to slow things down and put Herron at ease.

"Mister Childress, have you ever testified in a court before?"

"No sir, this is the first time."

"Would it be fair to say that you are nervous?"

"I expect it would," Herron replied.

"I understand. You just take your time and speak up so the jury can hear you, okay?"

"I'll do my best."

Garland began his line of questioning by asking Herron about his first memories of the Childress place. As if he was back in the barn at the grinding wheel, Herron shared with the jury how his father used to hook up a team of mules at the break of dawn and head for the fields. As a boy, hundreds of yards away from the work going on, he could still hear the gee and haw off in the distance. He recalled that when he was 11 or 12, his father gave him an acre and let him raise his own crop. He discoursed on the lessons he learned and his childish pride when the first fruits of the crop came in. Garland then led Herron to describe the terrain and the Childress system of crop rotation. Herron explained how his father had taught him to grow a cover crop every year between the corn and bean plantings. The Childresses had always used a three-crop, two-year rotation cycle with corn, wheat or grain, and a double crop of beans. This system allowed the family to manage soil fertility, reduce problems with soil-borne diseases, and keep the weeds to a minimum.

"How much did you buy the farm for, Mr. Childress?"

"I ain't never bought it. My granddaddy purchased 130 acres just three years before the War Between the States. The family struggled to keep it, almost lost it twice before the century turned, but we owned it free an' clear when I was still wearin' knee britches."

"Based on your cultivation of the land and experience with the land, what value would you put on it?"

"I can't give one. I might own that land on paper, but it really ain't mine to give to nobody or to set a price on it."

"Objection, Your Honor. I ask that his last comment be struck from the record and that the jury be instructed to disregard it. Fair market value assumes a price that a willing buyer would accept from a willing seller. His last statement is contrary to the legal definition of fair market value."

"Sustained. The jury is instructed to ignore the last statement made by Defendant Childress."

Feeling the sting of rebuke, Garland brought the examination to a close. "Well, Your Honor, those are all the questions I have for my client."

"Very well. Any cross?"

"Just a couple of questions, Your Honor." Morrison walked toward the witness stand and stood about one yard in front of Herron.

"Mister Childress, how far did you go in school?"

"Eighth grade."

"So we can safely assume that you do not have a high school diploma?"

"That'd be a fair assumption."

"Have you had any formal classes in valuation of property?"

"No sir."

"Since the eighth grade have you had any formal training at all?"

"No sir."

"Your Honor, those are all the questions I have for the Defendant." Morrison returned to his seat.

"Mister Childress, you may step down from the witness stand," Judge Atlee directed. "Gentlemen of the jury, this case will now move to closing arguments. As the burden is on the plaintiff, Mister Morrison will speak first."

Herron had barely gotten situated in the chair at the table when Morrison was on his feet and standing in front of the jury box. He carried no notepad and began to gesture with his hands as if he was the conductor of a grand orchestra.

"Gentlemen, Southern Railway Company appreciates your time and service on this jury. As Judge Atlee will tell you when he instructs you on the law, there is but one issue for you to decide today: just compensation. The law defines just compensation as the fair market value that a willing seller would accept in a voluntary sales transaction where the price represents the normal consideration for the property sold. I submit to you that the only evidence before you of just compensation is the testimony of Geoffrey Hughes. Mister Hughes lives here in Maxton and has been appraising property for years. You heard him describe the rigorous analysis he undertook and how he arrived at the price range of $260 to $275 per acre. The defendant has offered no evidence to rebut that. While we can all understand Mr. Childress' attachment to the land and we can agree that he is a fine farmer, his attachment and skill are not elements of the valuation process. In other words, you may not take into account such things as his family history, farming methods, etcetera."

As Morrison went on, Garland made notes on his legal pad. Garland listened as Morrison discussed the standard of preponderance of the evidence and what this means, the jury's job to find facts based on evidence, and the respect all parties should have for the judge and his role as master of the law. Morrison reminded the jury that Southern did not want a penny more than the fair market value of the property and how his client trusted them to determine a just price. After about ten minutes of argument, Morrison sat down.

Garland's heart raced as he took his turn with the jury. The conservative thing, he told himself, would be to ask the jury for the high end of the range. Morrison never suggested a figure, but spoke of the range of $260 to $275 per acre. Garland could argue that Southern's own expert had uttered the words two hundred and seventy-five dollars. That would be $600 more for the Childresses than a verdict on the low end of the range. They deserved far more than that, but ought to get at least the $275. So that's what he decided to do. He would point out what a dedicated farmer Herron Childress was and that his land, which had been so meticulously cared for, called for at least $275 per acre.

That was the plan. At least until Garland actually opened his mouth.

"Gentlemen, I agree with Mr. Morrison that the only issue before you is just compensation. I also agree with his legal definition of just compensation. It will be the same definition that Judge Atlee will give you when he charges you on the law. I want you to remember that the arguments of the lawyers are not evidence. Evidence that you may consider came from the witness stand and the exhibit entered into evidence. For example, Judge Atlee has instructed you to disregard Mr. Childress' statement that a price could not be set on the 40-acre parcel at issue. I am asking you to follow that instruction, just as you will follow his instructions on the definition of just compensation and fair market value.

"These terms have specific legal definitions that came about by the General Assembly's drafting efforts down in Columbia as well as interpretations given by the state Supreme Court that also sits down in Columbia. Here in the upcountry when we say 'value' we aren't usually talking about the Columbia definition. In the Chauga Valley, value, just like beauty, is in the eye of the beholder. We see it subjectively, whereas the legislature and courts see it objectively. And of course, when deciding this case you must, as the judge will tell you, follow the definition as given to us by Columbia.

"For example, I've got a photograph of me with my parents just before I went off to school. It was the last picture I ever had made with my parents, both of whom are gone. I wouldn't take ten thousand dollars for that photograph because of what it means to me. But under the Columbia conception of value, that picture is not worth two bits."

"Your Honor, I have listened to this long enough," Morrison interrupted. "This man is precariously close to causing a mistrial with his line of argument. I respectfully ask that you stop this and issue a curative instruction."

"Well, Mr. Morrison, the Court believes that what defense counsel has said is entirely appropriate. He is telling them to follow the law and explaining what matters they should not consider. Your objection is overruled. Please continue, Mister Breazeale."

"Thank you, Your Honor. As I was saying, although I would not agree to part with that picture for any amount of money, if a company was clothed with the power of eminent domain by the General Assembly and wanted that picture, say, to put in a public museum, you as the jury would have to value the photograph objectively, without regard to my sentimentality.

"The same reasoning must apply in the case before you today. Herron Childress views that 40-acre parcel much as I view the photograph. Considering that this farm has been in the Childress family since the 1850s, he grew up on that land, and his sons currently work that land, we can understand why he is so attached to it. But this 'upcountry value' is not what you are to base your decision on. No. This case is about Columbia value. All Herron Childress asks is that when you determine the Columbia value of the 40 acres, you use your best judgment and base your decision on the evidence in this case. On behalf of my client, we thank you."

When Garland sat down, Judge Atlee immediately charged the jury. The jury got the case at 11:45 a.m., ahead of the schedule predicted by Nelson

Morrison. They deliberated twenty minutes before the foreman informed the bailiff that the jurors had reached a verdict.

Herron and Garland sat at counsel table and watched as the foreman handed up a slip of paper with the jury's finding. Garland tried to keep still and to refrain from rocking back and forth in his chair. He caught a glimpse of Herron out of the corner of his eye. He appeared as comfortable in the captain's chair as he would in his rocking chair on the front porch of his home.

Garland whispered to Herron: "When the judge reads the verdict, no matter what the outcome—high or low price—remain in control. Judge Atlee does not tolerate outbursts. I don't want to be bailing you out of jail today."

Herron simply nodded and kept his eyes focused ahead.

Garland swiveled around to look at Mary. She clutched her purse in her hands. Garland tried to make eye contact but could not. Mary's eyes were tightly shut. Whether she was in prayer or could not bear to watch the outcome, Garland did not know.

Garland turned around and focused his attention on the judge. Judge Atlee held the paper in his hand and studied it as if the foreman had written a disquisition. After some time, Judge Atlee put the paper down on the bench and called the courtroom to order.

"Ladies and gentlemen, the jury has returned verdict. In the matter Southern Railway Company v. Childress, docket number 51-012, the jury has found in favor of the plaintiff and awarded the subject property to the plaintiff upon the payment of just compensation of $10,000 per acre. This court will now stand in recess."

Garland stood as the judge left the bench and returned to his chambers. He grabbed Herron by the elbow and ushered him into the gallery area where Garland motioned for Mary to follow them. As they exited the double doors of the courtroom, Nelson Morrison and his entourage remained seated and talked in low murmurs.

Once outside, Herron paused on the steps only to be met by a prod from Garland. "Keep going. We'll talk when we get to the truck."

In silence, Garland, Herron, and Mary walked toward the Blue Flame Café where the Childresses' had parked their pickup. Garland set a quick pace and gave no quarter as he expected Herron and Mary to stay in tow.

"Garland, son. What in the world is wrong with you? Didn't you hear?"

"I heard, I'm still not believing what I heard. I figure the best way for what I heard to remain true is to get as far away from that courthouse as we can. I'd hate for the judge to reconsider the propriety of that verdict."

"Boy, it's over. They jury did exactly what the judge told 'em to do. They awarded just compensation. Only in an amount somewhat higher than Mister Morrison and his folks thought. I don't suppose I'll be seeing a $400,000 check in the mail anytime soon. Southern will soon be reevaluatin' their 'need' for my property." With that statement, Herron pulled away from Garland and gave Mary a bear hug and lifted her up in the air.

Garland leaned back against Herron's black Ford pickup and fumbled for his cigarettes and matches. He lit a Chesterfield and inhaled. "Well, Herron, I suppose you can go ahead and plan to plant your corn on 'the Subject Property.'"

"What do you mean 'go ahead and plan?' I never doubted for a minute that you'd come up with somethin'."

While they talked on the street, a figure approached from the back of the courthouse. He was an older man in bib overalls and a crumpled felt hat. As he neared the trio, Garland recognized him as the foreman of the jury. The foreman seemed not to notice them as he approached the door of the café. He pulled open the door and removed his hat.

Just before stepping in he turned to the Childresses and stated matter-of-factly: "Ain't nothin' good ever come outta Columbia."

William J. Watkins, Jr., is relatively new to fiction, but has authored four books of non-fiction: Reclaiming the American Revolution *(Palgrave 2004),* Judicial Monarchs *(McFarland 2012),* Patent Trolls *(Independent Institute 2014), and* Crossroads for Liberty *(2016). He is an Assistant U.S. Attorney prosecuting white-collar crime. His articles have appeared in various publications including* USA Today, The Washington Times, *and* Forbes.

Little Termite

By Gary Ives

(This story was originally published in the May 2015 issue of The MOON.)

The *gringos* saw Bobby as retarded, a halfwit. But in Amazonia along the Upper Takchinga River, among the Ranawera, he was treated as special because he was different. The Ranawera know that at birth the spirits infuse certain babies with extraordinary vision and that they grow up in two worlds, this one and the spirit world.

Bobby's grandfather and grandmother, the Rev. and Mrs. Henry March, she a registered nurse, had begun building the Upper Takchinga mission in 1919, and had dedicated their adult lives to mastering the Ranawera tongue so that the Lord's word could be delivered in illustrated Bibles to be printed in their dialect. While the Rev. Henry March was a quick and decisive man of high energy, his wife was slow, steady and even-tempered. The Ranawera feared him but grew fond and trusting of his wife. She operated a very basic clinic where she instructed Ranawera women in simple hygiene, first aid and midwifery.

The Marches had raised their daughter Sarah until school age, when she was sent to live with Mrs. March's sister in San Diego. In her senior year of high school, with the help of her sailor boyfriend, Sarah got in trouble and the week after graduation was returned pregnant to the Takchinga mission. Damaged goods, as they say. Little Bobby's birth was difficult. Sarah suffered labor for a miserable three days until, under the full moon and kerosene lanterns, she at last dilated enough. First came the placenta, then the baby. Her mother and two Ranawera women she'd trained helped Sarah and the newborn. Under the lanterns amid swirling moths Mrs. March cut and unwrapped the cord from the baby's little neck and passed him to Pasqua and Natividad, whose actual names were Sha and Shoi, who gently washed and wrapped him in a cotton blanket, while Mrs. March tried to staunch Sarah's bleeding with gauze pads. Rev. March prayed, but on the second day Sarah died.

At the Reverend's insistence, Ranawera men dug the grave on the little rise behind the yuccas and bananas, a strange and ugly task, as only enemies were buried in the ground. When one of their own died the Ranawera properly cremated the body at night. There was feasting. Remaining bones were gathered in the morning, crushed with a mortar and packed into a bamboo vessel. Then at the next full moon another feast was held and the crushed bone dust sprinkled in the fermented yucca and drunk by relatives. Covering with dirt was what you did to something putrid, although Rev. March had tried unsuccessfully for twenty-two years to change this belief, along with so many other practices he reckoned as filthy and savage.

Just a few short days after her daughter's death, Mrs. March was felled by a fever. Rev. March sent a canoe downriver to the Catholic mission at Leticia for sulfa powder, but the return was days late for Mrs. March. And so it fell upon Sha and Shoi to wet nurse and raise Bobby. Again Rev. March sent two Ranawera downriver—this time to buy four milk goats for the baby. But before Mrs. March's clinic could be fenced-in as a goat shed, a big cat took two of the goats. Nevertheless, Sha and Shoi, Bobby's surrogate mothers, quickly grew to love the little baby. They would stroke his fine blond hair and kiss his fine long eyelashes while crooning Ranawera lullabies. He slept in their hammocks in the mission lodge where they called him, because he was so white, Talolowera, which in the Ranawera language means *Termite Person*.

Without the soothing presence of his wife, the Rev. Henry March soon deteriorated into a short-tempered, irritable, implacable alcoholic, who all but ignored his grandson. Without a father, mother, a birth certificate, much less a passport, and with a world war raging, it was impossible to send the baby stateside. Besides, who would accept a little bastard? Then, too, the Reverend was loath to leave the mission, even though half the Ranawera had already drifted away, returning to their semi-nomadic lives in the jungle. March had completed work on the Book of Matthew, and was halfway through the Book of Mark, which would take another two years. His sole purpose was to finish all the gospels in his lifetime, despite the burdens of his daughter's disgrace, his wife's death, and now the bother of raising this half-wit boy he viewed as God's test. But, by God, he *would* finish the books of Mark, and Luke, and John, and nothing would stop him, by Jesus Christ, nothing!

Bobby did not begin talking until his fourth year and, understandably, his first language was, to his grandfather's disgust, Ranawera. *"No Bobby, do not say 'pafwa' say 'fire.' Can you say 'fire'? "No Bobby. I am your grandfather, you call me Grandfather. Don't say 'Bui,' say G r a n d f a t h e r."*

Slow of wit and of speech, the boy found this utterly confusing and continued to blend his Bui's words with The People's when speaking with his grandfather. With the Ranawera Talolowera was not confused. Sha and Shoi told and retold the stories of The People and sung over and over again the songs all Ranawera learned.

When he was five years old Bobby fell ill with fever. The Rev. March, drunk, entered the lodge to check on Bobby and saw him in Shoi's hammock. She cuddled him against her, cooing the song for sick children, stroking his hot little forehead, and gently kneading his little penis, the Ranawera mothers' way of easing little boys to sleep. The Reverend exploded, roughly snatching the boy from Shoi and then slapping her face over and over again. "You vile instrument of Satan, get thee gone and never again show your filthy perdition. Go. I curse thy filthy name. Go, damn you, damn you, damn you, devil!"

A great wail went up in the lodge as Rev. March dragged the febrile boy to his own hut, placed him in a hammock and read aloud from the Book of Job, standing and weeping all the while. If Henry March had ever had any affection for Bobby, it was now gone. No, his grandson was to him as the boils God had sent down to Job. His burden was to feed, clothe, and bring Bobby up as a Christian while laboring on the translations of the Gospels. Whether punishment for a past sin or God's test, he would find a way to expiate this and complete the Lord's work.

By morning, many more Ranawera had slipped away. But Sha remained and, while the Reverend snored, a Bible and an empty aguardiente bottle on the puncheon floor by his hammock, she eased past and picked up Talolowera and returned to the Ranawera lodge on the mission grounds to care for him.

Tinka, Sha's brother, was fond of Talolowera and gave to him a baby spider monkey. In a short time the boy and the monkey had bonded and were inseparable. Mission supplies and mail came from Iquitos via small airplane to Leticia; thence three days upriver by canoe five times a year during dry season. After the war, the Winters Institute for Missionary Services sent a young man to the mission with a surplus shortwave radio and generator to set up a communications station. However, acquiring fuel for the generator was so onerous that Rev. March ignored the radio schedule and sent word to the Institute that the Ranawera had stolen the wire antenna and parts of the generator. That radio would put the Institute right here in the mission to interfere with his work, to spy on him. Hunters and rubber workers would drift in from the jungle wanting to use the radio. News of the outside world was of no interest to the Reverend now that the war was over. No, this mission did not need any damned radio interfering with the Lord's work.

Matthew and most of Mark had been translated without any radio, hadn't they?

At the Institute's headquarters the Reverend's translations of the book of Mark had raised skepticism. Rev. March seemed to have ascribed an Old Testament harshness to the apostle's writing; moreover, he appeared to be having difficulty completing his task. He was two years behind schedule. The Institute's Upper District administrators' concern for Rev. March prompted the Institute to insist that Rev. March visit the Institute's headquarters near Iquitos once each year. This infuriated the Reverend, but there was nothing to do but comply; they were impervious to reason. His chief argument was that the Ranawera would steal the mission blind in his absence.

For the first years of the required visits, the Institute sent one of the staff to temporarily replace Rev. March. Each time he was away the visiting administrator would get the radio station back online. But shortly after the Rev. March's return something always happened to take the station off the air.

The visiting administrators' reports always mentioned Bobby. "Reverend March's grandson appears generally healthy and happy, but exhibits mental retardation: difficulties with speech, inability to learn simple prayers or even the alphabet. He does, however function well in his assigned tasks, caring for the station's goats and chickens, as well as a pet monkey."

The Reverend took great care to dress up the station for these bothersome visits. The inoperable radio would be brought out and dusted off for repair. Empty aguardiente bottles were hidden in the jungle to be stolen by the Ranawera; Bobby would have his hair cut Christian style; and Sha was ordered to see that Bobby wore a shirt and sandals at all times during the administrator's stay and sleep in the mission house, not the Ranawera lodge. And he was to speak only English to the administrator.

Sha faithfully saw to this, not because she feared the Rev. but because she held her little Termite in such veneration and love. It was clear that Talolowera lived in both the spirit world and this world. The words of Ranawera songs sung by him differed because the spirits were directing messages to the Ranawera through this little Termite. For instance *"Na chagra, potchee tom..."* the song for fishing "Come fish to the spear" came out *"Ta chagra, hushee som"* which had nothing to do with talking to the fish; no this meant "Spear fly fast." Perhaps the Shibas, enemies on the Urulali River who fought with spears, were planning a raid. The Ranawera men then kept watch on the Shibas and days later a raiding party crossed into Ranawera lands and was ambushed. One Shiba was killed; the others driven off. The elders asked Sha to bring Termite into the forest for the singing of the dead enemy song. A hole was dug and the detested enemy buried while the song was sung. "Now the strength of this one is our strength. We see the spirit of the jaguar, he sees the worm." However, when Talolowera sang the song the words came out as "*Many worms monkey tree.*" On the way back one of the Ranawera brought down a howler monkey with a dart. The dead monkey fell across a huge rotting log filled with grubs, a splendid harvest for the victory feast.

Talolowera might be Bui's grandson, but to the Ranawera he was theirs through and through. At puberty he was ceremoniously adopted by The People and made son to Watchi, the tribe's shaman. As Henry March lay in drunken slumber every Ranawera of the Takchinga Band stepped before Talolowera and blew breath into his mouth. Watchi then lay Talolo naked across his lap and under the light of pine splinters with a large thorn and lampblack tattooed magic symbols on his buttocks and then huge images of owl eyes on his shoulder blades.

One hot jungle morning Bobby was in the shed dreamily milking Chichichiva. Squatting by the goat with his little monkey on his shoulder, his forehead against the soft, sweet-smelling fur, he repeatedly pulled her teats over the milk pot. Henry March happened by and heard Bobby singing *Jesus Loves Me* but in Ranawera, not English. "Damn that chuckle-headed little shit," he thought and stomped into the goat shed. There shirtless on the milking stool he beheld the two tattooed owl eyes. "God Almighty, what is that?" he yelled, startling the boy and the goat. He touched the tattoo, spit on his hand and tried to rub it off. "You heathen bastard, you fucking savage, God damn you!" he shouted. He tried to raise another curse but his anger was so great that his throat closed on the larynx and only a hiss of air escaped his lips. From a peg he grabbed a leather lead and began wildly thrashing Bobby's back, but striking the monkey instead. Bobby swayed and the leather lead cut into Chicichiva as she kicked the milk pot. Milk splashed up onto his grandfather's reddened eyes and on his face as goats bleated and panicked, chickens scurried and flapped, filling the air with dust. Bobby, his back cut and bleeding, lay in the straw, tears coursing down his dusty cheeks as he clutched his dying little friend. His grandfather stood over the boy thrashing his side, but soon the fire inside him subsided. He threw down the strap and strode out of the goat shed.

The continuing radio problems at the Takchinga station, suspicions of Henry March's drunkenness, and the mired and confused translations so perplexed the Board at the Institute that they sent a plane to bring in Henry March for a serious consultation. It was hoped that a good old-fashioned ass-chewing might bring Henry around. His sacrifices and many years of service to the Institute were highly appreciated and rendered him worthy of special consideration. Another factor affecting Henry's fate was the murder of five missionaries by the Chipavowera thirty miles away on the Nipo River two years earlier. The details of this tragedy had been widely publicized and a motion picture dramatizing the incident had been very well-received by audiences in America. This energized popular interest in the Winters Institute. Very large sums had been donated. Besides, the Rev. Henry March was the only clergyman fluent in Ranawera and trained in biblical translation.

Unexpectedly, the administrator arrived late one morning, shortly after Bobby's thrashing. The canoe bringing him from Leticia had been spotted by mission Ranawera and Henry had just enough time to hide his aguardiente and summon Sha, whom he instructed to dress Bobby in a shirt and sandals. The administrator explained the summons and assured Henry March that he would be returned within a few days. Henry, now paranoid, explained that the radio had been stolen, and persuaded the administrator to return to Iquitos with him; that his grandson could ensure the safety of the station for a few days. Before leaving he gave instructions to Bobby.

"This is the pantry. It is to stay locked. If Ranawera or anyone asks you for corn meal or beans you say 'no.' The pantry stays locked. No one goes into the pantry. No one unlocks the pantry. If an animal tries to get into the pantry, shoot it with the shotgun. If a person tries to get into the pantry, tell them to stop or you will shoot them with the shotgun. Do you understand?"

"Yes, Grandfather."

"If Sha or Watchi or anyone else asks you to get them beans from the pantry what do you do, Bobby?"

"I say no."

"That's right. What if a monkey or peccaries try to get into the pantry?"

"Shoot them with shotgun."

"That's right. What if some person tries to break the lock and get in the pantry?"

"Tell them 'stop.'"

"What if they don't stop?"

"Shoot with shotgun."

"Okay, Bobby. Do your chores and say your prayers. Sha has plenty of beans to cook for you and you can fish while I'm gone. I will be back soon. Do everything right and I will have a candy for you. Bye-bye."

Within a week Rev. March returned, in a rotten mood and very drunk. He had to be helped from the canoe to his hammock by two Ranawera. Bobby approached and asked his grandfather for the promised candy. "Get out of here, damn you. Didn't you hear me? Get outta here, you simpleton.

"I want candy, Grandfather."

"No candy. Now git!"

The next morning Bobby was carrying the milk pot to the kitchen when he saw Henry March fumbling with the key ring at the pantry.

"Stop," the boy dutifully said.

"Shut up and get that milk pot out of the sun," the Reverend snarled.

The boom of the shotgun echoed over the river until it was overtaken by the cacophony from the birds and monkeys. The Reverend March lay dead on his face before the still-locked pantry.

The Ranawera found poor Bobby trying to explain himself to his senseless grandfather.

You tell me, "No stop then shoot." I tell you to stop, Grandfather. You no stop."

The Ranawera deliberated how best to dispose of the Reverend's body: as an honored tribesman, by cremation, or as a putrid Christian, by burial. In the end, The People decided to follow the Reverend's own preferences, burying him in a shallow hole—his gospels with him.

Gary Ives worked in South America and became acutely aware of the terrible threats looming on the horizons of the beautifully simple folk of the Amazon. First the missionaries, then the miners, loggers, cattlemen, and land-hungry peasants— all of whom became agents of destruction for the indigenous tribal cultures and environments. Ives describes himself as a retired senior chief petty officer, now a recluse, who lives with his wife and two big dogs far, far away, where he grows grapes and writes. Read more of his stories at International Short Stories (garyives. wordpress.com).

Jealous of Daylight

By Madeline McEwen

(This story was originally published in the September 2017 issue of The MOON.)

"Insecure people only eclipse your sun because they're jealous of your daylight and tired of their dark, starless nights." —Shannon L. Alder

On a sunny Saturday in August, Babs McVitie, aged seventeen and of no fixed abode, shutdown her laptop in the air-conditioned library. Within twenty-four hours, under the cover of the eclipse, Dougal's release would change his life forever. No one had the power to stop her plan now.

"Closing in five minutes."

Babs checked the time on her phone dangling from its cable, recharging for free. She had half an hour to waste until work.

Shouldering her tote and carrying her ukulele case, Babs left her study carrel and headed for the elevator. When the bell pinged, she stepped inside and studied the report of a missing boy on a poster stuck to the metal wall on the way down: Jason Younger, 7, Caucasian, brown eyes, sandy hair.

A few moments later, she left the elevator, and then library. She passed through the ornamental gardens and park, across the street, and turned into a busy strip mall. Without wasting time, she took to the back streets and service alleys of the private houses, away from the traffic and the prying eyes of those on the lookout for shoplifters. Craig, her solitary friend, had taught her in the last month so many tips and tricks for living under the radar.

He was the one who told her about the solar eclipse, when total darkness would fall at precisely at two o'clock on August the 19th. He'd shown her a video on his phone about what to expect. That clip had given her the idea. She could do anything she wanted and no one would see a thing, better than a night Ninja, more like a cloak of invisibility bestowed on a knight on a worthy quest.

She walked along Butcher Boulevard, staying in the shade of the parched birch trees on the neglected street, until she reached the concrete, flat-roofed cube. It looked like a flop house or maybe a drug den. Either way,

Babs would never break into someone else's house. Better to sleep in the park or the station or down by the creek in the open air.

Dumping her belongings at her feet, she bent to spy through the knothole in the rotten wooden fence and scanned the ramshackle yard. She spotted him. Dougal—why had she given him that name?—lay sprawled in the dirt, fur matted, slack-jawed, tongue lolling over yellow fangs, listless in the baking, merciless sun. His tether, a twenty-five-foot chain, stretched to a hefty metal spike driven deep in the ground. A bowl, presumably for water, was upside down. No food visible. Bleached bones littered the ground, none within reach. The yard was scattered with detritus: cardboard boxes, several punctured balls, a few empty cans, a little kid's tricycle missing a wheel, and filthy furniture not fit for any purpose other than adding to the picture of a garbage dump.

Craig, who knew everybody and could engineer anything, had his friend rig up a makeshift night-vision camera in case something went wrong with the plan. She turned toward the blank, fisheye camera lens on a telephone pole on the opposite side of the street at shoulder height with a wide view of most of the fence. She raised a hand in greeting, smiled, and made a thumbs up sign. Everything was going to be okay.

"Dougal! Here boy." Did he know she was trying to help? She called him twice, that sweet-faced, sandy-colored mutt. On the third time, he raised his neck, his head too heavy and unsteady. A tremor juddered through his body. Would he stand? Could he walk? Crawl? How old was he? Two or ten? Dougal's paws and long ragged claws reached forward. He shuffled, rear legs struggling, scuffing clouds of dirt into the arid air.

She forced a smile on her face. "Come on, Dougal, you can do it." Uncapping the water bottle, she flipped one of the loose fence planks, reached through the gap and waved the bottle back and forth. Dogs could smell water. Dougal flinched. Straining, he raised his chest, stick legs supporting his emaciated torso, ribs visible through his loose hide. A thin line of drool spindled from his mouth. His floppy tongue swept over his black-button nose.

Babs swallowed instinctively. If only she could save him now. Why wait until the eclipse? Would he survive that long, another twenty-three hours? What if, miracle of miracles, the Humane Society came and saved him tonight, any time before tomorrow? Understaffed and underfunded, she knew they wouldn't. How long had she waited on hold? How many calls had she made? How many reports to so many different people? She'd lost count and lost patience.

She'd memorized Dougal's case number—MC—male canine—95124866—knew it off by heart, but that didn't help her navigate the labyrinthine bureaucracy. However, she had followed their advice: keep a diary of events, visit as often as possible, and don't challenge the human occupant of the property; not that she had ever seen a living soul in the vicinity of the house or yard.

Occasionally, she'd seen a light on in one of the upper windows, but no movement or sound. She wanted to meet the devils who hid inside. What kind of monsters were they? The same kind of monsters who could steal a child from his bed? She hoped someone would save Jason, just as she would save Dougal.

Dried kibble was expensive, but light, portable, and easy to keep in her pockets. It didn't taste half bad. She'd tried some out of curiosity—artificial bacon flavored. Gritty and crumbly it seemed to suck the moisture from her mouth. That's why she always began by tempting him to drink first.

Dougal edged toward her inch-by-inch, wide liquid eyes fixed on the bottle. She took the foldaway camping bowl from her pocket, snapped it open and laid it flat on the ground. The water splashed the base as she poured a couple of cupfuls, not too much or he'd vomit. She picked up the stick she had purposefully left behind on previous occasions, and pushed the bowl slowly forward. Drops of precious water slopped over the brim and soaked into the ground, disappearing in a second.

Lurching like a drunk, Dougal stumbled a few bow-legged steps, then a few more, staggered, paused, and staggered again until he reached the bowl. He collapsed in a heap and buried his muzzle in the bowl, the water flying in all directions. Empty.

Babs took a handful of kibble and lobbed single pieces through the air. They landed near enough for him to snaffle them into his mouth like a lizard stealing flies. She threw more, tossing them with care; she didn't want to exhaust him. Brushing the crumbs from her palm, she hooked the bowl with the stick, and pulled it back to the fence for a refill. Two more cups of water. Dougal watched her every move, patient, as if he had learned the routine.

Tires screeched.

Babs dropped the bottle, stood, and flattened herself against the fence. A truck came around the corner and barreled past her, horn blasting, music blaring from the windows. When it had gone, and Babs had caught her breath, she turned back to Dougal, undisturbed, eyes closed, still as a bearskin rug.

# # #

Babs caught her breath. Time? How long had she stayed with Dougal? Unzipping her bag, she grabbed her phone. Damn! She stashed the bottle and bowl into her bag, and pushed the loose plank back into position.

"See you later, Dougal." She took off at a trot, and jogged the ten-block distance to her court-approved part-time job. The sun still belted out heat, even this late in the afternoon, and radiated up from the sidewalk, hot through her thin-soled sneakers.

She shoved the double doors to The Holistic Healing Center, an out-patient mental health facility, and dumped her belongings in the knee-hole of her desk at reception. Ignoring the clients in the waiting room, Babs sat on the swivel chair. Kicking off her sneakers, she rubbed her dusty feet discretely on the carpet, and grabbed a pair of black pumps from the deep file drawer to her right. Powering up the laptop, she laid her fingertips on the keys and her eyes on the blank screen, the image of an industrious employee.

As the laptop sprang to life, Babs let her gaze wander over the clients: middle-aged, tubby woman in a tie-dye t-shirt, gray-bearded man with a flat cap on his bald head, and an acned teenager, with braces on her teeth and glasses on her nose. None of them looked miserable, depressed or suicidal. Why were they here?

Babs ran her eye down the sign-in sheet on the clip board on the edge of desk. This was how she had met Craig, reading his name upside down on the sheet—Craig Peterson—when he came for his weekly appointment with Dr. Schlesser. Patient files were password protected, but Dr. Schlesser, an old-school practitioner, often jotted down a few lines in a moleskin notebook, which she always kept close at hand—apart from one time, three months ago, when she left it on the counter by the sink in the restroom.

No doubt, Dr. Schlesser had thought she was alone in the cubicle chatting to her husband on the phone and not paying any attention to Babs. The doctor's handwriting, unlike many in her profession, was rounded, neat and legible. Craig Peterson's name was underlined three times. Babs memorized the word "recidivism" to look up later, but she knew it had something to do with crime. The other terms were familiar: OCD, ADHD, sibling rivalry, arson, and anti-social.

Babs had left the restroom, and the notebook as if untouched, and returned to reception. There, she found Craig perched on the corner of her desk, like a male version of herself, androgynous, slender, and middling height. He had a lopsided grin, a swathe of thick, blond hair hiding his right eye, and he spoke to her as if she were an ordinary, everyday person.

"Hi." He had run his fingers through his hair, tucking it behind his ear. "Dr. Schlesser asked if you could change my appointment next week. I have a clash in my schedule."

Babs had swallowed, flustered by his direct gaze. Taller than him, she folded her arms and slouched. There was no such thing as love at first sight. Just a crush, a sudden onset of irrational emotions, freezing her brain and stealing her powers of speech. He had waited patiently, didn't rush her, as if he knew how she felt, torn and overwhelmed. Craig had pulled a folded baseball cap out of his back pocket, snapped it open and held it by the brim, his thumb covering the letter "T" on the word "Taurus." Babs concentrated on the embroidered image of a stylized bull, and the sparkling constellation, little stars joined together by white stitches.

Babs could hardly believe that their first encounter was over twelve weeks ago in June. They had met again, often, and not just at the Holistic Center. She'd never have survived on the street without him. They had so much in common: values, history, and a dogged determination to survive. Babs was indifferent to Craig's obsession with astronomy, but tuned him out when he droned on about the subject.

However, Craig always listened to her. His enthusiasm for the plan, her plan, never wavered. She knew with absolute confidence that if she asked him to help, he would without hesitation. In fact, he provided the solution to the biggest problem—how to break the chain securing Dougal to the stake. Babs had elaborate plans to borrow a bolt cutter. She couldn't steal one. However, figuring out how to find one, hiding it until needed, and then returning it after carrying Dougal to safety, seemed far too complicated, especially when she explained to Craig.

They had sat together in a booth at a cafe nursing two coffees—Craig's treat. Babs wondered where he got the money, but didn't ask. She didn't question him about his clean clothes either, because he would probably tell a tall tale, and then laugh at her if she fell for it. Instead she watched the flat screen TV on the other side of the room broadcasting the news. They'd had a break on the kidnapped kid case, Jason Younger, abducted on the same night Babs had run away. Someone had phoned in on the anonymous tip line. A teary old lady pleaded for more members of the public to call in because she couldn't pay the ransom.

No one had reported Babs missing. Nobody searched for her. Then again, since she was already seventeen, practically an adult, the authorities had other priorities. Who'd worry about a selfish, spoilt, truant from high school, when a seven-year-old had been taken from his bed?

Craig snapped his fingers in front of her face. "You dumbass. You don't know the first thing about planning, or dogs for that matter." He rolled his eyes, and then spelled it out for her. "Douglas is wearing a slip-chain, like a choker. If he pulls, he strangles himself, simple, foolproof. All you have to do is open the chain collar, wider, and it'll slip right over his head and you can dump it in the dirt."

"How do you know he's wearing a slip-chain collar?"

"Maybe I checked out your story. Did you exaggerate? Might have taken him some dog treats. You're not the only animal lover on the planet, you know?"

Truth or lie. Babs couldn't tell.

# # #

After work, Babs rushed to meet Craig at the soup kitchen on Powell Street. On arrival, breathless, she spotted him, or rather his black baseball cap, near the front of the line. Taking it off, he stuffed it in his jacket and pulled up his gray-colored hoodie as always. Was he shy?

By the time she reached the bench behind the trailer at their pre-arranged rendezvous, his term not hers, Craig had already finished his food—soup in the winter, sandwiches in the summer. He grinned at her, face in shadow from his hat and eyes hidden by Ray-bans.

"Sunset in a couple of hours," Craig said. "Want to take in a movie before we split?"

Babs bit into her sandwich and shuffled her shoes across the dried grass beneath her feet. The movie theatre at the end of Powell had a broken fire exit door. Together they'd managed to slip inside unnoticed on more than one occasion. Craig always waited with his ear to the door, listening for the end of the trailers and commercials, just before the opening strains of the main feature.

"What's showing?"

"Dunno. What do we care?"

He rubbed his hands on his thighs. Why was he wearing black jeans, long pants, at the height of summer? Then again, knowing Craig he'd probably stolen them, or *borrowed*, as he often said.

"I'd kill for two hours of air conditioning, wouldn't you? Plus, you could wash up afterwards in the restroom. The place'll be emptied out by then. Have you still got that toothbrush I got you?"

"Yes, thanks."

"You don't have to keep thanking me. We're buddies. Brother in arms. Us against the world."

"Any more clichés stuffed up your sleeve?"

"I would say Thelma and Louise, but I'm the wrong sex."

"What, or rather who, are Thelma and Louise?"

"It's this great movie, my mom's favorite," his chin dropped to his chest, "before she died."

Babs took another bite, and tomato juice dribbled down her chin. Was he really sad? He had a habit of making stuff up and then when she offered sympathy or acted surprised, he would laugh—"Fooled you! Just kidding." This had happened so often that her reactions had become stilted and cautious. She didn't want to be the butt of another hoax.

Taking the napkin from his sandwich wrapper, he dabbed her chin. "You're getting better, Kiddo. It's good to be wary. You never know who's going to pull a fast one. When I think how naive you were at first—it's a miracle you've lasted. Still, not much longer."

"How do you mean?"

"Nothing." He stood and stretched his arms above his head. "Are you still going ahead tomorrow?"

"Do you mean, Dougal? Of course! I'm counting the hours, no the minutes."

""And you're determined to go it alone, you don't want my help?"

"No, this is all on me. You shouldn't risk getting into trouble again."

"Trouble follows me around, it's like I have a target on my chest. When in doubt, blame Craig."

Babs didn't respond. It always sounded weird when people talked about themselves in the third person, like a dictator of some god-forsaken, back-water country. Dad talked like that—"If I, Jonathan McVitie, ask you to jump, you ask how high."

"Hang on." Craig unzipped his backpack. "I got you this. Just think of it as Craig Younger's way of making a contribution to the cause."

"Younger? I thought your last name was Peterson."

"What's in a name? I use lots of different names for many different reasons. Haven't got time to explain them all now. Take these."

He handed her a plastic-wrapped, plaid, fleece blanket, a pair of black jeans, and a gray hoodie, all brand new.

"Thanks, but I can't accept them."

"Don't be a wuss. We're about the same size. You'll need them on chilly nights soon enough."

She spotted a second blanket in his backpack. Great. He'd got one for himself too, so it must be true about the cold.

"Plus!" He patted her knee, "wear them tomorrow to protect your legs from the piss-soaked, fleabag."

"Craig! Don't call him that." She was about to tear into him, but he cut her off.

"Use the fleece for carrying the dog. Make the whole escapade go so much easier. Trust me, it's the only way. He might struggle, scratch or bite if he's scared. This way I'll know you're safe. Remember, you're doing this for Dougal, right?"

Only later after Craig had left, Babs began to wonder. Had he really visited the dog on Butcher Boulevard? If he had, how did he find Dougal on that long, long street? Craig didn't know the house number. He had lied, bare-faced. Fooled again.

# # #

Babs struggled through the following day. She stole a shower at an all-female gym with poor security and sloppy staff. Brunch from a dumpster behind the Chinese take-out—moo shu pork and noodles. New shoes from the Salvation Army truck—closed to donations because it was full—the entrance piled with people's crap because they were too lazy to come back tomorrow. The rest of the day, she split her time between the bus depot in the morning, and then the library in the afternoon once the sun was too hot to tolerate unless you were a lizard.

She ran her plan through her mind for the umpteenth time: loiter around the corner of Butcher Boulevard and Cutler Street, out of sight from the camera, wait for the eclipse, as soon as darkness fell and everyone's attention, if anyone was around, turned toward the obliterated sun, then she'd pull off two fence planks, slip into the yard, roll Dougal in the blanket, carry him off and head for the Humane Society on Powell, four blocks away on foot.

Stuffing her backpack with supplies, dog kit and blanket, Babs filled her two empty bottles from the water fountain and tucked them into the net pockets on the side of the backpack. She'd kept her phone battery full since recharging it in the library and didn't plan to turn it back on until she reached the Humane Society with Dougal.

At the corner where Butcher intersected Cutler, she sat on the pavement with her feet on the gutter to wait. She didn't need to know the time, the sun's disappearance would tell her when to pounce. While she waited, she read a paperback she'd taken from the free shelf at the library. Babs hadn't like the way the librarian had eyed her at the time.

Minutes ticked away. Babs finished the first chapter and moved on to the next. Turning the pages, she soon reached the end of the second, and then the third chapter. Looking up, the sun shone back at her with no sign of a shadow in any direction. Had Craig got the time wrong? Had she misunderstood him? Should she text him and check? What if she missed the moment because her attention was on the phone? Would it be over that quickly? She should have asked him more questions, made certain that she had the facts down correctly.

On impulse, she picked up her rucksack and ran to Dougal's backyard. Maybe he was already dead. Perhaps the Humane Society had already rescued him.

Shutting one eye, she spied with the other through the knothole. Dougal lay in the same position as she had left him the evening before, ribcage rising and falling. Damn it! Why not do it? Do it now!

At the Humane Society on Powell, Babs carried Dougal in her arms for the last few yards and saw a woman locking the front door.

"Hey! Wait, I've got an injured dog here, he needs help."

The woman turned toward Babs, "Oh dear, you poor thing. Give me a second, and you can bring him inside." Her arthritic fingers fumbled with the keys. "I'll phone the doctor on call for emergencies." Hurrying inside, she snapped on the lights. "We close at five. Put him down on the couch for a minute."

She took her eyes off Dougal, and glared at Babs, assessing, appraising, and judging. "Everyone's gone home except me. What's your name dear? This is a clear case of abuse. Can you complete this form for me?"

Babs froze in the woman's cold stare. Did she think Babs was the owner? "I'm sorry." She grabbed her backpack and made for the door, "I've got to go."

# # #

Leaving the Humane Shelter, Babs didn't look back. As she ran she noticed a huge new billboard announcing the solar eclipse. Pausing, she shaded her eyes and read: the date—Monday, 21st August, 2017—made her blink. That couldn't be right. She jogged onward and stopped at a newsstand. The papers all ran the same story, front page news, the solar eclipse on Monday the 21st—all of them. Tears pricked her eyes. She'd picked the wrong day, or rather, Craig lied. Damn him!

Babs ran her hardest and fastest, all the way until she reached the creek, and relative safety. She leaned against a tree to catch her breath, anger and relief fighting for supremacy. Half of her wanted to share her story with Craig. The other half wanted to tear him limb from limb. Why had he lied to her about the eclipse? She had to find him. She wouldn't rest until she'd hunted him down.

She darted along a service alley to check out the first of his usual haunts. Although she had never accompanied him, he followed a circuit to make sure he never hit the same mark twice, or at least that was how he had explained it her.

"Never get recognized, keep moving, never go to the same place or use the same route. Don't let yourself be identified as homeless. Keep changing your look, your clothes, your appearance."

Craig said he stuck to his rules like a mantra, but had he? She'd caught him in one lie at least, had he told more? Babs had assumed that thievery featured high on his priority list, but had never had the guts to ask him straight. Had they ever met in the same place twice? No, apart from the soup kitchen. His ridiculous sunglasses and hoodie made more sense; when forced to break his own rules, Craig had tried a disguise.

Babs trekked through the town checking off Craig's list as best she remembered. She arrived at the parking lot behind a home improvement store. A huddle of day laborers sat along the curb. She walked toward them.

"Excuse me, guys, have you seen Craig Peterson today?"

"Who?" They looked from one to another, shaking heads. "Sorry, don't know him."

Pulling out her phone, she hesitated. Why didn't she have a photograph of Craig? In all the time they'd known each other, he had often taken selfies, and photos of her, but she couldn't remember any of them both together. She scrolled through the photos on her phone, roll after roll, album after album. None of Craig.

"Thanks, guys." She retreated across the lot. How would she ever find him? Did she have to wait for him to find her? They hadn't made any arrangements to meet. With all the worry over Dougal, she hadn't thought about what she would do afterwards. Hungry, exhausted, and close to tears, Babs returned to the creek to sleep under the bridge. Craig, his stories and the truth, could wait until tomorrow.

# # #

A siren blared.

Babs woke, rubbed her eyes, sat up and kicked off the sheet she used at night. Half a dozen cops, maybe more, approached the creek, stirring the occupants scattered along the bank. One man, she'd never learned his name, grabbed his cart and pushed it onto the road, but he didn't escape. The cops moved in, questioning each individual, flashing a tablet at them, "seen this girl?" She wanted to run, but she knew she had nothing to fear with her fake driver's license, another gift from Craig, to prove her age— over eighteen—an independent adult.

Sitting still and silent, Babs took a deep breath as the officer came toward her. He looked her straight in the face.

"Are you Babs McVitie?"

"Yes ... sir."

"I'm arresting you on suspicion of abduction—"

"—What? I didn't abduct him, I rescued him."

The cop spun her around and cuffed her wrists before she had time to think.

"Let me go!" She struggled, pulling away, but the cops closed in. "What are you doing?"

#

The cruiser fought through a barrage of reporters at the precinct. Cameras flashed. Hands pressed against the windows. Someone hammered on the roof. Angry faces snarled at her.

"What's going on?"

Nobody heard her above the noise of the writhing crowd.

Somehow, the cops dragged her through the mob and inside to a windowless interview room. She waited alone. A lazy fly crawled across the table. On the ceiling, a yellow fluorescent strip-light buzzed intermittently. For some unaccountable reason, as the minutes ticked by, she thought of the eclipse. What future did she have? She'd miss the whole thing. This once-in-a-lifetime event would pass her by. Why did she care, and why now?

The door opened. A sandy-haired man in a suit—a detective?—walked over, pulled out a chair, and slapped a dozen photographs on the table. "This is you, right?"

Babs looked at the pictures of her carrying Dougal wrapped in a blanket and then back at the detective's impassive face.

"You! In broad daylight."

"Yes, that's me."

"With a body wrapped up like a package for the mailman."

"I had to wrap him tightly to stop him escaping. It was supposed to be dark, during the eclipse, but I messed up my dates—"

"—Everyone knows the eclipse is on Monday, today, common knowledge, this afternoon. You'd have to be a fool or a lunatic not to know that."

"Craig said it was on Sunday."

"Craig who?"

"Craig Younger. He helped me, I mean, I thought he was helping me."

"Are you seriously trying to lay the blame at his door?"

"No, I'm just explaining what happened. How I got the idea in the first place."

"You're not denying you took him?"

"No." She sat up straight and met his gaze. "I saved him. Nobody else would."

"We'll see if the court of public opinion agrees, but I'm damned sure a jury won't buy your pack of lies."

"If you've got the photos then you must have the camera. It has a time stamp and will prove my story."

"What camera?"

"The camera on the telephone pole outside Dougal's yard."

"Who's Dougal? Are you trying to implicate someone else too?"

"No, I—"

"Listen! I don't know what's going on in your depraved little mind, and don't think you can play the Looney Tunes card and get away with it." His phone pinged, and he read the screen. "That's the only piece of good news today."

"What is?"

"They checked him over at the hospital. He's dehydrated but he's going to be fine. His Gran and his brother are by his bedside. No thanks to you."

"I don't understand."

He turned the screen toward her. Babs' lips parted. It made no sense. "What's Craig doing? Is that the missing boy in that hospital bed? Who's the old lady?"

"As if you don't know his name. He's been headline news for weeks." The detective stabbed the screen, "Jason Younger, his brother, Craig, and their gran. Why choose the park to dump him?"

"Park?"

"Did you think there wouldn't be cameras? We have recordings of you dropping him on the bench. That fleece blanket's at forensics."

Babs couldn't speak, couldn't think, couldn't process what she heard.

"And," the detective leaned forward and whispered, "we'll find a hair or some skin cells on that baseball cap Jason clung to when we found him."

The familiar sound of the constellation tune rang out. The detective shoved the phone in his pocket. "Wait here."

Babs knew where he was going and why. She had a million questions for Craig. But would she ever see him again? How could he have set her up like this? What had she ever done to deserve such treachery? She let her heartbeat slow and took a deep, sobering breath. Somehow she knew that if their paths crossed again, and she had another chance to ask him all her questions, the outcome would be the same: the chinks of her daylight obliterated by his darkness.

—

Madeline McEwen is an ex-pat from the UK, bi-focaled and technically challenged. She and her Significant Other manage their four offspring, one major and three minors, two autistic, two neurotypical, plus a time-share with Alzheimer's. She is a member of the California Writers Club and Sisters in Crime, Norcal. She maintains a blog with a loyal following. Her platform is associated with the Autism Hub [UK], as well as the usual Facebook and Twitter accounts, predominantly in the realm of disabilities.

Filmmaker

By John Betton

(This story was originally published in the February 2019 issue of The MOON.)

A little boy, kneeling on a chair at a kitchen table coloring, asks in accented English, "Where's Momma? I want to see her. When's she coming home?" His voice is straightforward, a bit demanding, but no different than any child wanting something missing. The camera brings in his drawing, shows his fingers grasping a crayon. He makes strokes of black, hair surrounding a narrow face. Camera backs to a long shot, whole kitchen, table with boy, dated stove and fridge, a man, slender, unshaven, standing at counter chopping vegetables, cigarette between his lips.

A girl, about six, comes into the scene, goes to the boy, pokes him. He makes a face at her. She moves to the counter, eyes the pile of vegetables, says, "Momma always puts in extra peppers."

The man, Hamid, sets his cigarette down, pulls her to him in a brief hug. "Leila," he speaks in English as well, accent thicker, "you and Jamal, set the table." Leila returns to the table, starts to push Jamal's papers aside. He squeals. Dad calls, "Hey." The kids turn to him. "What do you want to drink?"

"Coke," both answer.

He replies, "Do you think we are rich Americans?"

Hanna: "Jeez Dad, I knew you were doing this, but what the…"

Jeremy: "You're interrupting."

Tim, filmmaker and father, remote in hand, stops the film, rises from his chair, scans his family and the room, pretend camera in his hands.

"Daaad!"

The scene is Tim's media room, complete with projection equipment, large screen, subdued lights. Wife Ellen and fifteen-year old daughter Hanna sit on a sofa, twelve-year old son Jeremy is slouched beside them in an oversized, leather chair, his own similar chair on the other side of the sofa, empty. Photos and awards from his career as a documentary filmmaker decorate the walls.

The family waits, Ellen turning to Tim, eyebrows raised. He registers her impatience, wonders if asking his family to view this latest piece of his work is a good choice.

He lets his hands drop, "What's the problem Hanna, not your life?"

"Well noooo. You, your camera, your other guy, in their apartment every day, like, who would allow that?"

"Clearly not you," her mother says.

"Muuum!"

"C'mon Hanna, use your common sense," he answers in a chiding tone. "It couldn't be every day."

"Dad, I'm not a moron. What I'm saying is you were in their lives a lot."

"I was, but keep perspective. Remember you were ten when I started."

"Right!"

"And I had other projects, a living to earn, not to mention my own family to spend time with."

"As if you did a lot of that."

"Hanna!"

"Muuum! You're missing the point. Dad was away a lot. Even you had things to say on that. But what I'm talking about is having strangers right in the middle of your life. Not just in, but in and out. Like how many times? Totally crazy."

What is Hanna saying? Is she simply being fifteen? And why has he asked them to do this? Simple enough, he'd thought, when he finished the final edit. This is good work, maybe an important piece, and important that his family see it.

"Not so crazy, Hanna, if you know what you're doing and have a good purpose."

"Such as?" Jeremy asks.

"That should come through in the film. But look around. We live in privileged ways. Most people in those countries do not. Life is uncertain. I wanted to show that, the day-to-day reality. As for Hanna's question and the filming, it wasn't easy for them, or us. Every time we were in there shooting it was a balance – intrude, stay out of the way, get the everyday bits and then, when possible, intimate moments."

What more does he need? In part, he wants them to experience where he's been and have some sense of what kept him away so much. At the same time, he wants their reactions, family to family, as it were. What else? Will they see what he tried to achieve and how he was committed to that? Will they see that sometimes making good art requires sacrifices?

Hanna's eyes go to her mother, back to him. She says nothing. He waits another moment, returns to his chair, starts the film again.

A narrow street, lined with older apartment buildings, cars parked, some with one set of wheels up on the curb, people moving about, children playing with a soccer ball in the narrow path between cars. The camera swings around to one building, perhaps classy in another era but, like those around it, worn, a little run down. The stone facade appears dirty from decades of dust and pollution, the iron railing on one side of the stairs to the front door leans, curtains hang askew in some windows, garbage cans sit on the sidewalk.

Hamid comes out the door, down the four stairs, walks away. He nods to a man, passes two women in summer dresses, another in traditional garb, covered head to foot in black, only her eyes showing. The camera follows him, brings into focus a busy street beyond, a wide boulevard, traffic in both directions. A street car goes by, clangs.

Living room of the small apartment, older woman on a couch, green fabric faded showing white wear marks. Jamal and Leila, one on each side, all three looking at what appears to be a storybook. Jamal squirms. The woman doesn't try to hold him. He scampers away, brings back a photo, whines, "I want to see Momma too." He climbs back beside the woman, holds the picture up to her, does not return his attention to the book.

Sounds come from off-screen, footsteps on stairs, a door opening and closing. The camera swings in that direction. Hamid walks into view, goes to the older woman, pecks her on the cheek. He scoops up Leila and whirls her around. Jamal grabs for his knees, hugs, cries, "Were you with Momma? Did you see her?"

Hamid gathers him in one arm, holding Leila in the other, semi-dances around the tiny space. "I did."

Jamal demands, "When's she coming home?" Leila leans away from her father, watches.

Hamid, face and voice now serious, answers, "I don't know. Soon I think."

The older woman speaks, translation on screen, "How is my daughter?"

"Teta, she's okay."

Teta half turns her head, looks at him sideways, skeptical.

"Dad, I don't like where this is going."

"Why, big sister?"

"That should be obvious," Hanna answers, glaring at her brother. "Why isn't the mother there? Where is she? You can see in the looks that something's wrong."

"And you were expecting what?"

"Jeez, Jeremy, get a cell!"

Ellen, sounding concerned, "Tim, tell me again why we're doing this."

"I thought we had that settled."

"I'm fine, but how about Hanna and Jeremy?"

"You got it, Mom. Little snot-face here, well, who knows what it will do to him?"

"Thanks for caring, big sister."

"C'mon guys, give it a chance. This is serious work and I want your serious response."

"Tim, we're clear on that," Ellen's eyes now holding his. "But this isn't just about us. You're not sure of something, is that it?"

"For god's sake, Ellen, I'm not one of your students." He pauses, goes on, "Besides, what's wrong with wanting to share my work with my family?"

"Oh, don't patronize us. You always want something more."

Jeremy jumps in. "Yay, Mom and Dad. Give us a show."

"Jeez, Jeremy!"

"In any case, I'm with Hanna. So far this is heading down a darker path than I expected."

Tim turns away, picks up the remote; "Sorry, no reveal at this point."

"You're sure these two can handle it?"

"Really Ellen, this generation of video games and Harry Potter? C'mon."

Hamid walks towards forbidding building. Camera pans past him, takes in the structure, high concrete walls, windows with bars. In the near ground is chain-link fence topped with barbed wire, a gate, guard posts, uniformed men.

Hamid stops, shows papers, goes through, stops at a barred door; more guards, papers checked again and this time he is searched. Motion towards camera, words, questions, menacing looks, then camera waved through, follows Hamid into building, along corridor and into a room. Hand comes out blocking camera. Camera moves back, adjusts, and films from outside, through glass.

A gaunt, dark-haired woman enters. Hamid, still standing, leans into a glass partition, presses his lips to it. The woman meets his lips with hers. They sit, pick up black, old-fashioned telephone handsets. Hamid raises his eyes to the guard standing behind her, speaks into the phone, "Reem, are you okay?" Her mouth moves as though each word is an effort. They have a brief exchange, then he shows a photo, points to it. Parts of his phrases are audible: "Jamal … growing up… missing you. Leila helps…" She smiles wanly. We hear him say, "Teta," but the rest of the sentence is unclear. Reem turns away, mouth tight, hint of scowl.

"Oh god, the poor woman," Hanna cries.

Ellen reaches for her hand, squeezes it.

Once again Tim stops the film. He begins to speak, reconsiders. Instead, he rises and walks behind the sofa. Hanna twists to face him. He bends down, kisses her on the forehead, reaches, strokes Ellen's hair. Hanna, eyes still on him, frowns.

Unperturbed and maybe indifferent to his sister's emotions, his tone hinting at being impressed, Jeremy asks, "How did you get in?"

"There were hurdles," Tim answers, ruffling his son's hair.

"Like what?"

"Officials, documents, permissions and, yes, a little money changed hands."

"Cool. You bribed somebody."

"Small time stuff. The custom in those places."

Hamid reaches, his hand touches the glass. Reem shrugs, sighs, her forehead becomes creased. She turns away, rises, begins to leave the room, turns back, her face filled with something – resignation, pain, or perhaps just the gauntness we first saw.

"Look at her!" Hanna cries, voice almost shrill.

"I know, Hanna. It was a painful moment. I'm sure what I felt then was pretty much what you're feeling now."

Hanna, slowly shaking her head, "Her face! Oh my god!"

"I know. Three, maybe four weeks in that place, an awful toll."

"But why was she there?" Hanna, voice still pained.

"Politics!"

"Too simple, Tim," Ellen, giving a mild reprimand. "You can do better."

"Simple for me but not for her."

He pauses. Jeremy fills the gap: "C'mon Dad. Don't fudge the answer."

"No fudge. We're looking at a complicated place to live."

"Background, Tim," Ellen says pointedly. "The kids need help. They don't follow the news, and they aren't studying any of this stuff in school."

"A good reason for them to see the film, don't you think, a bit of contemporary history."

"Just the trailer, Dad," Jeremy chimes in.

Tim turns to him. "Okay, the brief version. What got Reem into trouble was being part of a group. Here it would be no more than a protest. There, anything like it was anti-regime."

"Just 'anti'? Didn't they stand for anything?" Ellen asks.

"As far as I knew they were just a loose collection of people, frustrated, agitating, speaking out."

"Seems pointless."

"From our position I'm sure you're right. There? A different story. In any case, police hauled a bunch of them out of a cafe one evening. That was it."

"Hardly, Tim! What else? What happened next? What about her family?"

He waits a moment, eyes still on Ellen, considers the demand in her questions, answers. "Hamid learned of the arrest hours later. He went searching and, of course, no one in authority would help."

"He must have been terrified."

"We hadn't started filming yet, so I didn't hear the story right away. Days went by, Hamid told me, before he even knew she was alive."

Ellen looks at her children, back to Tim: "Alive?"

"Yes. People disappeared, some never heard from again."

"Jeez, Dad, what kind of country?"

"We hear stories," Ellen says, "but how do people like us wrap our minds around conditions like that?"

"Out of our experience, isn't it? Even being there, you don't fully get it." He turns to the children. "How about you two? Can you imagine anything like that?"

"As in one of you being taken away?" Jeremy answers.

"You got it."

Both shake their heads.

"What they must have gone through," Ellen, tone now plaintive, "and that poor woman..."

"Hamid was in bad shape. We were ready to cancel, pack up and come home, but he said Reem really wanted us to do the film. So, we stayed and began."

Tim picks up the remote. Ellen says, "Wait a minute."

He turns to her.

"What about you? I assumed you faced risks, but you never said much. How serious was it?"

She watches, head tilted.

"We had moments."

All three sets of eyes are on him.

"You're sure you want me to talk about this now? I'd like to get back to the film."

"That, my dear husband, is a dodge. Fess up. What happened?"

He shrugs. "We were harassed – officials, police – nothing we hadn't expected. Threats? Yes, a few. All part of being there and you can never tell whether they're serious." He hesitates, sighs deeply. "Once, early on, we were taken into custody."

Ellen, angry: "You never told me."

Hanna: "Daddy!"

"It was brief, not as bad as it sounds. And I didn't want to worry you."

Ellen, shaking her head, "Christ, Tim!"

"But what if?" Hanna asks.

Jeremy: "Were you scared?"

Tim looks at Jeremy, answers, "We were. It was intimidating. But they released us the same day with no explanation, in the same way they took us in. We *had* been cautious, but were a whole lot more so afterwards."

"Does that mean she wasn't—cautious?"

"No. The only caution in that country was to keep your mouth shut, something they weren't willing to do."

"Why?"

"She said there was no future for them and even less for the kids, too oppressive, too corrupt."

"So what was she charged with, being a good parent?"

Tim laughs, "Maybe nothing. In all likelihood Reem never knew."

"They can do that?"

"There, yes, and in many other countries as well—even our own in certain circumstances."

Jamal grins, cries out. He is facing four candles on a cake, puffs, blows, extinguishes all four. Two other little boys are at the table. One pokes his finger into the cake and then into his mouth. He laughs, a deep caricature, as though he were some cartoon figure. The other boy and Jamal follow suit, licking the icing off their fingers in exaggerated ways. Leila, standing to one side, complains, "Papa, don't let them. It ruins the cake."

Hamid, smiling, shakes his head. "Leila, they're just boys."

The camera swings away, finds Teta. She is standing to the side, steps forward, knife in hand, ready to cut the cake. Jamal reaches again with his finger. Teta catches his hand, holds on a moment, releases it and, with her own hand free, scoops up a finger of icing. The boys giggle.

"Sweet, Tim," Ellen comments, "a softer touch than in your other films. Is there more like it?"

"A good moment, yes. We had others but I haven't included many."

"Why?" Hanna asks.

"Balance and focus. Families are families wherever you go. The real story I wanted to tell is the circumstances they live in. I want the viewer to experience the impact of that."

Ellen: "But you haven't made a propaganda film."

"Of course not," he answers, sharper than he intended, "unless you see something I haven't."

He pauses, lets his annoyance settle, continues.

"This film was harder than I expected, hard to stick with and hard emotionally. I never felt part of the family; I couldn't let that happen. But you can't spend as much time with them as I did without feeling invested. Their life was difficult and I wanted to document that. At the same time I did care about them. So, I need your reactions, your take on how well I did on both counts."

"Yeah, and he wants us to know how good we've got it," Jeremy says.

Tim nods to Jeremy, looks at Hanna and Ellen. Did they hear his plea? And what was it anyway? All three wait, watching him. He glances at Ellen and

Hanna once more, receives no response, turns back to the remote, re-starts the film.

Camera shot, framed by a window, shows an outside view, rooftops, TV antennas and, beyond those, the soaring peak of a mosque's minaret. The scene holds for a moment, background beyond the minaret unclear. Then, the sound of far-off explosions. Camera brings into focus distant, rising, plumes of smoke, pulls back and returns inside, pans the room, the living room, settles on Hamid and Reem standing in the middle, holding one another. Jamal is at their knees, Leila sitting in a chair, Teta on the couch, both watching. Hamid strokes Reem's hair, presses her to him. She turns her face up, puts a light kiss on his lips, settles her head on his chest, reaches down with one hand, pulls Jamal against her thigh.

Leila calls, "Dance, Momma, dance like you used to."

Reem smiles at her, wrinkles her nose, pulls Hamid close. They begin to shuffle around the tiny space, Jamal hanging on to their legs.

"Good stuff Dad," Jeremy comments, "but how did she get out?"

"Often what happens when civil wars start. Many guards just leave their posts and prisoners walk away."

"Really!"

"Yes."

"Were you there when she got home?" Hanna wonders. "It must have been something."

"I wish we had been, but no. When we arrived the next day, Jamal ran to the door yelling, 'Momma's home! Momma's home!' We filmed the scene right after."

"So, how did you feel?"

Tim meets his daughter's gaze, turns the question back on her, "How do you feel now watching it?"

Hanna smiles. Tim adds, "Me too, not only good but something more, a real sense of relief."

Family, sitting in living room, Hamid on couch, Leila, beside him, taller, more grown-up, less a little girl, watchful; Jamal on the floor at his feet, making engine sounds as he pushes toys, a car and a truck, back and forth. Reem, in a chair away from them, appears separated, on her own. The camera closes in on her. Her eyes move as if she is seeing something, but her face is vacant.

Pot clanking, whistle of kettle comes from off-screen. Camera swings in that direction. Teta's face appears in doorway. She scowls at camera. From somewhere, closer than before, a whump, the unmistakable sound of an explosion. Jamal whimpers. He looks up at his father who remains motionless, turns to his mother, starts toward her. Her eyes are elsewhere, not seeing him, or seeming not to. Crying now, he redirects and heads off camera. We hear Teta cooing to him.

Hanna: "Dad, this is gonna get worse, isn't it?"

Leila on the floor in corner of living room, playing with dolls, talking to them. Reem comes into view. Leila turns to her. "Momma, why don't we have a TV?"

The camera swings outside through window, pans rooftop skyline, shows, among other things, plethora of TV aerials, but no smoke, nor any sounds of explosions. It returns inside, sweeps the room showing no evidence of a TV.

"Papa and I don't like TV."

"Why?"

Reem pauses, her eyes search the room before coming back to Leila. She answers, her voice serious: "We're like Teta in a way. She doesn't like a lot of modern things. She thinks TV is no good for traditions. Papa and I don't agree about the traditions, but we do about TV, especially all the stupid American stuff."

"But other kids watch it."

Reem smiles at her, sits on the floor, picks up one of the dolls, talks to it. "TVee, Leila beeee, every little girl just wants a mommeee." *Leila, falling into her mother's lap, more little girl for the moment than she is, laughs.* "Don't be silly, Momma."

Reem, holding Leila, falls backwards to the floor, nuzzling and kissing her daughter who starts to giggle. Jamal comes running from off screen, yelps as he worms his way into the heap, both children's hands searching for ways to tickle their mother.

"This is the set-up, right Dad?"

"Meaning what, my smart-assed son?"

"Simple. The filmmaker getting us ready for what's to come. Like Hanna said, it's gonna get worse."

"Well, fancy that. Little snot-face agreeing with me."

"Hey big sister, you taught me well."

Hamid and Reem in the kitchen, Reem preparing food. Hamid comes up behind, encircles her waist with his arms, pulls her to him, kisses her ear. She swivels, hugs him, but returns to the food. He holds her for a long moment; she makes no further response. He shrugs and moves away.

"Look at him," Hanna says, voice raised. "All he wants is sex. He has no idea what she's been through."

"Hanna, don't be so black and white. Love is more complex, and so is the situation."

"I don't think so, Mom. There's no sign they've talked or that he knows what happened to her in prison. Sure he wants his wife back. But Dad cuddles you the same way."

"Hey, you're too young to notice those things," Tim chides.

"As if you guys are ever subtle."

Jeremy: "Be careful of these innocent ears."

Hanna: "Yeah, right!"

"But isn't what we saw just affection?" Ellen persists.

"Mom, look at how he turned away from her. He wanted more, and that's sex."

"Alright, point conceded. But give them time."

"Well nooo. Time has passed. Dad?"

"Several months."

"And this is edited. What are you trying to show? And what have you left out?"

Reem sitting, camera on her, Tim's voice from off-screen:"Reem, life has been difficult for you since you came home."

Reem's mouth turns up, she shrugs: "Yes, hard, very hard. Prison changes you."

Tim: "The hardest part?"

Reem: "Being mother." She appears to be about to cry. Turns away for a moment, turns back, face stoic. "I want to, and I try, but..." She goes silent.

The camera brings in Hamid, "And for you?"

Hamid, perplexed, shakes his head, mutters, "Those bastards. What they do to us."

The camera comes to the children, sitting together on the couch, both serious.

"Leila, Jamal, we've been here in your home for a long time. What has it been like?"

Leila turns to Jamal, waiting for him to answer. When he doesn't, she speaks: "Sometimes it's strange. You're here and then you aren't."

Jamal: "But after you come back, well, in a little while I don't notice you."

Tim: "And how has it been since Momma came home?"

Both children look away from the camera. Jamal slides off the couch, the camera follows as he walks the few steps across the room, sits beside Reem, leans into her. The camera swings back to Leila. She is watching, turns to the camera, her voice grave and grown up: "It's different."

"An odd twist, Tim. What made you insert an interview?"

"For a couple of reasons, one being to acknowledge our presence in their lives. You can edit a film like this to make it look like no filming was going on and no film crew was in the room. That creates a false impression. The second reason is all gut. I felt it was important for the family to speak to the viewer, give you a different view of the toll prison had taken on her and on the family."

Reem and Hamid once more standing side by side at the kitchen counter, both silent. She reaches for a cigarette package, takes one, lights it, walks over to a window, stands staring out. He goes to her, leans against her back. She turns, pushes him away. He is quiet for a moment, studying her and then half-yells, "What's wrong with you?"

Reem meets his eyes for a moment then turns her head away, from him and from the camera. Her shoulders rise. When she turns back she wipes at her cheek, but her face is now filled with something else. She utters a sound, stops, brings her hands up, speaks almost to herself, "I have to get out of here."

"And go where? To some fucking refugee camp," Hamid's voice raised, not quite yelling.

Reem glares at him. "You go wherever you want. Or stay. It doesn't matter to me. I don't care anymore."

He shifts away, suddenly turns back. For a moment it seems he might strike her. He hesitates, glares. "Sure, go to your political friends, get locked up again. Leave the kids. They won't miss you."

She stares at him, her eyes hard, black. "Yeah, you and your girlfriend can take care of them, or did she leave you too?"

The children come in carrying school things, backpack, lunch bag. Jamal is taller, older, perhaps seven. Leila stares at her parents; Jamal, eyebrows bunched, looks around. A moment of stasis, all four standing, watching. Then Reem turns to the camera, yells, "Get out of here!"

Hanna, in tears: "You have to stop, Dad. I can't take this."

"There's not much more, Hanna. I know this is tough, but your reactions are important."

Hanna is quiet for a moment then almost explodes: "But you didn't do anything. You could have."

"What was he supposed to do, big sister?"

Hanna turns on her brother, indignation, rage: "Can't you see anything? The mother needed help. Whatever happened to her in prison must have been awful."

Jeremy, ignoring the emotion: "Like what?"

"Even a little runt like you can figure that out. How about torture? How about rape? How about watching people die?"

Ellen: "Tim, what Hanna is saying is important. I think it deserves an answer."

"What's the point?"

Ellen, voice raised: "The point? The point she's making is, as a western raised and educated man, you would have known Reem was in deep trouble. If you didn't, you should have. If you did, then you made choices."

Tim sighs, eyes first on his wife then on his daughter: "Let's watch it through to the end."

Camera pans a street scene, a wide boulevard with store fronts, cafe patios, a few people walking, parked cars but none moving. The sounds of explosions and gunfire come from nearby. Reem, sitting at a table on one of the patios with two men and another woman, in heated discussion. Their voices are raised, not quite shouting. Reem stands up, throws her hands in the air, walks away.

A second scene, this a line of tents, people wandering about, trash scattered, kids kicking around a soccer ball. The camera zeroes in on one tent; Hamid emerges, searches, calls. The camera swings to the children, Leila and Jamal, bigger and older, leaving the group of kids and coming to him. The camera follows them a moment then turns to the tent, zooms in on it. The flap is partially open, the camera peeks inside. Teta, sitting on a folding chair, chin on her chest, appears to be in a deep sleep.

"Oh shit. I knew this was coming," Hanna cries.

"Tim," Ellen calls, her voice sharp.

Hanna near tears, voice full of indignation: "How could you? How could you just do nothing? She needed help. You knew."

"Not my job, Hanna."

"Your job? She's human, you're human. She needed help."

"Big sister, you're so first-world."

"Fuck off."

"Hanna!"

"Mom, you don't get it. None of you do, just like the husband. How could she return to being a wife? We don't have to know what happened in prison. It's obvious."

Ellen, worried, meets her daughter's eyes, turns to her husband, frowns, glares.

Tim takes in the glare, turns back to his daughter: "A huge part of the story, Hanna, and why I was there. Families are destroyed in those situations. Sure I might have helped one. But even that isn't certain, given all that was going on. And then what about all the others?"

"You did nothing!"

"I did a lot."

"Fuck you, too."

"Hanna!"

Hanna, in full tears, turns away from her family, holding herself, sobbing. Tim goes to her, sits, puts a hand on her shoulder. She shudders, jerks free. He puts his hand back, is able to place it so she can't move further away, pulls her to him. She seems to resist and then allows herself to collapse against him. He wraps his arms around her. "It's alright baby. It's alright."

He looks past Hanna to Ellen. Whatever he is seeking, she doesn't offer. Her face is serious, perhaps accusing.

Hanna, her voice close to a whimper: "You didn't do anything."

Tim turns back to his daughter, "I did a lot, baby. But I couldn't do what you think I should have done."

Hanna pulls away, her voice regaining some of its indignation. "Right, your film came first."

"Dad, she's got you on that one."

Tim's eyes go from Jeremy to Ellen and then back to Hanna. They all wait.

He says, "Do you think so? Do you think that's true?"

—

John Betton is a retired psychologist, living in St. Albert, Alberta, Canada, where he co-founded Saint City Writers. He continues to explore through fiction his lifelong fascination with the way people think, feel and interact. His story, A New Old Love, *appears in the February 2019 edition of* Spadina Literary Review.

The Rakan Kembar

By Charles Albert Joseph

(This story was originally published in the May 2018 issue of The MOON.)

Deeyaitch looked with contempt about the train car. Peering over the top of his *London Times*, he took in the dense hodge-podge of grubby fellow Malaysians. Jammed into the tête-à-tête benches were entire families of wild, ill-behaved children, parents who were still children themselves, odiferous crones clutching rotting bird carcasses or bundles of rags...an old man sat in the front of the car, wispy gray hair sprouting from a dozen moles about his face and neck. He held a large eviscerated snake, the hideous thing no doubt due to be boiled up for some teenagers' wedding dinner.

The Express Service had again been interrupted, which was why Deeyaitch was forced to shuttle in the Local with the great unwashed masses. He buried his carefully groomed head back into the world of his *Times*, wondering just how far along this backward little land was capable of coming. It galled him that he could not even commute from his well-to-do suburb north of Kuala Lumpur to his office in the financial district without having another immaculate seersucker suit endangered by the grubbies.

He had only felt this disdain since his return from England and University. If any of his old Queen's College fellows could see him now, on the slow train, surrounded by riff-raff, he should fairly faint from mortification.

It took several hours in the cool, hushed corridors of his office building at Athercrombie and Jones (est. 1737, exactly three hundred years old!) and two piping hot cups of tea before the creases eased on his young forehead, and Deeyaitch was able to put the morning's unpleasantness behind him, immersing himself once again in the cerebral world of international trade.

By eleven twenty-six he had recovered serenity through his assessment of the Borneo poultry industry, and was therefore composed despite the surprising apparition of Harris, a rather quirky colleague (although, Cambridge!).

"I say, old bird! Free for lunch, today, then?" Harris said, poking his head in the door.

Deeyaitch raised an eyebrow without looking up from his tables. "Of course I'm free, silly duck."

Silly indeed: the staff of the Near East Commodities department always ate lunch together at the nearby Albion Club, an indispensable milieu of rumor and prognostication that could make or break an investor. Indispensable, that is, unless a particularly important client was in town. Those were dined at Chez Julien.

"Grand. Well, you see, the Old Bull himself is here. Asked about dining with one of the natives. So, there it is. We had to pick between you and the Great Faker. Well, Julien's it is. Pick you up at one, then?"

Deeyaitch nodded his head, and Harris's vanished from the doorway. Well! Lord Athercrombie himself! The Old Bull, the last heir to the Athercrombie family fortune, a stout man of fifty given to the occasional round-the-world jaunt. Rumor had him headed to India. Evidently, the shuttle to Calcutta had been waylaid, or perhaps inclement weather had forced a detour. A bit of luck, that! Nothing improves one's career like personal acquaintance with the founding family. And protectionism was rampant in this company.

On the other hand... Deeyaitch wrinkled his nose in disdain of being called a "native." Even worse was to be invoked in the same breath as Mastapa Ma'lagway, known in the office as The Great Faker, a preposterous, portentous buffoon, not even a native of Malaysia but instead a rootless drifter originating from the Indian subcontinent, an undisciplined megalomaniac whose affectation of bemused paternal worldliness was surely to compensate for his inability to get a proper English education. That they had chosen Deeyaitch over Ma'lagway was not even gratifying; quite simply, the man was insufferable.

When he arrived at Chez Julien, Deeyaitch blushed with honor to be seated only one away from Lord Athercrombie. What is more, Deeyaitch immediately felt a mystical bond with the man. An invisible connection. This sort of feeling was known among the grubbies of his people as soul-brotherhood: Deeyaitch and Lord Athercrombie were *rakan kembar:* twin souls. He lost all resentment of being chosen as the token native and found himself looking forward to an epiphanal luncheon.

And then the Great Faker came.

And was seated between them.

If Ma'lagway was aware that he was coming between two *rakan kembar*, he was only the more pleased to draw the attention of both to what he considered its rightful place: himself. For that matter, he exhibited no concern for the desperate feelings of others of the party who were English and therefore desirous of engaging Lord Athercrombie in the possibility of being returned one day to the mother country.

For Ma'lagway, the entire room was there to be entertained by his portentous bombast, and he delivered one ego-centric monologue after another in that lilting yet sonorous voice of the Indian. The deference of the silly English to Ma'lagway reminded Deeyaitch in great annoyance that the buffoon was regarded within the firm as a seer of Eastern culture. Preposterous indeed since Ma'lagway had had to flee several of these backwater countries under threat of death, so profoundly inept was he in understanding anything except his own magnificent self-worth.

Ma'lagway's indiscreet recounting of a scandal involving a corrupt local businessman, one of Deeyaitch's uncles, capped the meal.

"You are all intelligent men here, of course," Ma'lagway was saying. "Our work does a marvelous job of winnowing out the chaff, doesn't it, Lord Athercrombie? And so I can give you the actual details of the case without fear of misinterpretation. For this is a very delicate matter; it involves a terribly important businessman, well-connected to the highest levels of government and so on. Well. He has used our services on a number of occasions for the underwriting of his timber concerns, and we have found him to be of the finest caliber of credit risk.

"However, it was only two months ago at the child-marriage of the governor's son to three lovely daughters of the various politicians, in which I was asked to read some benedictions from the *Kama Sutra*, that I discovered that this lumber company did not exist at all, and that in fact, he was exporting not trees, but aboriginal virgins, to the brothels of Japan!

"Well, that may indeed be a more profitable venture," he paused here for the laughter that he knew would follow, and continued, "but it is hardly a realm in which our company engages, and so I regretfully declined the last request for loan... despite a private offer made to me in the denomination of twelve- and thirteen-year-olds!"

The laughter exploding from around the room galled Deeyaitch so much that he could not finish his filet of sole. How presumptuous of these men to despise this practice, when half of the men in this room were customers of

Deeyaitch's uncle. Ma'laway must realize this; what political maneuvering was he attempting here before the Old Bull?

Athercrombie looked askance at Deeyaitch's uneaten sole as a waiter carried it off. This only upset Deeyaitch the more. Worse was Ma'lagway's patronizing observation that Malaysian "boys" had trouble digesting dairy products and that perhaps Deeyaitch's mouth was bigger than his stomach.

"I'm rather afraid that the size of *my* mouth isn't the problem," muttered Deeyaitch darkly, a comment generally unnoticed due to Ma'lagway's chatter. Unnoticed, except by his *rakan kembar*, who smiled faintly, a twinkle shining in his paternal eye as he rose from his chair, interrupting the oratory at last.

"Well, well, a most excellent repast. Good old Julien. The French are quite incompetent at anything except cooking, but there, they are the last word in civilization." Deeyaitch smiled at that remark, which he had heard often in University. "And I suppose a brandy and cigar would help the digestive process along." He turned toward the club room as the others at the table sprang from their seats to follow him.

Some fortuitous delay in the serving of the brandy had them lighting cigars immediately, and Deeyaitch was overjoyed to see the Old Bull insisting on lighting the cigar of The Faker, particularly in light of the latter's utter intolerance for tobacco. Within a few minutes, Ma'lagway was quite green.

"I—ulp!—think I'd better go back to the office; these bloody things don't agree with me," he blurted, his smooth palaver coarsened in panicky concern for his own bloated stomach.

"Quite right of you; beastly habit, that," said Deeyaitch triumphantly, between puffs. As the Great Faker fled from the room, an onerous veil lifted, and suddenly everyone else's conversation became gayer, more animated. Harris and Barnaby bantered witty gossip about their respective clients, Japanese silk makers. Marlowe told an engrossing account of a factory venture in Singapore in which the locals had tried to produce a batik seersucker.

"Doomed from the start!" he ended, laughing. "Can you imagine it, chicken keepers in suits on the Malacca Straits?" The company snickered; although this was precisely the sort of thing Deeyaitch would have found terribly amusing before today, after the ridicule of his own family moments ago, it disconcerted him, and in his twill seersucker he supposed that he looked the ridiculous chicken-salesman to his mates. In the face of the slurs of

Ma'lagway, and in the light of his invitation to the lunch based solely on his nationality, he felt an unfamiliar sense of guilt about his intolerance on the train this morning.

He became, then, rather withdrawn, and finished his cigar quietly. His desire to converse with his *rakan kembar*, rekindled with the dispatching of Ma'lagway, was again at an ebb. Besides, the rest of the room was now filling the Great Faker's void.

Well, let them! Let them show their cleverness by laughing at Malaysians in seersucker. What was so ridiculous about his adopting English culture? In this enlightened age, it was not acceptable to call Malaysians an inferior people, yet it was still permissible to mock the anglophiles among them. And how fair was that? Wasn't it also prejudiced and hypocritical to dictate to him whose culture he should adopt, what clothes he should wear?

At last the lunch party was breaking up; Deeyaitch headed with the others toward the door, but found Lord Athercrombie motioning to him.

"If you aren't too terribly busy this afternoon, I should appreciate your company in a drive. Let us walk to the Rolls. Deejay, is it?"

"It—it's Deeyaitch, my Lord."

"Curious name. Not traditional Malaysian, I think."

Deeyaitch considered Lord Athercrombie's visage as he decided how to respond. He generally avoided questions about his name, but his *rakan kembar*'s face had such a familiar aspect to it—something in the eyes, perhaps—that made Deeyaitch want to be direct.

"Indeed. My mother is a great admirer of the works of D.H. Lawrence."

"Well, that was quite, hmmm, liberal of her, then, wasn't it?"

"Quite, milord. But then she is a liberal spirit. Not very many Malaysian women took a liberal arts degree from Oxford in seventeen."

"Did she indeed! Well, well. You know, I finished in fifteen." A curious look came into the Old Bull's eyes. "I was quite the admirer of Lawrence myself, at the time. I say, what did your mother look like back then? I wonder if I mightn't have met her?"

"I really couldn't say. I was only just born in nineteen-fifteen."

As he said that, Deeyaitch noticed the older man's expression grow even more strained. He seemed to be noticing Deeyaitch's face for the first time, and his bushy white eyebrows raised in an arch that Deeyaitch recognized from the mirror. Lord Athercrombie was muttering, "It's impossible. No, it's not possible; she told me she was a coolie servant, not a student!"

"Sir? I'm sorry, I don't believe I quite caught—"

"Never mind, never mind." The Old Bull made another strangely familiar expression, this time as he struggled to compose his features. Deeyaitch wondered what thoughts the older man had about this connection, but it was not his place to ask such questions, and he waited for the Old Bull to speak again.

They had reached the Rolls-Royce, and Lord Athercrombie's chauffeur started them off in the direction of the textile entrepots. The stately car made its way painstakingly through fantastically thronging alleys of hideous poverty, and along teeming pock-marked boulevards of rickshaw, bicycle, ancient mule-drawn omnibus, and thousands of hobbling pedestrians, merchants, children, thieves, and old women. Deeyaitch marveled at the strange sensation of being a part of the street traffic, and yet being comfortably isolated from it. With the noises dampened, the stenches stifled, and the burden of negotiating through crowds left to the chauffeur, one had only to relax and enjoy the ride.

Deeyaitch began to sense that he was under scrutiny of his *rakan kembar*, and in that instinctively frank way of the non-English, turned and looked at him directly.

The Old Bull, taken aback, blurted, "Deeyaitch, my boy, one would almost say you were looking at your hometown for the first time."

"Well, my Lord, I suppose this is the most tranquil trip I have ever made on my soil."

"Ah, yes. A private carriage is a marvel. Of course, it has its limitations. I personally feel that close contact is absolutely vital to our industry."

"Indeed?"

"Yes, Deeyaitch. Unless one is out there, cheek-by-jowl with the hordes, one is losing contact with the motive forces of humanity. Oh, I can see in your eyes: the great unwashed hold no fascination for you. I suppose you came to this job because of exactly the opposite inclination, eh? Quiet office, pleasant account ledgers, intellectual exercises."

Deeyaitch inclined his head.

"But you see, Deeyaitch, empires are not made abstractly. Someone had to wade into the morass in order to provide you with your account-ledgers. Someone has to verify the assets, to ascertain each facility's actual state."

Deeyaitch began to divine the direction this was going, and he didn't like it.

"Deeyaitch, my boy, we need more people with a native understanding of this city, of this culture, to be out in the field. We need to be more diligent in our fact-gathering before we make the larger decisions. Don't you agree?"

Deeyaitch didn't want to be in the field. He had only wanted to make the larger decisions! That was the whole point of University.

"I'm not quite sure I understand, my Lord...."

"You have shown quite a clear distaste of this task. Indeed, the entirety of the field work in your office has been left to Ma'lagway."

The enormity of this sank in. It was an inescapable truth, however unpalatable, that the Great Faker provided the only in-the-field verification of the ledgers that Deeyaitch so lovingly consulted.

As he mulled this, it dawned on Deeyaitch that the Rolls was approaching the Wan Fat Chu textile warehouses, which he had only the month before evaluated as a potential investment. Their inventory had seemed to him too slight, and their margin too scanty. And yet, already from a distance, he could see a bustle of activity at their docks. The business was clearly doing much better than it appeared on paper.

"Ah, I see you recognize this location. Do you know, Deeyaitch, that Chu has just obtained new financing? A miracle; he has quadrupled his volume of business."

"But—but how could that be? I personally rejected the proposal."

"The financing wasn't from us. He got the money from Lloyd's." Frozen silence. Lord Athercrombie let his single deadly point sink in before continuing.

"They sent a few inspectors round and could see a serious business in the making. We, on the other hand, did not send anyone, because Ma'lagway was elsewhere… and on paper, they did not look like an attractive risk, I grant you."

Deeyaitch stared at the bustling warehouses. The Old Bull's point was now obvious. They wanted to send him out into these noisy, smelly, crowded, uncivilized warehouse areas, to the stench and filth of the agricultural hinterlands, to be plunged once again into the ugly throngs of humanity that he had thought to escape through academic diligence. The realization of this and the resulting distaste showed clearly on his face.

The Old Bull considered him with impatience and demanded in a rather sharp tone, "I say, young man… are you *afraid* of the lower classes?"

Deeyaitch, startled, took a moment to answer. "No, my Lord, I don't believe I am. I am simply ill at ease with them."

His *rakan kembar*'s eyes softened, and his voice took an understanding, paternal tone. "Well, I certainly share that condition. But it is hardly conducive to our business. Why, almost all of our investments are in the world's great cities. It is time you grew to know them, as I have done. You have apprenticed long enough behind the ledger-book. You must prove your true worth to the firm now. You can see for yourself the disasters incurred by a lack of this diligence." He paused briefly, and continued, it seemed, in spite of himself. "Deeyaitch, my boy, I can't—won't—tell you why, but I feel you are almost like a son to me. I will make certain you are amply rewarded for this difficult next phase of your career. Your salary, for example, shall be doubled."

The Old Bull and Deeyaitch both gulped at the same time; neither of them had expected this. They turned to look out opposite windows, surveying in silence Chu's lucrative traffic.

At last the Old Bull continued. "I dare say that you, too, are a sensitive lad, as I was when I was a student at Oxford. Oh, yes, I found the hurly-burly of the masses unpalatable for tastes as refined as my own. But I knew that one day, I would have to take the helm of the family business and that such intractability as mine was doomed to a quick death. Nevertheless, I was quite beside myself with agitation when I was sent to Bombay to apprentice. The stench! The crowds! The unspeakable living conditions! It was all…" here the old gentleman's eyes drifted out over the crowds outside the Rolls, and Deeyaitch sensed an unsettling flicker of emotion.

"It was worse even than here." He leaned close to make certain Deeyaitch was attending and continued: "And the reason is that the Indians have not fully embraced the English aristocracy. But here, all goes well: we oversee the lower classes, we coerce the work out of the crude beasts. Look about you! That is what these throngs here crave most of all! To be placed under the benevolent control of us, the leaders of the great British Empire!"

Deeyaitch struggled to keep from becoming sick.

"And make no mistake..." He turned to look at Deeyaitch significantly, with all the authority he could muster, "...only a proper class system can keep the lower classes *in their place* and maintain world peace. Look at India! They worship this Gandhi, and now they are chaos!"

Deeyaitch searched the Old Bull's visage for signs of a joke. But none showed in his face.

"You see, all of these uneducated beggars, all of these mindless drones, they are only happy when a gentleman is in control. The Japanese understand this! Only country in Asia that does it properly. Mark my words, boy; by nineteen-fifty they will be undisputed masters of Asia. And Athercrombie and Jones will be the ones who helped them get there."

Deeyaitch deliberately did not peer at him as he continued, but instead froze his gaze out the window to disguise his alarm. Oblivious, Athercrombie continued pontification as the Rolls turned back toward the office.

"Yes, quite. The highest point of civilization is the gentleman's class, is it not? Therefore, all of the distasteful hullabaloo that surrounds you must necessarily surround you because they exist for you! The stinking chicken vendor and the noisy factory men and the ill-mannered urchin take on a holy importance, because, don't you see, they are all striving and sweating and sacrificing so that the miracle of you can exist in the manner to which you are accustomed. That is why we eat at Chez Julien and they eat there!" He motioned to a street vendor spooning noodles into disposable clay bowls before a throng of customers.

"Ah, thank God the perversity of classlessness never assailed gentle England, what?"

Deeyaitch was now staring openly at the lunatic seated across from him like a Dickensian specter of brokerage future come to warn him of a horrible fate to come. For the scariest part to Deeyaitch was not that the old man was rambling incoherently. It was exactly the opposite, that his maniacal logic was accessible to Deeyaitch, that Deeyaitch was already halfway to the same point of insanity himself.

***

Three weeks later, Deeyaitch stepped off of a train and strolled through a small town in a strange land. He could feel his shoulders relaxing, his agoraphobia dissipating. The energy of the place suited him: cool sunshine, ancient stone buildings, cobblestone roads—it all added to a delightfully bucolic kind of run-down disorder to the place. Although he had only just been sent here by the firm, he now began to conceive an irrepressible intention to settle here. Indeed, it seemed quite the obvious thing to do! And with that, his step grew lighter and he swung his briefcase more cheerfully. He would resign from Athercrombie and Jones and become a private investor. He would do it; he would move here, invest his life savings in the factory, join its management, and do whatever was in his power to avoid the madness that had seduced his *rakan kembar*. And what better place to free himself of that poisonous elitism than here in the land that Athercrombie had expressed the greatest aversion to: India.

‒‒

Charles Joseph Albert runs a metallurgy shop in San Jose, California, where he lives with his wife and three boys. His poems and fiction have appeared recently in Quarterday, Chicago Literati, 300 Days of Sun, Abstract Jam, The MOON Magazine, Literary Hatchet, *and* Here Comes Everyone.

Fourth of July

By Arthur Carey

(This story was originally published in the July 2018 issue of The MOON.)

Ahmad jerked awake, dragged from uneasy sleep by the wail of a siren on the street below. In his dream, he had been back in the desert in Afghanistan, firing an AK-47 at targets stuffed with straw to resemble men. He was exhausted, worn out from non-stop travel. Was it only days before he had been living with his mother Ameena in a mud house in a village?

Now he was deep in the land of the infidels. Ahmad had just turned 17 and didn't expect to live to be 18. He shut his eyes and thought of his companions, six men and a silent, dark-haired girl. Were they also troubled in their sleep?

Morning revealed the full ugliness of the third-story flat to which they had been brought. Arriving in a truck, he had glimpsed the soaring, glass-eyed towers of Manhattan. But here ripped wallpaper dangled from scarred walls. The main room had two folding chairs, a table, an old TV, and a battered couch with broken springs.

Beyond lay a grungy bathroom reeking of disinfectant. In the kitchen, insects scurried from sight when the light was flipped on.

The day passed slowly. The small television blared in one corner. Ahmad stared in distaste. Women in shorts hit small white balls across a net. Had they no shame, clothed like that in public? When one hit the ball back and the other missed it, people in the stands clapped politely. They encouraged the disgraceful display!

"Afifa! Serve the food. You... boy! Help her!"

Ahmad's eyes swung to the speaker, a lean, muscular man with glasses, named Fazil. Unlike the other five men, he still had a beard, but it was neatly trimmed. Fazil was the leader, and from the way he treated the watchful, silent girl wearing a kerchief, Ahmad assumed she was his wife. Introductions had been brief when the group met—first names only.

Hatchet-faced and cold-eyed, Fazil had supervised the training in the desert and watched keenly as they boarded the first of several planes. They flew first to a Latin American country and then to Canada, using false identification. Then he had led them to a truck that waited on a deserted road. On a dark, overcast night, they crossed an unguarded section of the border into the United States.

Ahmad followed the girl into the kitchen. She had prepared pilau, rice cooked in meat juices, the way his mother did. The girl filled the plates and he carried them to the hard-eyed men who sat cross-legged on the floor. Dusk fell. As they ate, some of the men touched their chins unconsciously, feeling for beards no longer there.

Ahmad had been 15 on the day that changed his life. A frightened teacher had pointed him out to the men in uniform as the smartest boy in the class, the one who read and reread the books sent by Americans before the Taliban had seized the village.

"So, you read the filthy lies of the nonbelievers," the leader had said, fingering a children's novel in English. He threw it to the floor in disgust.

"I..." began Ahmad, expecting a beating.

"Never mind," the man said. A scar furrowed his right cheek, and he had a dirty, black patch over one eye. "I have told the teacher to give you more books. Soon you will be schooled with other boys, watch tapes on the television, and study the language of our enemy, the Great Satan."

And he had. Ahmad had joined other boys, older boys, whose names he never learned, listening to endless lectures about the sacrilege and crimes of unbelievers in the West. At night, before shuffling off to sleep, the boys huddled before a TV screen and watched the lives of the enemies of Islam unfold. Such extravagance! Women without respect! But he noticed something else that surprised him. Many of the people smiled and laughed, even the adults. His lips curled. Only children at play laughed. Life became serious too quickly.

The boys talked when the teachers were gone. Jihad! They were being trained for jihad! A cold uneasiness settled in Ahmad's stomach.

One night after he turned 16, a man came and took him from the school. After a hurried goodbye to his tearful mother, he boarded a rickety bus and rode over rutted roads to a dusty camp in the desert. There he learned the skills of a warrior: firing rifles, exploding bombs, slashing the throats of sheep to steel him to the sight of blood and death. There were always books and worn newspapers in the infidel language to read. He mimicked the way the nonbelievers spoke English on a flickering TV screen, learning words repeated frequently.

Now, in the land of the unbelievers, he waited again.

Hours passed slowly, tedium stretching into more tedium. The five men and Ahmad sat about the humid flat, bored. They found a sports channel and watched the football matches the Americans called soccer. Fazil studied a New York City street map. The woman vanished into a room.

Fazil's cell phone rang. He talked briefly, turning his back so the others couldn't hear. The other men's cell phones had been confiscated at the desert camp. Ahmad had never had one. Fazil directed three of the men to go to the street and pick up a delivery. They returned bearing worn cases for musical instruments and two canvas vests.

"You…boy…go downstairs to the front door," Fazil ordered. "There is one more thing to get. Bring it up."

"My name is Ahmad, not boy," Ahmad shot back, sticky from the heat in the airless room and tired of the leader's curt tone. He squared his spindly shoulders, thrust out his chin, and rubbed the faint beginnings of a mustache for reassurance.

Fazil's face flushed. "Go! Now!"

Ahmad walked down the stairs to the street. He saw and heard no one. When he opened the door, an unshaven, dark-haired man handed him a shopping bag without speaking. Ahmad took it back upstairs and gave it to Fazil, who dumped out the contents, a pink backpack adorned with pictures of kittens.

"This is for Ah…Mad," Fazil smirked, pointing to it.

Ahmad shook his head. "This will not do."

"Why will it not do?" The question, asked quietly, came from a gray-haired man named Aaban. He was the only one older than Fazil. He rarely spoke, but when he did, Fazil listened without interrupting.

"This is for children," Ahmad said, waving the pack. "No adult would use it. People would notice and wonder."

Fazil scowled. "It is too late to obtain another."

"No, we can buy one," Ahmad disagreed. "I saw a sporting goods store on the street when we arrived." He was tired of being in the flat. "Also, we need more food."

The leader hesitated. Food was running low. The men grumbled.

Fazil nodded. "You speak English. Buy a pack and more food. Afifa will accompany you."

The girl looked up in surprise.

"There are some other things we need," Fazil said. "It is better a woman should buy them."

"What?" she asked.

"A baby carriage, also blankets and a doll." He did not explain.

Fazil paused for effect, doling out words as if they were precious coins. "Allah has willed that we strike the infidel at a public place where they honor their history. You will know more when it is time."

Afifa held out a hand. "Give me money."

Grudgingly, Fazil opened a worn wallet chained to his belt and handed her a thin roll of bills.

She shook her head. "More. This is not Kabul. Americans do not haggle over prices in the marketplace like housewives buying fish."

Ahmad watched the exchange, puzzled. The girl didn't act like a dutiful wife. There was tension between the two.

They left. Upon reaching the street, she said, "This way, boy!" and set off briskly.

"Do not call me that!" Ahmad said. He spoke sharply as a man should when admonishing a woman. Afifa smiled, eyes flashing, and pulled off her kerchief. Glossy, black hair tumbled down to her shoulders.

"All right, Ahmad." She pointed to a glass-fronted building on a corner. "Look, it is a McDonald's. I have seen pictures. Let us get a soft drink. They will have ice."

"Your husband Fazil didn't—."

"Fazil is not my husband," she snapped. "He is my sister's husband. She hates him. He is a bully. I do not let him bully me." She laughed scornfully. "He is angry because I will not sleep with him. Come."

After they entered and ordered drinks, Ahmad tried to pay with some of the money Afifa had given him to buy the backpack.

She pushed him aside. "No. This was my idea. I shall pay. Women are the equal of men here." He stared at her.

They lingered over soft drinks in the cool air, sucking on the delicious fragments of ice, sneaking glances at the other customers. Men wore dark suits and seemed in a hurry, glancing at watches or cell phones, shifting their feet impatiently in line. Others dressed casually, the women in shorts, revealing t-shirts, and cropped, uncombed hairstyles. Boys wore jeans ripped at the knees and shirts with sleeves cut off at the shoulders.

Such freedom! Ahmad thought enviously. He chafed in the greasy jeans and worn cotton shirt he had been given.

Afifa's cool green eyes studied him. "How old are you, Ahmad?"

"I am 19," he said, inflating his age. "How old are you?"

"Older," she replied, a superior expression on her face.

He doubted that.

She swept up their cups and napkins. "Let us purchase your backpack."

They found the sporting goods store and bought a green backpack that Ahmad slipped over his shoulders. Back on the street, he marveled at the surge of people. What did Americans do when they got to where they were going? Wouldn't they be tired? And if they were so rich, why didn't they dress better?

They walked several blocks to a huge, brightly lit store. Inside, wide aisles overflowed with shelves of goods: plastic toys, metal cooking utensils, gardener's tools, lotions and soaps, colored socks and white handkerchiefs, and a dazzling array of glossy magazines.

"Look around," Afifa said. "I'll be back." She shook her head at his expression. "Try not to appear like a cow stunned before slaughter. This is what Americans have all the time. To them, it is not unusual."

After wandering about, he waited at the front of the store, beyond the cash registers. She met him there, holding two small plastic boxes. She handed one to Ahmad. "Here."

"What are—" he began.

"Cell phones...one for each of us. The service is prepaid. My phone contains a camera. We won't tell Fazil."

"Why do I need a cell phone?"

She shrugged. "Maybe you'll pick up a girl and want to call her later."

Ahmad's eyes widened. "Pick up a girl? I would never touch one!"

Afifa laughed and punched him lightly on the arm, something he had never seen a woman do. "You must listen to the conversation and learn slang. 'Pick up' means to meet someone new and hang out with them."

"Hang out...?"

She sighed. "Never mind."

"Look around," she continued. "Almost everyone has a cell phone. Most of these people don't know we exist. Pretend to talk on the phone, and they won't notice you."

They stopped at a park and sat on a bench. "Take out your cell phone," Afifa said. "I'll set it up and show you how to use it. One of the counselors at my school, where I learned English, let me use hers. Then we must get the baby buggy, purchase food, and return. Fazil will be angry at how long we have been gone. He is always angry."

Patiently, she showed him how to use the phone and insisted they exchange calls. Ahmad looked at the screen one last time and buried the marvelous device deep in a pocket.

Before they left, Afifa said, "We must record our first time in New York. I shall take a selfie." She laughed at his expression. "It is a picture people take of themselves with their cell phones."

She positioned them in front of a fountain and held the phone at arm's length. "Smile," she said. For the first time in days, Ahmad did.

They found a department store that sold children's clothing and supplies and bought a baby carriage. Afifa selected the cheapest. "We do not need to worry about repeated use," she said. He didn't need to ask why.

Next came food. They looked for a Middle Eastern market without success, finally settling for a small neighborhood grocery, tucked away between a shoe repair shop and a dentist's office. Afifa bought several baguettes of French bread, rice, vanilla yogurt, peaches, pipe tobacco, and fresh mint to add to the doogh, an Afghani drink made with water.

When they returned, Fazil complained about the few dollars she gave him back and demanded receipts. "You didn't ask for receipts," she said. "I told you things were more expensive here."

That night, after the men had retired to thin sleeping pads and blankets in other rooms, Ahmad and Afifa took control of the TV. They watched the late news and looked for movies. They watched a cops and robbers film in which the gang leader, pressured by the FBI to be an informer or go to jail, "dropped a dime" and made a telephone call to betray his comrades.

Over the next few days, tension in the flat grew. Fazil brought out a small computer device—Afifa told Ahmad later it was called an iPad—and passed it around. They viewed terrorist attacks with trucks exploding, fires spreading, and close-ups of victims, eyes staring but not seeing.

Ahmad swallowed and looked at Afifa. They had never been shown videos so graphic, so detailed, during training. Her face was stone, but she blinked several times.

Fazil unrolled a map and taped it to a wall. "This is where we shall strike our blow against the unbelievers," he said. "It is a park where they gather once a year to celebrate their atrocities. This time we shall celebrate—with their blood!"

"We shall enter the park from both ends, north and south," Fazil said, pointing with a bony finger. "Ahmad and Afifa will follow. This object," he pointed to a black square, "is a bandstand. We shall take up positions around it. Watch me. When I begin firing, it is the signal for our attack. When they hear the gunfire, Ahmad and Afifa will detonate explosives near the entrances. The park will be crowded because it is a holiday marking the founding of the infidels' country."

Ahmad swallowed. A park! They were going to set off explosives and shoot down people in a park. He imagined the shock, the panic, and the screams as gunfire chopped down families, and bombs sent a metallic rain of death and destruction everywhere. No, he could never do that, murder innocent people who had done him no harm.

Fazil noticed his expression. "What is the matter, boy?"

"Nothing. Nothing is the matter."

"Perhaps you lack the stomach for jihad."

Ahmad's lips tightened. "I said it is nothing."

"Good," Fazil replied. "Then I have another errand for you. We are drinking too much water in this accursed heat. Go back to the store and buy a case of bottled water. The water that comes from the tap here smells like warm donkey piss." He thrust a wad of dollars into Ahmad's hands.

Dusk had fallen. Lights appeared in buildings, and fewer people hurried along the street. Ahmad stepped under an awning at a closed shop. He breathed deeply and reached into his pocket, retrieving the cell phone, and punched in 411, the number Afifa had told him provided information.

"Hello...Hello..." he said, "I need to call the G-Men!"

"The who?"

"The G-Men," Ahmad said impatiently, "the ones who catch the bad guys."

"Oh, you mean the police?"

"No, no...the government ones."

"The FBI?"

"Yes, yes, those are the ones."

She rattled off numbers.

He made the call, shifting back and forth nervously.

"Federal Bureau of Investigation, Agent Gonzalez," a male voice responded.

"I want to report bomb plot in park." The words gushed out.

"Bomb plot? What's your name?"

"Ahmad. I am one of the peoples...people...with the bombs."

And then he blurted out the story, the words running together: Afghanistan, the training camp, Fazil, backpacks, and an unnamed green swatch on a map.

"You must stop," he said desperately.

"All right, Ahmad," the man said calmly. He asked for more details. What type of weapons? What did the vests look like? How many people were involved? Sex? Ages? And finally, what park? When?

Ahmad pressed the phone to his ear. "I don't know. We haven't been told yet. But soon...soon!"

Silence. "All right, Ahmad. My name is David. Call back when you know more and ask for me. Tell whoever answers the phone that David needs information about Greenbrier. Have you got that? David and Greenbrier."

"Yes...Yes, but—"

"And tell them your name is Tango."

"Tango? I don't—"

"Tango will be your code name. Thank you, Ahmad." The line went dead.

Ahmad found a convenience store and bought water. He trudged wearily up the stairs to the flat. Fazil grabbed the first bottle and grimaced. "No cold water?" he complained.

"They do not chill the cases," Ahmad replied. He wiped sweat from his forehead. The air was close, and the body odor of eight people was making it more so.

The explosives and weapons—AK-47s—were delivered the next day. The explosives were placed in the two canvas vests, one of which was inserted into Ahmad's backpack. Afifa's vest was placed in the baby carriage. A doll, its face hidden by blankets, was placed on top. Fazil dismissed the men to clean the AK-47s and briefed Ahmad and Afifa about how to detonate the bombs.

Morning. They sat eating bread and drinking tea, a last breakfast. "Bang... Bang...Bang."

Ahmad jumped to his feet. "Gunfire!" he cried.

142

Fazil smiled. "Relax, boy. You hear firecrackers. The infidels are celebrating their day of independence. For some, it will be the last."

The mood in the flat had changed from sullen irritation to silent anticipation. Conversation died. There was little left to say.

Ahmad couldn't eat. He drank only water. How was he to alert the FBI about the location of the park and time of the attack?

A van arrived, driven by the same unshaven man who had made earlier deliveries. They piled into it, leaving behind garbage, plastic bottles, torn playing cards, and dirty blankets. The ride was slow and silent. The interior of the window-less van was like a tomb, dirty, barren, foreboding. Perspiration ran down Ahmad's forehead, and he swallowed repeatedly.

Fazil noticed, observant as usual. "Peace be upon you, brother," he said. "Soon you shall be with the martyrs."

The van stopped at a passenger drop-off at the park's north entrance. Three men clambered out and joined the throng passing through a stone gate. Afifa glanced at Ahmad, hesitated, and joined them, pushing the baby carriage. The van moved slowly to the south entrance. Ignoring a no stopping sign, the driver discharged Fazil, Ahmad, and the remaining men.

"Don't hurry, boy," Fazil whispered. "Enjoy this moment before paradise beckons."

The backpack carrying explosives felt like a heavy rock crushing Ahmad's shoulders. He imagined a giant sign above his head flashing the words: Terrorist! Terrorist! But no one gave him a second glance. He was swept up in a stream of people who waved flags, wore red, white, and blue shirts, toted picnic baskets, and tried to control excited children.

Was there still time to give a warning? Ahmad pulled out the cell phone, checked the scrap of paper in a pocket, and called the FBI.

The line was busy.

He staggered to a tree facing the path and slumped against the trunk, placing the pack at his feet. Above, through a canopy of green leaves, patchy white clouds drifted across a blue sky. Birds chirped, and the shrill voices of children rose in the humid air. And then he heard a familiar sound muffled by distance: a single gunshot.

He imagined Afifa positioning the baby carriage, reaching into her pocket for the detonator, gazing at the world for the last time and...

"Hey, kid, how about some ice cream?" A chubby man in a white jacket and hat stood behind a cart on the path.

"No," Ahmad said, waving him off.

"Sure you do," the man insisted. He reached into a freezer and pulled out a pistol. "FBI! Don't move! Show me your hands!"

Before Ahmad could comply, another man wearing sunglasses and a woman in shorts sprinted from a nearby bench and jumped on him. They wrenched his arms behind his back and handcuffed him. They took him to a police station, where he was questioned for hours.

Ahmad yawned. He slumped in a chair. Panic and fear had given way to fatigue and boredom.

The door opened and a sandy-haired man carrying a folder and a can of Coke entered.

"Hello, Tango, or should I call you Ahmad? I'm David." He sat down and pushed the can across the table. "Thirsty?"

Ahmad picked up the cold can and gulped down half the contents without stopping. He licked his lips. "What happened to Afifa? She is dead?"

"She's fine," David said. "You'll see her soon, and she can explain everything."

"How did you find me?" Ahmad asked.

David flipped open the folder and extracted a photo. He shoved it across the table. It showed Ahmad and Afifa standing by a fountain. "We knew what you looked like. We'll talk more later."

He left and Afifa walked in. "Hello, boy."

She laughed. "Kidding, Ahmad. That is what the Americans call pulling someone's leg."

Ahmad winced. Where did Americans get those strange expressions?

"You didn't set off the bomb," he said.

She sat down opposite him. "Kill Americans? No. I want to live here. There is more opportunity. That is why I bought the cell phones and 'dropped a dime' to call the FBI like in that film we watched."

"They were waiting for us."

"Yes...All around the band platform. As soon as Fazil pulled out his AK-47, a marksman shot him dead. The others were arrested."

Ahmad was silent. "What about us?" He really meant what about me, but didn't want to say it.

She sat back. "I think they will hold us and try to get all the information we have about the terrorist training and the desert camps. Then my guess is they'll let us go and we can stay here."

Ahmad absorbed her words. The corners of his mouth turned down. "We can't go home, can we, Afifa? I'll never see my mother again."

She looked away for a moment. "No, Ahmad, we can't go home. Not now anyway."

* * *

Ahmad's mother wandered through the busy stalls of the Afghani market, examining the pale-green melons, clusters of grapes, and eggplant. Ameena flinched as a bearded man in loose pants and a faded tunic bumped her and slipped something into her shopping basket.

"Do not look," he hissed. "Read later."

In her dimly lit room that night, she unveiled the object. It was a small, tattered notebook. On the first page, she read, "Dear Mama..."

Her hand trembled. A photo fell out. It showed Ahmad sprawled on a grassy lawn near a massive granite building with twin colonnades. He wore a white t-shirt and tan shorts. Next to him sat an attractive young woman with short, curly black hair. She appeared to be listening to something through earphones. Ameena wondered what she heard because the girl was smiling.

—

Arthur Carey is a former newspaper reporter, editor, and journalism instructor who lives in the San Francisco Bay Area. He is a member of the California Writers Club. His fiction has appeared in print and Internet publications. His short stories, novella, and novels are available at Amazon.com.

Making Peace

Everywhere Stars

By Laura Grace Weldon

(Published in the January 2019 issue of The MOON; originally published by *Cleveland Scene*.)

The weary face behind her in the bathroom mirror startled Lia. Her mother usually slept in after a late shift at the bowling alley.

"Don't go getting any big ideas," her mother's reflection said.

"Uh huh," Lia answered.

Lia's morning routine, bathroom to hallway to kitchen, was slowed by her bathrobed mother who exhaled loudly in irritation at each contact. Finally her mother lit the first cigarette of the day, clicked on the TV, and sat down. The heavy plastic couch cover crackled as she leaned back.

"You're not something special. You hear me?"

Lia left the apartment without answering. She hurried down the stairs knowing she'd have to run to the bus stop. She should have figured her mother would pay her more mind today. When Lia attended Lincoln West her mother scoffed at good grades, at homework done. "Won't do you no good," or "Don't stick your nose in the air," she'd say.

Lia excelled at escaping notice. Back in school she dreaded teachers who paid attention to her. Her English teacher, Mr. Laurent, was the worst. He used to ask her to meet him after school, where she would stand awkwardly by his desk watching him cut an apple. He'd offer her a piece. She'd shake her head. He asked her to do things she'd never do, like enter poetry contests or write for the school newspaper. He told her she was gifted. He said she should go on to college. Sometimes he brought brochures from universities in different parts of the country. They unfolded, all thick expensive gleam, into pictures of students who were nothing like her. They all smiled and leaned on one another with confidence she'd never known. The week before graduation Mr. Laurent gave up. He helped her get a job downtown instead.

But today after work Lia was starting her first college class. It had taken a few years to gather herself. She watched new hires in the office. The ones with college degrees became managers. They had offices with doors that shut. They cluttered their desks with personal things and freely went out to lunches that lasted for hours. Plus they had something else, an extra layer of the assurance that everyone else seemed to have been born with, a quality Lia studied like an immigrant to the human race. Maybe a degree would free her from a tiny cubicle, even if it couldn't give her the ease she saw in faces everywhere around her.

The way she counted the credits, she'd be well over 30 by the time she graduated. If her mother wanted to get the last word in, Lia let her have that. As she settled on the half-full 45A bus headed downtown she watched people as she always did.

A heavy woman with hands older than her face had an expensive baby carrier next to her. She unfolded a magazine from the diaper bag over her shoulder. The tiny blonde baby slept, its lips puckering as if tasting the air, the woman's dark arm over the carrier like a roof sheltering that new face.

An elderly man sat across from her. He had the powdery skin that some old people get, the kind that looks dry and soft. He was wearing a raincoat and had an umbrella on his lap, although there was no hint of rain. His hands trembled so much that the fabric of the umbrella shivered. Lia decided to look up diseases next time she went to the library. That way she'd know if the tremors stopped when he slept.

The bus jerked to a stop and new riders got on. A young couple walked down the aisle, his arm on her shoulder as they sat down. The girl had complicated bracelets twining up her wrists and her skirt looked as if it was made of fabric from far away, from a place so interesting that Lia knew she wouldn't recognize the language spoken there. Lia noticed that the girl had acne scars and the boy wore jeans that were scuffed and frayed. The couple didn't face straight ahead but turned to look at each other as they talked. Then the girl put her head on his chest and closed her eyes. Lia wondered if she might be listening to his heart.

This was her only skill. Lia could observe freely without anyone noticing. That's what she'd done all through school. She studied the popular kids and the loners. She listened to what they said and the expressions on their faces and especially how they acted when they thought no one was around. She'd read many times that people sense when they're being watched. But no one ever looked back at her. Sometimes she felt like a shadow.

This didn't always work to her advantage. Lia might be standing at the counter of the used bookstore and the clerk wouldn't look up from his phone. Or she'd be waiting in line at the corner grocery only to have people cut in front of her like she wasn't there. She rarely said anything. When she admitted it to herself, she was sure that her problem wasn't shyness; it was something worse, a kind of invisibility that didn't have a name.

As soon as she headed off the elevator she knew the office had been fumigated again. She didn't smell it so much as feel it, a choking fog that settled in her chest making it hard to breathe. Her eyes watered as she sat down.

Around her cube other employees were arriving, chatting freely. Lia kept snippets of small talk memorized for emergencies although she hadn't quite mastered the casual look that seemed to accompany conversation. Occasionally people spoke to her but they usually turned away to talk more eagerly to someone else soon after. These moments were becoming less exhausting for Lia. Still she preferred the comfort of invisibility. Whenever she saw someone make a gaffe or slip on the sidewalk she knew that they would like a temporary taste of the oblivion she knew so well.

She opened a dull gray folder next to her keyboard to start the morning routine. She liked to work while listening to what her co-workers had to say. Andy talked about a late night with friends and Maria chided Andy for not taking better care of himself, as usual. Then Darnell said he was going to check out another used car after work and hoped his wife liked this one. Allison flipped through a catalog looking for something to wear to a wedding, showing Maria her favorite outfits. Her co-workers reminded Lia of teacups in an amusement park ride. Their lives twirled around and around with such bright colors that Lia felt glad to know they were on tracks, sure to be coming back the same way when they talked the next day.

Krystal, whose cubicle was next to hers, came in last. She wore tight outfits and heavy make-up. Her laugh was harsh as she stood looking past Lia to talk to Allison, complaining about late support payments for her two-year-old. She called the boy every day at lunchtime before she went out to smoke. "Put him on," she'd say to her grandmother. Then her voice would change. "How's my big man doin?" she'd practically sing into the receiver. "Whachoo havin for lunch, baby?" She'd tell him what they'd do when she got home that day. Sometimes it was just a trip to the laundromat, but Krystal talked like it would be the best thing ever. She told him what they'd pass on the street and how he could carry a bag like a big boy if he wanted, and that he could put money in the gumball machine when they got there, and then they'd watch cartoons till the clothes were dry. Lia couldn't help but imagine the evening being perfect as Krystal described. She wondered if her own mother had ever used such a voice.

A rustle spread across the office like an incoming wave. It was the sound made when Judy was sighted. Workers sat quickly, swiveling their chairs forward and clicking to the correct screens. Judy operated on many levels at once. She could chat conversationally while looking over a worker's attire, desk, and computer screen; fitting comments about job performance into an apparently innocent remark. Lia noticed that people managed to seem friendly, even unguarded around Judy, as if they genuinely welcomed her. But they hated her. Not her power over them, which was understood, but something more. No personal details about Judy were known, only that her toothy smile never matched her eyes. That made everything about her the subject of intense speculation. Although no one solicited Lia's opinion, she had nothing to offer. There were only a few people she never really looked at. One of them was Judy.

Today Judy's progress through the office was unusually speedy. That was bad news. Everyone's attention was heightened on days when Judy came down to watch the goings-on in each division. She would stroll around in no predictable pattern, sometimes spending the morning getting through all areas. Everyone strained to perform at top efficiency until she retreated to her spacious office upstairs. But when she headed directly from the elevators to a particular division it meant only one thing. Layoffs.

Judy was hands-on about such things. Lia could feel her co-workers' tension, more toxic than the fumigant, and could sense their relief as Judy passed. They didn't dare look up from their workstations but still, in the seconds it took for Judy's heels to go by, they'd gone from potential victims to rubberneckers at the scene of an accident.

Lia muttered the only prayer she knew. It wasn't a Christian one. Her father used to take her to church when she was small. He was a large stern man. He and his new wife had a collection of children, hers and their own newborn twins. In the pew Lia sat at the end of the family like the last bead of an unlatched necklace, straining to hold her leg away from the child next to her. The only thing she liked was the church music. People in the choir wore the same robes, swaying in unison and singing as if they were one person, only mightier. She imagined joining the choir when she got older. But her father moved to Seattle and a few months later, died in a car accident. That ended her desire to sing.

Lia's mother had no use for churchgoing. Sometimes when her mother was at work Lia would watch evangelists on television. They talked a lot about prayer, but not how to do it. They talked even more about sending in money. Then one Saturday Lia found a paperback introduction to Buddhism at the used bookstore. She kept it on the shelf in her bedroom for a while, having second thoughts about the foreign-looking cover and the unknown places the contents might lead her. When she did start reading she stayed up half the night to finish it. She read about detachment and wondered if she'd been Buddhist all along without knowing it. She read about cultivating compassion, then looked out the window into the darkness, staring at nothing for so long that she wondered if she had unknowingly meditated for the first time. Near the end of the book she found a prayer to repeat throughout the day, a prayer for the happiness of all beings. This prayer moved silently across her lips now.

Judy's heels made a softly carpeted warning as she approached. Lia hadn't considered that her own job might be in jeopardy. In fact, her job kept getting more burdensome as other employees were laid off. The more she was asked to do, the harder she worked, until her head ached with the effort to get everything done and still get on the last express bus out of downtown. But Lia could see Judy approaching the cluster of cubicles that made up their shrinking division, now down to seven of them. Maybe she'd be let go.

No attachment, she reminded herself. She vowed to keep the prayer on her lips. Her thoughts went to the bowling alley. Her mother always said they'd find a job there for her. Well, her mother usually accused her of thinking she was too good for the work they'd find for her. Lia knew she'd make a lousy Buddhist, because she kept thinking of herself even when she tried to pray for everyone else's happiness.

Lia heard a collective intake of breath in the surrounding cubicles. Judy had halted, her presence an announcement that the layoff would be in their division.

She was standing behind Darnell, who was a recent hire. He was fast, efficient and had the kind of graceful charm that went along with his soft Carolina accent. He made the work look easy. Everyone liked him. Lia couldn't understand why he'd be fired.

Judy lingered for a long moment. Then she leaned down and spoke into his ear. It looked like she was sniffing Darnell's shirt. When she straightened he turned in his chair and looked at her without the smile subordinates usually show a boss.

Barely pausing, Judy stepped over to Lia and leaned over the same way. "I'll need to put an extra helping on your plate," she said quietly. "I know you're up to taking this on."

Extra helping, as if workers were being served more food at a banquet instead of given someone else's job to do. Lia steeled herself, then copied Darnell, turning to gaze at Judy without smiling. What she saw beyond the distance in Judy's eyes surprised her. It was the look of a dog chained too long.

Lia forgot the prayer, forgot to act busy, she just stared as Judy walked a few steps over and asked Krystal to come into the conference room. As if the privacy there made any difference. Nearly everyone in the office watched the two women walk away. Krystal's generous backside rolled in her thin green pants and her hair swung sideways at each step. Next to her, Judy's tailored suit and stiff hair seemed ridiculously prim.

The moment the door shut behind them a hum of conversation started up in the office. It was subdued, watchful, aware that the conference door would open in a few minutes.

"Thank God," Allison said to no one in particular. "I thought for sure the bitch was after me." She gave a little laugh that sounded like a doll's cry.

"Corporate squeeze in action," Darnell said. He put his hands behind his head and swiveled around as if announcing to the room, but he spoke in a near whisper.

"What's Krystal going to do?" Maria said. "She supports her granny and the little boy. It isn't right to just toss people out, more all the time."

"Yeah, what are you gonna do about it?" Allison said. "I'm sure as hell glad to keep my job. Maybe Krystal shoulda worked a little harder."

"Harder?" Andy spoke up from the other side of the cube wall. "They keep adding to the workload. They take away benefits and still cut jobs. Pay attention, the execs upstairs get loads of bennies plus huge salaries. Ever looked at the cars they drive?"

"Arnie in accounting told me about some of the receipts Judy submits in her expense account," Darnell said, just as quietly as before. "One lunch would cover my family's groceries for a week."

"My father said it's always been this way," Maria said. "He said owners would be happy to make us pay for the right to breathe. He should know, he tried to start a union back in El Salvador. It didn't end too good for him."

"You're talking like a bunch of radicals," Allison said. "I for one am glad to have a job. And I work damn hard at it."

Andy snorted at that.

Darnell said, "Yeah, we all work hard. I'm just seeing that it's impossible to get ahead here."

Lia never thought about any of these things before. She went to work, puzzled about the behavior of her co-workers, then went home afterwards. In the evenings, while her mother was gone, she read novels and then puzzled about the behavior of those characters too. Or she watched movies. But in movies and books the conversations were too exact, problems too easily solved.

Lia imagined the whole moment backing up, then starting over as a movie scene where her co-workers would agree to go on strike if Judy didn't reinstate Krystal. But she didn't say anything.

She knew by mid-afternoon Judy would send a memo giving instructions to redistribute Krystal's workload. Lia and Darnell were the chosen ones this time, so their jobs were probably safe from the next round of layoffs. Krystal's vacant cubicle would be would be taken apart, *deconstructed* they called it, leaving no space where they'd once heard Krystal's two voices, the one she used at work and the one for her son.

Lia still felt sick from the fumigant. Her stomach roiled with nausea. She stood up, telling herself that she would head to the bathroom. But her steps didn't veer to the right. Instead she found herself walking directly to the conference room door. For the first time in her life she knew everyone was watching her. It felt strange.

After she knocked on the door and swung it open it was easy as Darnell's charm, Allison's anger, Andy's smarts, Maria's spirit. It took one sentence.

She told Judy to give Krystal another chance because she was planning on quitting, right then, that moment. Then without waiting for an answer Lia walked to the elevators and left.

All the way down to the lobby Lia thought of Mr. Laurent. The last time she saw him he didn't slice his apple in pieces as usual. He cut it in half crosswise, then held it up to show her that the core and seeds formed a perfect star in the center. He apologized for being a sentimental old man. Then what did he say? Something about a star hidden in each person. She'd forgotten the exact phrase.

As Lia stepped outside, late morning sunshine glinting off One Cleveland Center, she decided to tell her mother that she'd been fired. It would make her mom happy to have Lia "knocked down a few pegs" as she called it. And making her mom happy made things easier for both of them.

But right now Lia had all day before class with nothing to do. The feeling was satisfying as the warm sun on her face. Office workers hustled by. An unfamiliar spicy odor caught her attention. Her brown bag lunch was still in a desk drawer on the 4th floor. She followed the scent to a push cart at the corner and without any of her usual hesitation looked right at the man wearing an apron lettered "Amir's Falafal" to ask what he recommended.

"Oh, do I have a treat for you," he said cheerfully. "First customer of the day." He talked to her while he piled and then rolled fillings into a foil-covered offering she couldn't pronounce. When she held out money to pay he insisted on giving her the drink of her choice for free. She chose a bottle of lemonade, keeping her head up and looking into his brown eyes as she thanked him. He smiled broadly as if giving drinks away was the best part of his day.

Lia held the cold bottle in one hand and warm bag in the other. Then she began to walk against the crowd on the busy sidewalk, seeing stars everywhere.

—

Laura Grace Weldon is a book editor and edits **Braided Way** *magazine. She is the author of the poetry collections* Blackbird *(Grayson Books 2019) and* Tending *(Aldrich Press, 2013) and of a handbook of alternative education titled* Free Range Learning *(Hohm Press, 2010). She lives with vast optimism on a small farm where she'd get more done if she didn't spend so much time reading library books, cooking weird things, and singing to livestock.*

The Peacemongers

By Mitchell Toews

After a summertime ballgame, we sat in the shade of the playground's toboggan slide and somehow the conversation wandered from baseball to the philosophical.

Our Mennonite elders taught us peace and how to live in a congregation and a community. Our greatest collective efforts as a people were directed at prevention and resolution. Other, less noble, efforts concerned denial and a refusal to face the conflict that found us. Sometimes this denial worked its way deep down into the compressed community until, like ice in a rock fissure, the pressure was too great and the rock broke along the hidden fault line.

I'd fight you but it's against my religion, was a statement that would not be laughed at and might even command some respect. Turning the other cheek and "love thine enemy" were taught in Jesus' name and, in many cases, practiced. At our young age, however, such Sunday school principles were discarded when the blood ran hot. While we knew and accepted these higher ideals, the rules of the jungle applied in the schoolyard and the hockey rink.

Our conversation on that day was this: "If there was a war tomorrow... and you were old enough, would you go?"

Many in our group admitted that they would not. Others were inclined to bravado – at least there in the familiar shade of the slide – and said they would go to war.

I thought of my dad and my grandparents and how they all became quiet when we sat in front of Grandma's TV and the announcer discussed the growing crisis in Cuba. The international emergency was distilled into a simple formula by the CBC newscast. The US had found evidence of nuclear weapons in Cuba; Russia was steaming ships to the island loaded with more weapons and soldiers, and President Kennedy was all but openly accusing them of preparing to wage war on the USA. Cuba was close to the tip of Florida; close to the famous Cape Canaveral launch pad and millions of Americans.

All of this seemed plausible to my parents. Dad said Cuba was only as far away from the Florida coast as Hartplatz was from Pembina, North Dakota. This reference made it real to me. Pembina was where one of the TV stations was re-broadcast from, reaching us at the dim northern edge of its range. It was also a place where Roger Maris, of the Yankees, had played high school and minor league ball. Maris was from North Dakota, born just a few beet fields south of us. A man from Pembina who looked a lot like Maris, but with a suit and thick eyeglasses, read the news each night on the Fargo station. My parents often listened to him in addition to the CBC telecast, despite the snowy screen, to hear about what Kennedy and Khrushchev were doing.

#

There were other signs that everything in the wide world beyond was not quite right. One of the Loeb brothers had just built a house near the new elementary school and it had a special room in the basement: *a fallout shelter.* Atomic bombs, we were told, were giant explosives that could be aimed at various targets, like the cities in Japan that were destroyed at the end of WWII. They were now delivered by rocket, not dropped from a plane. Upon landing in a brilliant flash ("Put your heads down on your desks and don't look up!") the bomb released a toxic, radioactive "fallout" that lasted for days or even weeks. The bomb shelters, containing food, guns and other implements of survival within their dense concrete walls, were—to us kids—the ultimate fort. Still, we were disquieted by the presence of one of these doomsday shelters here in tiny, peaceful Hartplatz—even if it was only the indulgence of an ostentatious man.

The US aimed its weapons at targets in Russia and the Russians aimed theirs at US targets, including air bases and missile launching sites. Nearby Grand Forks had a massive air base and their planes' contrails were common – they could be seen far, far above Hartplatz, specks of silver spewing a faint watercolor plume of white. My grandpa and Mr. Vogel would stand on the sunny sidewalk outside of the post office and look up at the faint parallel lines etched high in the sky. They held their palms up to shade their eyes against the glare of the sun and sucked their teeth, estimating how high the planes might be and if they were "fighters" or "bombers."

I had a hatbox full of brightly colored plastic disks I'd collected from Nestlé cereal, tea and chocolate milk powder containers. The company promoted its goods by including two free disks in each package. The colorful disks had the company's logo molded into the back, while the front carried an image of an airplane. Hundreds of models were in the collection, such as

Von Richthofen's red tri-wing, muscular P-51s, futuristic flying wings, and obscure Fokkers. The last, a name I whispered for fear of being chastised for cursing, were German war planes that carried the name of a Dutch aeronautical engineer. Like Mennonites, the Fokker possessed a convoluted Northern European ancestry.

I pulled out a handful of Nestlé airplane disks from my pocket and showed them to Grandpa and Mr. Vogel as they peered at the US planes far above us. "They are either B-29s or F-10s," I offered, handing them each an illustrated disk. "When they get to Russian airspace," I continued with authority, "the Russians will scramble MiGs, like this." I handed them each a disk showing a MiG and its sleek, swept-back wings. In the picture, the dull gray fighter stood out against fluffy white clouds with the red hammer and sickle insignia the focal point of the image. The pilot, his football-like white helmet visible beneath the streamlined, clear canopy, looked ominous and resolute, if not ruthless. Besides the Billy Bishop Sopwith Camel, I had more MiGs than any other single disk. There was one in almost every package—an orange pekoe warning about those insidious Russkies and their mighty war machine.

Grandpa stared at me, incredulous for a few seconds, as Mr. Vogel chuckled, still looking up at the distant jet trails. "We're gonna scramble you!" Grandpa said, snatching the disk I held and pulling me into a gentle hammerlock in one motion.

#

It was my turn to answer the "would you be a soldier?" question. I thought of the people huddled in their fallout shelters as the brave soldiers climbed into tanks and airplanes and jeeps to fight the war. I imagined the people in Miami (and Moscow), skin hanging from their burnt bodies like torn fabric as they wandered in a daze among flattened buildings in a Hiroshima landscape. I imagined one of my comic book favorites from the Rexall Drug Store wading ashore in a hail of bullets. (Vip! Vip! Vip!) I thought of my Uncle Barnie, who had joined the Winnipeg Rifles and had made it as far as Halifax before Hitler was defeated. I recalled the great gray battleships tossing on the *War at Sea* film—stark, grainy images projected on a white sheet in the Kornelsen school basement, at a National Film Board evening sponsored by the local Arts Council.

"I think I would do whatever my dad said to do. I think my grandma would say to help by going to the CO camps and working extra hard. I think my dad would fight – he'd be a General, at least," I stated, without guilt or doubt.

"What's a CO camp?" said Corky.

"It's what you can do if your minister will go to Winnipeg and say that you are baptized. The government sends men a letter saying they have to join the army. If they don't go, they are put in jail. But if they are members of a Mennonite Church, my grandma says that the government promised they didn't have to be in the army," I explained.

"Just Mennonites?" asked Ralph Reckseidler, a Lutheran boy who lived on Barkman Avenue on the other side of Main Street. No one answered.

"Dunno," I shrugged. "My grandma says that in the Second World War, lots of Canadians fought and some Mennonites went and some, lots from Hartplatz, went to CO camps instead of the army."

"What's CO again?" Corky asked again. He was a little older than us and he came along with his brother Paul, who usually played in our ball games at the park.

"Don't know," I replied. "But my grandpa went to a CO camp. He said he worked in the kitchen and they had a big bread oven. Grandpa learned about baking in the camp. The camp was by a lake and a forest and lots of the guys worked as lumberjacks."

"Neat!" said Scotty, who sat cross-legged, his ball glove on the ground beside him and his hands holding an elm leaf, which he stretched between his thumbs, blowing against the leaf to make a squawking, reed instrument sound. "I'd like to be a lumberjack and chop down trees instead of shooting guys in the war. The war is neat too, especially the tanks and stuff, but lumberjack is really good. I would sign up for camp," he concluded, sighing, happy to have made his decision.

"I don't know if it was the same thing or not," Corky said, "but my uncles went – my mom's brothers. My dad wanted to go too, but his minister told the army that he had to stay to run the farm. My uncle John went to the camp and he learned how to sawmill there. After the war, he got a job in Loeb's mill and worked cutting trees in Sandilands too."

"My great uncle Walter was in a POW camp. That's for prisoners in the war. He was in Hong Kong. He said he was a cook and he smuggled eggs and lumps of butter out of the kitchen by hiding them in his armpits," I offered, trying to help solve the mystery of what kind of a place a CO camp was.

"I didn't know Japs ate butter," Willie Warheim said. He was a quiet boy with blonde hair and more freckles than everyone but me. He had showed me his dad's war keepsakes—a knife with a swastika embossed in the handle and a German phrase book with intricate sketches of common things like bicycles with the names printed in German, Russian, French and English. The Warheims were from East Germany and they had fled to Canada after the war. A Mennonite church from Switzerland had helped them get away.

Sometimes Willie got into fights because guys called his dad a "Nazi." Kids called Willie "Kaiser Wilhelm." My mom told me never to call him those names. She said that everyone is good but everyone also has some bad in them. The Nazis had just got carried away, she said. "No one knows exactly how it happened. They did horrible things. But I do know that they were kind to the Mennonites they came across in Russia."

"Why were they nice to the Mennonites?" I asked her.

"Because the Mennonites spoke German and they were peaceful. My grandparents let German soldiers sleep in their barn and your grandpa remembers getting a ride on a motorcycle. He rode in the sidecar," she explained. "The soldiers left them food. Not every German was bad – but there was a war and people on all sides did things that were terrible. We shouldn't judge others – we weren't there and we don't know what we would have done."

# # #

Hartplatz people went out of their way to avoid "trouble." I tried too, but because my hair was bright orange and my ears stuck out like that motorcycle sidecar in Grandpa's memory, and because I was small and hot tempered, conflict often found me. Grandma counselled to avoid it as long as you could, but that if you were going to fight, then you did your best and the other guy had to be ready. "He starts it, you finish it," she would say, her body in constant motion in the tiny kitchen of the house where she raised a baseball team worth of children, mostly boys.

"That's what I told your uncle Barnie when he joined up for the army," she said, her eyes far away as she shelled peas with a machine-like cadence. "It is serious business, not just marching and uniforms. If you go, it has to be to do what they send you to do. Come home alive and we can work out everything between God and you once it's done."

162

"Once you go," she said, pausing in her chore, "then there is no more peace. Then you fight, Barnie. Fight to come home."

# # #

We sat in the hazy light as the afternoon waned; some boys climbed the gray back side of the wooden toboggan slide. It was a 16-foot-tall slide, sloped to 45 degrees, and in winter the neighborhood garden hoses brought water to the top and it sluiced down to create a magnificent slide that carried us on sleds and sheets of cardboard down the iced plywood ramp and out along a bumpy trough on the ground that ended in a fanned delta of ice at the end of the run. After hurtling down, we pulled our sleds behind us and ran back up the 2X4 cleats to the top of the ramp.

As we languished in the shade of the slide—which appeared to my active imagination like a great, grazing brontosaurus of spruce, pine and fir—two cars pulled up across the park at the ball diamond. Seven or eight teenage boys, most of whom we knew, piled out of the cars. There was Johnny Fehr, a big tough hockey player; Corny Haerder, a cousin of mine from my mom's family; Dennis Fehr, Big Johnny's younger brother—a natural goal-scorer in hockey; Fats Fehr, a cousin to Johnny and Dennis; and Tracy Lord, one of the toughest guys in town.

Two more were in Johnny's car in the back seat. One was Erdman Reimer, a big square-shouldered boy who was almost as big as Johnny and who played a solid defense on the town hockey team. Beside him was Richard Lord, Tracy's older brother.

The Lords were from the neighboring hamlet of Ste. Remaud, but they both had jobs in Hartplatz and so they hung around here with the high school boys. The Lord boys were fighters – often getting into "rumbles." They came from a family where the father was most often absent, having moved to Brandon for work as a welder and seldom visiting – although the family depended on him for money and lived in his house in Ste. Remaud. Richard was a wonderful diver and he spent hours at the swimming pool diving off the springboard – precise jackknifes, spinning somersaults, and towering swan dives. He wore leather jackets and pointy black Beatle boots that slipped on with elastic patches on the sides to allow a foot to go in or out. These boots were dreaded as he was rumored to be able to kick – "shoot the boots" – to a height of nine feet. Indeed, he had kicked out a light bulb outside of Fred's Lunch and that was a good eight feet above the sidewalk, give or take a toe.

His younger brother Tracy was the one we feared most of all. He terrorized us, and even though many of my friends' more wide-bodied older brothers could take him in a fight, they did not dare to take on *his* older brother, "Rebel Richard" (or, Reb, as he liked to be called.) So Tracy was left unchallenged and he took particular delight in torturing us little guys, who feared him without shame. I dreaded going to my grandpa's distant shoe shop on an errand for Grandma because it would take me past one of the restaurants where Tracy hung out, drinking innumerable Pepsi-Colas and smoking Export "A" cigarettes.

On one such trip, he saw me and pulled me by my sleeve into a vinyl upholstered booth, where Scotty already sat, likewise kidnapped. Tracy pushed me in next to Scotty, then lit a wooden match with his thumbnail and held the orange flame under the heel of his hand. "Just getting' ready for Hell, boys, jus' gettin' ready," he said, grinning at us. Then he cuffed us each and said we'd be taking a ride soon, "so stick around you little shits!" Scotty and I were his favorite victims.

We snuck away when he went to another booth full of girls and turned his back to us. He later caught us at the A&W and pulled us into the front seat of his 1949 Ford Fordor sedan, our exit blocked by big Johnny Fehr, who sat eating a burger against the far door. Tracy held the car keys up in front of my face and said, "Hey Zehen. Did you know this car is a magic car? *This car is a LIE DETECTOR, Zehen, and you are gonna be tested right now."*

Johnny snickered, elbowing me a little but without Tracy's psychopathic attitude. Tracy continued: "OK, Zehen. Here's the first question: Do you like girls? Eh, Zehen? Do you like girls?"

I stared at him dumbfounded and then looked at Scotty who shrugged his shoulders and turned his palms up, his lip quivering. "C'mon Zehen – time's up," Tracy cooed, prodding me hard with the car key. I sucked in my breath and stiffened, involuntarily leaning against Johnny Fehr (Johnny *Fear* to us) and making him spill a bit of his root beer. He shoved me back hard, back into the key point which tore my shirt.

"Answer, little turd!" Johhny growled. "No!" I answered. "No, what, *schnudda-nase*?" (snot nose) "No, I don't like girls." I sputtered back.

"Ohhhh. We'll see," Tracy said, gesturing with the car key. "Car," he intoned mechanically, "Does Zehen here like girls? True or False?" Then he pointed at the gas tank gauge, the red needle lay inert pointing at the E. As he put the key in the ignition and clicked it once, the narrow needle animated and rose steadily past ½ and then stopped, pointing at the F.

"F!" Tracy yelled, making the family in the car next to us stare. Johnny Fear waved a hand at them in annoyance, shouting sarcastically, "Take a picture!" They responded by looking away, except the small children in the back who stood on the seat staring unabashedly.

"F stands for what, Johnny? F stands for . . ."

"FALSE!" Big Johnny barked, despite a mouth full of food. "F stands for False, m' Lord."

"False, eh, Zehen? The lie detector Ford says that your answer is false. So, I asked if you like girls, you said you did not, and the car says your answer is false. So that means you DO like girls."

Johnny chimed in roughly, "Good thing; don't want no homos in here."

Tracy laughed just a bit *too* hard, bringing looks from the family next door, which Johnny waved away angrily, gesturing with pronged fingers for them to point their eyes forward.

"OK, Zehen. Here's the next question. The lie detector Ford is all warmed up now. Tell us, Zehen – do you like ME, Zehen. Eh? Do you boys like me, Tracy Lord?"

To say yes, we liked him, was a lie – too easy for him to insert the key and generate the F response. Then what? If we didn't like him, what would happen?

"No. We don't like Tracy Lord." Scotty interjected, to my horror.

"What's that? What is THAT?" Tracy erupted, as Johnny Fear laughed, wheezing and spitting onion and saliva on the worn steel dashboard in front of him. Johnny clapped Scotty on the back and coughing, eyes tearing, said, "Good one kid, good one!"

Spotting a pair of girls arm in arm, coming out of the bowling alley across the street, Tracy lit a cigarette with a flourish, gestured at Johnny to look and jumped out of the car.

#

I remembered all of this as we drifted across the field to the ball diamond. We steered towards the edge of the group, away from Johnny Fear and Tracy and the two young men in the car. I went behind my cousin, who was tagging along, quite far out of his weight class here. "What are you guys doing?" I asked him. He looked down at me and explained that Erdman had been in Fred's Lunch delivering cheese for his uncle when he had come to the attention of Tracy, Reb, Johnny Fehr and Corny.

Tracy had said, "Who's the queer?" in a loud voice. Erdman, apparently oblivious, had continued counting out change to the restaurant owner. Reb had jumped up when Erdman ignored the comment and had walked up to Erdman and inquired loudly, "Hey! Didn't you hear what Tracy said?" to which Erdman immediately replied, smiling broadly back at the booths, many of which held high school girls, "Tracy? Which one is *she*?"

Corny whispered all this to me, with my friends listening intently. At the conclusion of the story, we unanimously exclaimed, "whoa!" or "oh, but!" and Corny winked. He said to us, "Now Johnny and Reb are gonna make Erdman fight Tracy. Tracy wanted to fight him right away, but Erdman was chicken. So the other guys grabbed him and made him come here."

Just then, Johnny Fear yelled, "Shut up!" We did and then he said, in a ring announcer voice, "Erdman called Tracy a girl. Tracy wants to fight but Erdman says no. Either Erd fights Tracy or me n' Reb are gonna pound the shit out of him."

"End of story!" Reb shouted from the car, where he sat next to Erdman. Then he suddenly began pushing Erdman out, as Johnny reached in and began pulling, skidding Erdman out on his back onto the sandy lane.

Grimacing, Erdman rolled onto his side and like a bear woken from hibernation, was not pleased. He kicked out at Johnny's legs, who jumped back and yelled, "Now we're cookin'!"

Tracy stood snapping swift, showy kicks near the pitcher's mound, waiting with obvious relish for the chance to defend his honor.

Erdman was a big man. He had outgrown his boy's body and many years of farm work had given him a chunky squareness that made him hard to get around, even on skates. He rose, slamming the car door so hard it sounded like a gunshot, and Corny, who had been talking to me, whirled around like he had been yanked by a chain. So, too, did Tracy. He stood near the mound in some kind of a martial arts pose as Erdman, pulling off a white cheese factory delivery jacket, approached him.

"Alright," Erdman said, "fist fights are against my religion, but you crazy guys are making me. So let's fight."

We all knew Erdman could fight. When one of his clumsy but powerful checks sent a rushing opponent into the boards, he sometimes had to defend himself with his fists. But hockey fights were different and the legendary Lord brother's boots were much scarier than sweater-tugging and off-balance hay-makers. But now something had happened and, like the weather after the first frost of September, things felt different.

Tracy made some threatening kicks, leaping into the air as Erdman came forward. Approaching the mound, Erdman started instinctively stepping back and to his left, quartering his body and raising his hands in front of his chest, fingers loose, palms down.

"C'mon, L'il Reb!" cheered Johnny Fear, earning a loud, "Yee-haw!" from Richard, the elder Reb, who reclined on the car hood, his hands clasped behind his head, fingers interlaced.

Starting with a pronounced lurch, Tracy ran forward and jumped, pedaling his legs in the air. Erdman stopped, watching the striking foot coming at him and threw a forearm over the outstretched leg. Catching hold with both hands, he twisted Tracy over in the air and forced him down, like bulldogging a calf. Tracey landed hard and could not prepare, so his left cheek hit the pitcher's mound, dirt first. He came up moaning and reaching for his neck, a handful of gravel and grass pressed into his red cheek.

Erdman shouted, "Ha!" as surprised as anyone, and Reb sat up on the car hood, his fists clenched.

Erdman backed off a step as Tracy scrambled up, wiping his face with a swipe of his hand, checking for blood. Seeing none, he hitched his shoulders and threw his hands in front of him, hissing swear words. He danced forward like a fencer, then led at the big man with a careless, straight right hand. He left himself open and Erdman leaned back to slip the punch and slapped his flat palm against Tracy's unprotected right cheek. The wallop sent Tracy to the ground again, this time falling on his shoulder, ducking his head to prevent another scrape on his bruised cheek. A cut opened and a trickle of blood ran down through the hair on his temple and onto his jaw, dripping off the tip of his chin.

Erdman, seeing the blood, dropped his hands and the smaller man rushed forward, this time jabbing well with his left and then sweep-kicking at Erdman's shin. The jab knocked Erdman's head back and he threw his arms around Tracy in a bear hug to keep from falling when the kick knocked him off balance. They fell as one, with Tracy taking the landing on his unprotected left side, his head, and again his cheekbone. He pushed free and regained his feet, blinking and rubbing at his injured eye, which was already bloodshot and showing puffiness. Erdman rose, clapping dust from his hands.

Reb stood watching. He had moved in front of the car now, his feet spread wide apart, arms crossed on his chest.

Panting, Tracy mimicked Erdman's boxer stance and waited for an advance. Seeing this, Erdman lowered his heavy arms and said loud enough for all to hear, "I thought you wanted to fight. C'mon." He beckoned with a crooked finger.

Enraged, Tracy leaped forward and Erdman used his superior reach to copy Tracy's earlier jabs, hitting him with two sound blows and opening a cut that bled freely from above the smaller man's right eye. Tracy's left cheekbone was fiery red, with some blue and purple showing. His eye was completely bloodshot. Facing Edman's bulk, Tracy was being exposed as a thin, unpolished scrapper who was more reputation than skill.

He regrouped and swung wildly, missing with his left hand and pulling himself forward. As he fell past Erdman, the larger man raised an elbow into Tracy's path, catching his top lip and nose. The collision made an audible crunching sound and beside me, Scotty and Cork said, "Ohhhhh" at the same time. The blow stopped Tracy short and he fell to all fours in front of Erdman.

"This fight is over," said Johnny flatly, stepping forward to slap Erdman on the back and hand him his white delivery jacket. "C'mon big fella, I'll take you back to your truck. Let's go." He waved Reb away from the car and hopped in. Vindicated, Erdman strutted around the front of the car, a grim smile on his compressed lips as he walked by Reb, who watched him in silence.

Erdman stopped and looked over at Reb, who had backed up a step to let him by. Sensing Reb's wariness, Erd hesitated, and then flashed a fake jab. Reb stumbled as he ducked, throwing his hands up and falling in a cloud of dust on the third base line.

I frowned with mock sternness at Scotty who beamed back at me. "Do you like Tracy?" I asked him, my finger feigning the motion of the gas gauge "lie detector" needle.

"No, I don't like her at all," he grinned.

Mitchell Toews lives and writes at Jessica Lake in Manitoba. When an insufficient number of "We are pleased to inform you..." emails are on hand, he finds alternative joy in the windy intermingling between the top of the water and the bottom of the sky, or skates on the ice until he can no longer see the cabin. His writing has appeared in CommuterLit, Fiction on the Web, Literally Stories, Red Fez, SickLit, Voices Journal, The Machinery, Storgy, Alsina, *and* Rhubarb *magazine. Details can be found at his website, mitchellaneous.com.*

Harbor From the Cold

By Laura Widener

(This story was originally published in the December 2017 issue of The MOON.)

The diner was a chorus of chatting patrons, clanging dishes, and yelping kitchen appliances when the young man in the tattered coat took a seat at the bar that morning. Baltimore's winter mornings were unforgiving, and chilled bodies craving warmth occupied most of the diner's seats. Despite the activity, the waiter behind the bar with the nametag "Eric" noticed the young man instantly: the hair styled in dirt and grease stemming from beneath a frayed knit hat, the way body odor mixed with the crispness of cold air embedded into the fibers of the young man's jacket.

As if wanting to be small and unnoticed, the young man slumped in the seat—the one at the end of the bar's L shape. He studied the specials flyer intently with stone eyes, his lips pressed together and framed by a thick brown beard. His hand trembled as he moved toward his pocket, jingling the coins within. He withdrew a handful of tarnished copper and silver, and then set it on the bar top in front of him, his lips moving soundlessly as he slid the coins into piles.

I watched from two seats down, barely curling the corner of *The Baltimore Sun* and peering above reading lenses to watch the exchange between the men. I gave up reading over my horoscope again after losing my place three times just to watch Eric's upper lip curl at the sight of the young man calculating his chances at getting a hot breakfast. His lip trembled above the beard in a way that made me want to stroke my own chin, smooth by choice, one that I wondered when the young man had last had the chance to make.

Eric finally approached the young man, but didn't hold up his pad as he did for the other customers.

"Come on, man, you've got to get out of here," Eric told him.

"I haven't ordered yet," the young man said, still focused on his coins. "How much is a side of toast? I think I've got enough for that."

"This isn't the place for you, buddy. Try the soup kitchen four blocks down."

The short exchange demolished the levy retaining memories that flooded over me in a fierce rush. A knot seemed to swell in my throat as I saw myself in this young man, nearly a decade ago. My beard was grayed and the light was snuffed out of my own stone-like eyes, too. I wasn't supposed to outlive Betty. I wasn't built for the overwhelming pain that came with being a widower. Weakness terrified me as much as being alone, but drugs and alcohol were the right kind of numbness to make it day to day. Ironic, since the driver who struck Betty was intoxicated.

I didn't think anything was capable of making me warm again, bringing back the light again. Not after the darkness that blanketed my life after Betty died and I'd let go of everything that reminded me of her. Only the cherub-like face with brown curls and a toothy grin, and the words, *Dad, this is your granddaughter* in the surreal voice of my estranged daughter, were able to end my six years on the streets.

When I looked at the young man, I thought *what did he lose to get here?*

I set down my black and white paper curtain and retrieved my wallet, thumbing a twenty from the bills.

"Sir," I extended the bill toward Eric and cleared my throat, "you bring this young man whatever he wants."

"What?" he asked under a raised brow.

"You heard me," I said as I folded my wallet, the leather somehow warmer in my hand.

Eric muttered a "Be right back," before disappearing. I thought he'd better return with a cup of coffee and a menu if he knew what was good for him.

The young man stood to leave, and as I began to form the words to keep him here, he stopped beside me and extended his hand. "Thank you, sir."

I grasped it and offered a firm shake, noting how his breath smelled of mint, not of alcohol as mine had. When our touch separated, he sat in the chair next to mine. I wasn't one for conversation, so I resumed my reading while the young man ordered and slowly munched away at a plump omelet and a heap of pancakes between three cups of coffee. His face seemed a shade brighter when he pushed the empty plates away and wiped his lips.

When I folded up the paper and fingered the wallet again to pay my bill, two faded tickets with dog-eared corners slipped from their tucked spot.

My eyes scanned over the text, *Lyric Opera House,* and the date of our 25th anniversary, just a month after Betty died. Tickets I never had the chance to give her. We never had the chance to use them. I'd carried those tickets around in a worn black backpack while I looked for a place to sleep every night. They were a reminder of a life not fully lived, one that I needed to live for her.

I paid the bill and rose to leave, needing a change in scenery, but unsure of what the day held. The young man sprang up from his seat and faced me. "Thanks again, sir," he said with a quiver. As if the words were inadequate for sharing his gratitude, the young man moved forward hesitantly, and then embraced me. My thoughts moved to Betty again, remembering how her embrace felt, how she tapped her fingers against my back when she'd wrapped her arms around me. She was a hugger; the type of woman who would embrace anyone like her own family.

I wrapped my arms back around him and tapped my fingers on his back. When we parted, I clapped him on the back one last time. "Pay it forward when you get on your feet, son."

He nodded, and by the glisten in his eye, I could tell that he would.

"What was your name?" I paused before I walked away.

"Evan," he said. "Evan Billings."

The floor felt like quicksand, swallowing my very will to move as I stared back at the young man. The name was etched into my memory with the precision of a laser. I'd seen it in print, I'd even seen it accompanied with a black and white photo, with eyes less human, and a face not shrouded by hair.

In the years since Betty's death, I'd wondered countless times what I would do or say if ever confronted by the man who had extinguished the love of my life. I never imagined we would share a meal and an embrace.

Laura Widener is a coffee-loving introvert living in rural Georgia. She is a professional writer and editor, with an MFA in writing from Lindenwood University. Her previous work has been published online and in print with publications such as The Sunlight Press, TWJ Magazine, Rathalla Review, Spider Road Press, *and more. Read more at laurawidener.com.*

The Bell Tower

By DC Diamondopolous

(This story was published in the December 2017 issue of The MOON. It originally appeared in the literary journal, *Children, Churches and Daddies*.)

Reverend Langston Penniman sat on the edge of his bed, stretching his black fingers. Everything had either twisted up on him or shrunk except his stomach. Once six-foot-five, he now plunged to six two, still tall, but not the imposing dignitary he once was standing behind the lectern in front of his congregation.

His parishioners aged, too. So hard nowadays to attract the young, he thought, standing from the bed he shared with his wife of fifty-two years. His knees cracked. He'd gotten his cholesterol under control, but at seventy-five, his health headed south as his age pushed north.

Born and raised in Montgomery, Reverend Penniman had a hard time staying relevant, what with tattoos, body piercing, rap music, not to mention homosexuals getting married and reefer being legalized. For a man his age, changing was like pulling a mule uphill through molasses.

The smell of bacon and eggs drifted down the hall. He heard the coffeemaker gurgle. How he loved his mornings with the *Montgomery Daily News*—not Internet news—something he could hold in his hands, smell the ink. He even enjoyed licking his fingers to separate the pages.

Off in the direction of the Alabama River, he thought he heard a siren, not far from his church.

"Breakfast ready," Flo shouted from the kitchen.

Flo was the sweetest gift the Lord ever bestowed upon a man. Oh, he was fortunate, he thought, passing her picture on the dresser bureau and the photo of their three boys and two girls. Proud of his church, he was even prouder of their five children. Three graduated from college, all of them respectable citizens.

"It's gonna get cold if you don't come and get it."

"I'm a comin. Just let me wash up."

The siren sounded closer.

The Alabama spring day was warmer than usual. At nine in the morning, it was headed off the charts, as the kids say nowadays.

Reverend Penniman washed and dressed. At the bureau, he brushed back the sides of his white hair, his bald crown parted like the Red Sea. When his kids teased him about looking like Uncle Ben, he grew whiskers just as white. His boys joked he looked like Uncle Ben with a beard. He chuckled. He would have preferred Morgan Freeman.

"I'll feed it to the garbage disposal if you don't come and get it."

"I'm a comin now, sweet thing."

He heard the siren turn the corner at Bankhead and Parks.

Reverend Penniman looked at the cell phone lying on his dresser. He'd yet to master how to get his thick fingers to press one picture at a time, or type on that itty bitty keyboard. He couldn't even hold it in the crook of his neck.

He hurried down the hall. The floorboards of the fifty-year-old house creaked just like him. Not quite shotgun, his house did have a similar layout what with add-ons for the three boys.

The siren was upon them.

"Lord have mercy," Flo said as she put the food on the table. "That sure sounds angry."

"Sure does. Let me take a look," the reverend said from the kitchen's entrance.

He went to the living room window and saw a police car pull into his driveway, the siren cut-off. Two uniformed police officers, one black, the other white, got out of the cruiser and headed up his footpath.

He opened the door.

"Are you Reverend Penniman?"

"I am. What's the problem?"

"There's a girl up on the bell tower of your church. Says she's gonna jump," the black officer said.

"Good Lord!" Flo cried, standing behind her husband.

"Let me get my keys," the reverend said.

"No time, sir. Come with us. You'll get there faster."

Flo took off and came back with the reverend's cell phone. "Here baby. I'm gonna meet you there, soon as I shut down the kitchen. You should at least have your toast. I can put it in a baggie for you."

"No time," he said as he hurried out the door with the officers.

Reverend Penniman sat in the back of the car with a screen separating him from the policemen. "Who is she?" he asked.

"Don't know," the young white officer answered.

"What's she look like?"

"Black teen, skinny, baggy pants, chain hanging from the pocket, hoodie pulled over a ball cap."

"Akeesha."

"You know her?"

"Like one of my own." The reverend looked out the window as the car pulled away. He clasped his hands together and said a quick prayer for the troubled girl. Lord, help me help her, he repeated to himself. "Did she ask for me?"

"No."

"How'd you find me?"

"Your name is on the marquee of your church."

"Oh, right."

"I'm Officer Johnson," the older man said. "This is Officer Perry."

Officer Perry reached forward and turned on the siren. The noise deafened everything, including the pounding of Reverend Penniman's heart.

They drove toward downtown Montgomery along the banks of the Alabama. The RSA tower soared above the city's skyline.

The speed limit was forty. The reverend guessed they were doing twice that. His right knee pumped like the needle on Flo's sewing machine.

The siren screamed. The lights blinked and rotated, flashing red and blue on the hood of the car. Reverend Penniman felt like he was up on that bell tower, on the edge, with his arms stretched out, his body holding back the weight of all his parishioners who had wept in his arms.

At the corner of Graves and Buckley, the cruiser slowed, the siren cut-off. Officer Johnson made a right turn. People rushed along the sidewalk their cell phones pressed against their ears.

Halfway down the block, Reverend Penniman saw more people standing outside his church than he ever had inside. A fire truck parked in the lot with men unloading a ladder.

The police car jumped the curb and drove to the side of the brick building. He saw Greaty, Akeesha's great-grandmother in her burgundy wig, mussed like a tornado whirled through it. She cupped her black hands on the sides of her mouth screaming and crying at the roof. Her pink housecoat hung open revealing her cotton nightie.

Before the car came to a stop, the minister jumped out.

Greaty saw Reverend Penniman and ran to him. "You get my baby off the roof, you hear, Reverend? She done gone and have a meltdown."

"We'll get her down. Just craving attention like all teenagers."

"She cravin' nothin' but death. She gonna jump. She all I have!"

He ran to the front of the church. Greaty followed. The reverend gasped. "Good Lord." Akeesha teetered on the edge of the bell's shelter. Her baggy pants flapped in the breeze.

Two firefighters carried a ladder to the roof. They propped it against the gutters.

"Get away," Akeesha screamed. "I'll jump, you try to get me." Her voice carried over the mob.

"I know the child. I can get her down."

"Don't think so, Reverend."

The minister turned to see Officer Johnson standing beside him. "Then why'd you get me?"

"It's your church. I thought you'd be younger."

"I'm young enough and I'll get her down." He gazed up at the girl. "Akeesha!" he shouted using his pulpit voice. "I'm coming to you, child." He sprinted around the side of the church, to the back, amazed at how his body complied with his will. Officer Johnson's leather holster crunched with each matching stride.

Akeesha had broken the frame of the door and busted in.

"If I have to cuff you Reverend, I will," Officer Johnson said.

"You really want to save this child?" Reverend Penniman asked. "I've known her since she was four. I'm the only father she's ever known. Now you let me do my business."

He pushed open the door when he heard car wheels on gravel.

"Langston," Flo yelled out the window. "Where do think you're going?" She slammed the driver's door.

"Good Lord, woman, I don't need you pestering me too."

Flo ran up to her husband. "Officer, you arrest this man if he so much—."

"You gotta save her . . . she my baby—she all I have!" Greaty screamed coming around the corner.

"Calm down," Reverend Penniman said.

Greaty wiped her face with the sleeve of her house coat. "She never been so upset. She so angry. Them girls who beat her up. Them punks who tried to rape her."

The reverend looked at Officer Johnson. "Get all those people away from the front of my church. And tell those firemen to take down the ladder."

"I'm the one in charge here, Reverend."

"How about we get Captain Martinez?" Officer Perry asked. "They can secure the reverend with a rope and harness." Before his superior had a chance to argue, young Perry ran off.

"Thank you," Reverend Penniman shouted.

"She a good girl except for her sin," Greaty sobbed.

Flo put her arm around Akeesha's great-grandmother.

"Flo, take her to the car," Reverend Penniman said. "I'll be okay."

"Keep him safe, Officer. Don't let him do anything foolish," Flo said as she led Greaty away.

Reverend Penniman heard the whirling blades of a helicopter. "Good Lord. A child's life is at stake and this is turning into a circus," he said entering the back of his church.

"How'd she get up to the bell tower?" Officer Johnson asked.

"There's a room with pulleys. A stairway curls around leading up to the bells." Reverend Penniman could kick himself for letting Jake show Akeesha the inside of the tower.

Officer Johnson shot up the stairs.

"Wait! You can't go that way. You'd come out behind her. I swear, man. You let me handle this my way or that girl is going to die."

Officer Johnson turned on the landing.

The reverend had him in an eye-lock. "Please," he said, not used to the sound of the word or the helpless feeling that it carried.

"Why is she up there?" the policeman asked.

"She's a homosexual."

"My brother's gay," Officer Johnson said.

The minister watched how the cop's eyes captured a memory, something powerful enough to soften his features.

Reverend Penniman climbed the fourteen steps to the landing. He'd always been proud of his bell tower, right now he'd wished his ancestors never built it.

Officer Perry returned with Captain Martinez and a boyish looking black man. Both men held gear as they took the steps in three strides.

"Well Johnson, your call," the captain said.

"We'll feed Reverend Penniman below her, on the roof."

"Thank you."

The reverend led the men around a corner to a loft with stairs to the church roof.

"Got your Nikes on, I see," Martinez said. "Good."

"Now put that contraption on me and let me out there."

The firefighters held the harness for the reverend to step into. They hooked the cloth rope to the straps, gave it a tug jolting the reverend backwards, then tossed the rope to another man who waited below. "Side-step going down the incline. It's not steep, but we got you no matter what."

"Get rid of the ladder and the looky-loos. And stay well below. I don't want her knowing you're around."

"We'll be down on the first landing," Captain Martinez said.

"I've had enough talk, gentlemen."

Reverend Penniman took the steps to the roof praying as he went, for Akeesha, for Greaty, but most of all for himself. That he'd say the right thing, be sincere, because Akeesha had the gift of honesty. He prayed, asking the Holy Spirit to fill him with wisdom.

The door to the roof was ajar. He gently touched it. He felt the rope tug the harness. The door swung open.

The roof slanted and leveled out several feet down. The area around the tower was flat.

He smelled the fumes from the asphalt as he stepped sideways onto the shingles, planted himself and managed the incline. He took his time placing his right foot, then his left, and held for a moment. He did it again until the roof flattened out.

Applause and shouts broke out. "Get back!" Officer Johnson shouted. "Everyone!"

The reverend glanced at the Alabama River. The spectacular Montgomery skyline like a masterpiece God painted. Then he looked below. He saw the van of a local TV station, the helicopter off in the distance; the crowd herded across the street by young Perry, and so many cell phones held up to the bell tower it looked like Beyonce held court.

He heard sniffles, then crying.

"Akeesha. I'm here to talk, child."

"Won't do no good."

"Well, I didn't climb all the way up here thinking it wouldn't do no good. You and I have a way together, now don't we?"

"Prayin' don't work. I'm still gay."

"No reason taking your life." He thought back to the convention when one minister said, let the gays kill themselves. We need to protect our children. Only problem with that was all the molesting he knew came from men with little girls. He left those conferences feeling tired and old, the same men year after year with their stale jokes and self-righteous rhetoric. He felt trapped by the old ways and frightened by the new.

"Everyone knows. It's on Facebook." Akeesha whimpered. "My girlfriend broke with me."

Reverend Penniman made his way around the side of the bell tower feeling the tug of the harness. He looked up at the teenager.

Her hoodie covered all but the bill of her ball cap. She wiped her tears with the black leather band she wore on her wrist. "I wanna die." She inched forward to the lip of the shelter. Her hand left the arch.

"No!" Reverend Penniman yelled his arms stretched out as if he could catch her.

The crowd oohed.

He moved slowly around the tower until his back was to the mob. "Sit on the ledge baby."

"I'm goin to hell when I die. Bible says so." Her voice quivered. "Greaty found out. Said I'd bring shame on her house—more than my mama in jail. Said a woman's body parts were made for a man to make babies." Her voice trailed off.

"Greaty loves you, child. She's running around screaming and bossing, telling us to get her baby off the tower. You hear me, child?" He watched horrified as she balanced herself on the rim of the tower. A slip and she would die.

"They callin me a freak."

"Sit down now. We need to talk."

"Jump, faggot!" someone hollered across the street.

Reverend Penniman looked back at the crowd. Officer Johnson grabbed the man. Perry hauled him away.

"They all stupid." Akeesha sobbed.

"We can work this out."

"Don't dish with me, Reverend. Talkin's no good," she shouted.

He lifted his head up to see her lip quivering. "Can be," he said.

"I'm goin to hell. Might as well get it over with."

"Now, don't talk like that." He thought of all those times they knelt together holding hands. Their eyes shut tight, the way Akeesha repeated his words to rid herself of the sin of homosexuality. When they were through, her face was wet with tears. He'd never forget how she'd wipe her fingers several times across her jeans like she'd been holding hands with a leper. He knew then she'd yet to be cured.

He talked to his daughter about it. Rose told him the gay people she knew said they were born that way. She told him his generation treated the Bible like a deli, picking and choosing what to live by, who to hate, and the nonsense of fearing God. His conversations with his middle child made him reflect. That's all it did. He loved his children equally, but Rose had the gift of benevolence.

"Akeesha."

"What?"

"You jump, I'll try to catch you. Then I'll die trying to save you. You know that'd make Flo mighty mad, child." He took a careful step back to get a look at her face. She gazed out at the Montgomery horizon. Her calm scared him.

He remembered the first time Greaty brought her to church. She was four, always carrying her dump truck and running it along the pews. During the sermon, she'd nestle into Greaty's bosom, thumb in her mouth. Her short hair braided. When she got older, she sang in the choir. For extra money she gardened around the church. He'd take her to McDonald's afterwards. They talked. She was a good girl—even if she did look like a gang banger—thoughtful and quiet, never swore, didn't do drugs. But she suffered at school. It showed in her grades, and she finally dropped out. He was the only man in her short life, and she clung to him like a daddy. Her great grandmother looked after her like a one-eyed cat watching two rat holes. She ain't goin to end up in jail like her mama, or dead like her granny. She gonna be respectful, yes, indeed, she gonna be a fine woman when she grow up.

"Akeesha," he said with a stern voice. "You want to give Greaty a heart attack? I told you how worked up she is."

"She always worked up."

"She loves you."

"Quit lyin!" She spread her arms out.

"I'm not lying. You've seen her below. Running around. Now you hold onto that post." The noon light threw no shadows. The wind rippled his shirt. He felt the sun beating down on his bald spot. "God loves you."

"Then how come we pray to change me?"

"Cause you wanted to be like other girls. Remember? I'm not a psychiatrist. Praying is all I know."

Reverend Penniman took out his handkerchief and wiped his brow. In the 1980s, he buried a young man who died of AIDS. He'd never forget how his boyfriend threw himself on top of the casket crying and shouting the dead boy's name. He never thought homosexuals had feelings until he witnessed that young man's grief.

"We prayed to make your life easier. So you'd be happy."

"Didn't work. My life be easier if people left me alone."

"You're probably right, child." The reverend wiped his mouth with the handkerchief and put it in his pocket. Even if his heart struggled with what he was going to say, perhaps he could save her. "Maybe God made you perfect the way you are," he said, thinking of Rose.

"You lyin so I don't kill myself."

"No child. I'm saying it 'cause God has a reason for you being here." He heard sniffles. Then he saw her skinny hand swipe across her face. "Oh baby, come down and let's have a good cry together."

He watched for any movement from her feet.

"Quite a view up here," he said, trying to sound casual. "We live in a beautiful city. Don't you think?"

"I wanna go to California."

"Now, why would you want to do that? What about Greaty?"

"What about her?"

"Girl, I'm getting a crick in my neck looking up at you. I haven't eaten today. At my age, I'm on a schedule, and I get awfully tired if I'm hungry. We can talk better down here. Sit behind the tower. Alone. I want to talk to you like a grown-up."

"I am grown up." She shifted and pulled the hoodie off her head so it fell around her neck. "Jalissa broke with me. Who gonna love me?"

"Child, there's a whole lot of people in the world. There's got to be one just for you."

"You not being honest." She tugged the hoodie back up. "You wanna boy to love me. I don't wanna boy."

"Darlin baby, I admit I don't know much about such things. All I know is that I love you, and that love is greater than any judgment I cast upon you." He hesitated, and thought about the words that flowed out of him so effortlessly. It sounded like something coming from Rose's lips, not his.

He looked up. "Akeesha!" Where'd she go? He held onto the tower. He circled it fearing she jumped from the other side. "Akeesha!" he cried. He didn't dare to take that part of the roof. The slant angled too steep. He felt weak, a little dizzy but his adrenalin rushed. He went back the way he came, the harness tugging. Sweat poured into his eyes.

The door to the roof creaked open.

"What you wearing Reverend?" Akeesha stood in the archway.

"Lord have mercy, child!" His heart felt like a bowl of confetti. Instead of fearing the worst, she had climbed inside the tower and took the stairs to the roof. "You could have answered me when I called. You done scared the daylights out of me, child."

"What you mean, your love greater than your judgment?" Akeesha asked.

"Oh, oh, my darlin baby—we should enjoy this magnificent view of our city and thank the good Lord for the beautiful child that you are."

"I'm not beautiful."

"In God's eyes and mine you are."

"You lyin'."

"I swear on my sweet Flo's life."

"Then why we waste all that time prayin when I'm already okay?"

He caught a glint of the stud that she wore in the center of her tongue.

"You not as smart as you think, Reverend."

Reverend Penniman let out a hearty laugh. "Well, I'll tell you a secret, Akeesha, I don't have all the answers. Sometimes I have to make it seem like I do or no one would come to my church."

"They won't come anyway, lyin and all."

He thought about what Rose said, how the young have turned away from religion. "You know my daughter, Rose? She'd agree with you. You know she's studied in India. Traveled the world. Says God is always expanding—not sure what that means." He walked slowly toward the girl. "You know something, Akeesha?"

"What, Reverend?"

"You taught me something." His voice fractured. "You taught me, child. And I'm truly grateful."

"Taught you what?"

"Can we sit here, for a minute? I'm really tired." He slid down the wall. The harness grabbed at his thighs as he sat.

Akeesha walked like she'd been on the roof a hundred times, maybe she had, he thought. She sat next to him.

"You taught me to accept you." He slowly pulled the hoodie down so he could see her face. "I've always thought of you as one of my own. Flo, too."

Akeesha took his gnarled old hand. She spread each of his fingers to include hers. He felt love in her fingertips.

The confetti in his heart flung out over his beloved Montgomery. It showered like a vital rain. "I think there's only love in God's house," the reverend mused. "So much of life is good."

"Can we go to KFC?"

Reverend Penniman smiled. "Not McDonald's? We always go to McDonald's."

"No. KFC."

"Sure enough. My treat," he said. "I could take you to a fancy place where we sit at a table with a white cloth and linen napkins. We can order ribs. They have finger bowls with water so our hands don't get all sticky. Eat as much as we want."

"No. KFC," she said, standing and holding her hand out for the reverend to grasp.

DC Diamondopolous is an award-winning short story and flash fiction writer with over 150 stories published internationally in print and online magazines, literary journals, and anthologies. Her stories have appeared in: So It Goes: The Literary Journal of the Kurt Vonnegut Museum and Library, Lunch Ticket, Raven Chronicles, Silver Pen, Scarlet Leaf Review, *and many others. She was nominated for Best of the Net Anthology. She lives on the beautiful California central coast with her wife and animals. dcdiamondopolous.com*

A Show of Strength

By Rodolph Rowe

(This story was originally published in the August 2017 issue of The MOON.)

Sabine greeted the last of the lingering parishioners at the front door. As she came past the *Welcome!* kiosk on the way to her office, she picked up a handful of brochures that had been prepared to introduce her to the church and community. She'd meant for many, many months to send some of the extras to her mom in Gainesboro, who would distribute them to family and friends with the zeal of a brand new Amway salesman. The reason she'd put it off was because the brochure was still a painful reminder of her first conflict in this new church.

At thirty-five years of age, after serving for a decade in staff positions at large churches, this was her first parish where she was on her own as the pastor in charge.

Clive and Warren Parcher, bachelor brothers, large donors, senior men of considerable influence, had let it be known that they were personally funding the development and printing of this introductory brochure as well as underwriting a mass mailing to every home within five miles of the church. Generous indeed.

* * *

She had given the introductory brochure committee a nice color photo of herself presiding at the communion table, arms spread in welcome and some basic biographical information. The catch tag, "Come Home to a New Beginning," had been readily agreed upon by the administrative board, hoping to appeal to many of the young people buying their first homes, who might consider returning to the churches they'd left behind, as they started families of their own.

She had been pleased with the drafts, but then Clive passed around the final galley like he was giving out one hundred dollar bills at the end of a Staff-parish Relations meeting. She felt a dull ache in her breast when she saw that one word had been added on the front panel underneath her picture. Instead of the agreed upon, "Come meet our new pastor," it read, "Come meet our *beautiful* new pastor."

She blushed with anger and shame and fought back tears. She had tried to convince herself that the comments she overheard in the first few days were harmless--just people trying to get a sense of her. Yet, the phrase, *Moves like a lioness,* which slipped free from a group of young husbands loitering outside the nursery as she came past them on the way to the sanctuary, entered her breast like an arrow. Or just yesterday, when she was stopped by laughter outside the door of a classroom room used for a women's book study, and felt slightly nauseous, when hearing a disembodied voice claim, *I'm telling you she's in the Sophia Loren mold, but tight ladies, eve-ree-thing tight as a marathoner!*

Now, as people around the table looked to her and saw her distress, they went very quiet trying to sort out whether she was genuinely touched or very hurt. The only sound was a dry shuffle of the impressive three-fold being opened, smoothed out, closed. After a few moments, Clive moved that the brochure be accepted as is and printed for distribution. His brother Warren offered a friendly amendment. "Let's print five hundred extra brochures to put in the pews and for people to take home and give to their neighbors."

Clive nodded and smiled.

"Remove the word, *beautiful,* and I'll be fine with it." This was greeted with quiet laughter around the table. "I'm serious. It's inappropriate."

"Rev. De Luca, surely---."

"Nonnegotiable, Clive."

Always the peacemaker, younger brother Warren jumped in. "The picture's right there. The word is not even necessary. One picture is worth a thousand of them, right? Everyone can see for themselves."

Clive Parcher was just over five feet tall. Retired now from a long career teaching young women in Catholic day schools, he always dressed like a bank president or Wall Street lawyer, expensive, immaculate. He was tightly wound, supercilious, and like some small men, met every perceived challenge with all out disdain that he only half-heartedly tried to mask as kindly condescension. He was sourly displeased to ever be confronted by an opposing idea, but to be even mildly challenged in public by his jug-eared, lanky, let's-all-get-along, *Up with People,* younger brother, made him instantly apoplectic--a state that those who had known him a long time found sadly amusing. *Who's got the nitro?* Was code for *Clive is about to stroke out over something again.*

Struggling for composure, Clive said coldly, "The reason, my dear brother, the word is important is that to most people, this is junk mail. But beautiful! Beautiful? The soul is hungry for beautiful."

Warren cringed as usual, but to everyone's surprise, possibly because he knew something about his older brother's conflicts with women in his past, murmured, "It's sexist, Clive."

"Oh, pleeese! We are always grousing on about what a grace-based, inclusive, generous, progressive gospel of hope we have. How attractive it would be to new generations of young people if they only knew us, right? Well, we have "attractive" embodied for the first time in a gifted person. Sabine, surely, I mean honestly. Is it really too much to ask not to have you hide your light under a bushel?"

She wanted to tell them all about the dark side of being female and clergy. Explain how adding "attractive" to that mix often simply made things worse. She wanted them to know about the man who, when she offered him bread at the Lord's Table, forced her fingers momentarily into his mouth and sucked. Or several men and even one woman, who used the excuse of needing pastoral care to hit on her in her office, even though her secretary was just a few feet away. Or the series of increasingly explicit, sexually violent anonymous notes left in her inner office mailbox that led to involving local police and the costly installation of surveillance cameras, putting an end to the notes but not the chilling sense of violation. Or just have them imagine what it's like every Sunday to gracefully disentangle themselves from men who held on just a bit too long at the passing of the peace, and feel cutting into their souls the cold eyes of jealous wives. She wanted to tell them all this as well as challenging their understanding of the community of Jesus. Is our center the Spirit of a present Savior, or a personality cult focused on the pastor? Instead she just said again, very slowly, very quietly and very clearly, "No, Clive, absolutely not."

She hoped that was the end of it, until three days later when she came into her office to remove her robe after the eleven o'clock service and found Clive tucked into the visitor's chair. Seeing the dismay on her face, he raised a hand, "I come in peace," and chuckled. "A compromise, pastor." He pointed to a copy of the brochure he had laid on her desk.

"Clive, it's been a long morning---."

"It's a way for both of us to win. I mean the church to win. See, it says, come meet our lovely pastor and tour our beautiful facilities. Surely you can't object to 'lovely', for you are lovely."

"Mr. Parcher, please."

"Sabine, look. Just take off your robe, sit down and relax a minute." When she kept still, not bothering to conceal a look of contempt, he said, "You really don't get it, do you? How very sad."

"What don't I understand, Mr. Parcher?"

"Well, for starters that for any man, but especially us older men, even watching you take off your robe is one of life's rare pleasures."

She suddenly felt chilled. Wondered for the briefest instant how rage could be so hot and yet so cold. "Clive Parcher, do you. . . . *Breathe so you don't cry.* . . .have you any idea at all . . . .*breathe.* . . . of how that makes me feel? To be turned into an object for your pleasure?"

"Now you are being ridiculous. You'd think you were---."

"Were what Mr. Parcher? Nude? Nude under my vestments?"

"Now again that's just----."

"Ridiculous, right? What's ridiculous is thinking this deeply offensive behavior is acceptable. It's not. Let me inform you of its proper name. Sexual harassment."

Suddenly, his whole body hiccupped as an electric jolt cut deep into his chest and he made a gargling sound. Then Parcher started to use the arms of the chair to try to rise. "Naaa," he reached for his throat with both hands as he toppled toward her. She caught him under his arms and helped him to the floor. Then, kneeling beside him loosened his collar button and tie. Seeing the raw terror in his eyes she said, "Clive, try to relax. I'm calling for help right now." Then, with trembling hands found her cell on the desk and punched 911.

* * *

Rehabilitation began immediately at the hospital ICU and, putting personal feelings aside, she visited faithfully. When this initial emergency was followed a few days later by a series of mini-strokes, she organized lay visiting, and a couple weeks of evening meals for Warren, remembering he'd once admitted to her that he was pretty incompetent in the kitchen, and Clive did most of their cooking. By mid-summer, Clive had settled into a private, corner room with a view of the sound in the Fidalgo Nursing Facility and was holding court every day with church friends and business associates.

* * *

So this morning, she had already removed the large, silver pectoral cross hung from her neck and the green eel grass patterned stole that yoked her shoulders and fell to the bottom hem of the alb, when she entered the outer office absently unfastening the top collar buttons on the robe. She looked forward, as she always did, to her small, cozy office, a welcome refuge decorated with bright African prints and filled floor to ceiling with her beloved books. The focal center point of the eight by ten room was a battered, wooden end table she had rescued from a dumpster at the end of a college term over twenty years ago. This "old friend" had served since then as a prayer altar, holding her collection of sea shells and antique keys scattered around a palm-sized icon from the Roman tombs depicting Christ healing the woman with the flow of blood.

Though close to eighteen months had passed since the incident with Clive Parcher, every once in a while, like right now, a sense of dread came over her as she approached her office, an adrenaline "flight or fight" rush that made fireworks out of her nervous system. Sabine touched the doorknob to her inner office as if checking to see if it was hot. "Hello?"

"Oh, hello." A female voice. Then the sound of a chair pushed back. Someone standing. Sabine let out her breath. Put a smile on her face.

"Hello? I hope I haven't been keeping you long." Pushing open the partly closed inner office door, she looked down upon a mid-twenties, fair, blue-eyed woman, with a slightly off-center up-turned nose, who gave Sabine an initial impression that each smile or frown would be intriguing. She had clasped her hands tightly in front of her, and colored as she awkwardly stood.

"I've startled you. I'm so sorry. One of the ushers said I could wait. Maybe he meant the outer office. Anyway, I'm Carly Soderholm."

"You're fine. No apology necessary. Nice to meet you. Please call me Sabine." The young woman nodded. "And make yourself comfortable." With relief, the young woman smoothed the light blue cotton dress under her as she sat and crossed her long slender legs. "Give me a moment, and then we can visit." Sabine turned away from her and opening the closet door where she kept her vestments, hung the cross and stole together on a hanger. Then she unzipped the alb from top to bottom, gracefully turned out of it and placed it on a hanger.

Sabine settled herself in a chair opposite as Carly said, "I love seeing you in the robe! You look so. . . . I don't know. We've always had men pastors and they all wore black."

"Too academic for my style, and to me white hints at all things new.

"Anyway, the robe is also supposed to serve a theological purpose as well, masking my individual personality, and reminding everyone that I represent Christ. For women religious leaders that is especially important."

"Sexism?

"Yes, that, but on a more practical level there's the whole wardrobe issue." Sabine comically crossed her eyes and bobbled her head. Carly, wide-eyed, laughed. "Like this morning. After I spent twenty plus hours preparing my fifteen-minute message on the critical importance of forgiveness, and still I get two comments on my shoes, and at least a half dozen on how nice I look. But you're not here to learn about the challenges in being a clergywoman."

"No." A shiver passed through Carly. She hugged herself.

Sabine saw the change. Felt the young woman's tension in her own body.

"You know about us? My family?"

"No. But now that I think of it, I saw you, or someone who looks a lot like you with an older man in our Easter crowd."

"Yeah, that was us. My dad teaches in the English Department at Skagit Valley College. I'm finishing a two-year program with a focus on social work at Whidbey Community College, and now I've been accepted at the University of Washington—criminal justice. Actually, we've come in, sat in the back, and slipped out quick a few times. Like to keep a low profile. Well, Dad does more than me, because of this other thing, this thing that happened a few years ago. You've been here how long?"

"Just finishing my third year."

"Okay, well this was a little over six years ago." Carly looked anxiously past Sabine to the inner office door that wasn't completely shut. Sabine followed her gaze, got up, quietly pressed the door shut and sat back down. "Trying to put some distance between us and what happened. So have wanted to find a church off the island, where not many people know about us."

"I'm glad you're here," Sabine said quietly.

A big sigh. "So, here's the thing. I had a high school sweetheart named Jason Wentz. First love, earthquake stuff, you know. But once I decided to go to college and he stayed in town and worked for his dad, Chevy dealer, things changed. We grew apart; no longer spoke the same language. Macro cliché right?"

"First love? Very real, very precious, and intoxicatingly overwhelming."

"Yeah, well anyway, at some point I just realized we were making one another unhappy. I found the courage to finally end it. He dealt with it badly. Things got ugly. My family had to get a restraining order."

"Oh, Carly, I'm so sorry."

"Yeah, so." Suddenly, Carly stood up, a stricken and confused look on her face.

"Carly?" She had turned away from Sabine. "How can I help?"

Without turning back she said, "I could use a glass of water if it's not too much trouble?"

"You bet. Just be a sec." In moments she was back.

Grateful, Carly took a sip and sat back down. "So. One night." Then she stopped, looking unsure.

"Take your time. I'm in no hurry."

Carly allowed a sad smile. *A little girl smile,* Sabine thought.

"Okay, okay, so, one night my mom and dad were going to go to the symphony. This was the once a year fundraiser that includes dinner and an auction. Anyway, Jason's mom was in charge of the silent auction part. So, I guess he went through the dinner list and saw both my parents were on it." Carly's voice had gone so soft, Sabine found herself leaning forward. "At the last minute, my mom got one of her infrequent migraines and begged off, so I took her place with my dad. Thinking my parents would both be out, Jason took the opportunity to mount one last grand plea. I was nineteen at the time. My mom had me young, so she was only thirty-eight. People were always saying she could pass as an older sister, and she could for sure." She took another sip and her hands shook.

"Anyway, Jason knew where we kept a spare key. Had a dozen red roses, a ring, brochures of possible honeymoon destinations. So, shit, shit, sorry."

Sabine stayed very still. Her voice breaking, Carly pressed, "Jason found my mom in the bathtub. Probably thought it was me, at first." She paused again. Then stood up again and stared out the windows. "Most likely scenario is that pretty quickly things got out of hand." She placed a hand on her stomach. "He drowned her and then went into my room and left the roses and ring on my pillow. Then went back out to his car and shot himself in the head. That's how we found them when we got home."

Sabine stood and started to move to her. Carly hugged herself, and over her shoulder gave Sabine a quick look full of anguish. "No, wait. Sorry, sorry. If you touch me, it's all over for sure. I'll start crying and sometimes I can't stop for a while. I'm almost done." Sabine sat back down and Carly turned back to face her. "I'm beginning to put my life back together, but my dad. Not so much. And see the thing is, we both like you. Think you're the real deal. He even said you are a comfort. That's just huge for him."

"How old are you now?"

"I'm twenty-five now. Therapy on and off ever since. But this morning?"

"What about this morning?" The young woman's vulnerability and earnestness touched something deep in Sabine. A trickle of current sparked up her spine as the word *daughter* entered her mind by a secret wish of a doorway she had always left unlocked.

She came back and sat. "I feel like you wrote this sermon just for me." She reached into her purse and unfolded the morning bulletin. "See, I made lots of notes." Sabine smiled encouragingly.

"Okay, okay," she said studying her scribbles on the borders of the bulletin. "I get the first two. Forgiveness takes time, maybe a very long time, and is very hard work. I've known that in my heart, but it's a comfort to have it confirmed."

"Good."

"But could you say more about it being a strength?"

"Sure. So remember the purpose of forgiveness is not to let anyone get away with abusive behavior. Not to ignore the unfair hurt, but forgiveness is a gift to help put back together people that are broken apart. So it's a way to leave behind the horror and pain your boyfriend caused you. Not to excuse him, but to no longer let that pain consume your life, or drain your capacity to love so you can enjoy life again."

"But what to do about the anger? A couple months after the murder Jason's dad had a new Camaro delivered to our house. Title, keys, free and clear. Dad spent a maniacal day with a sledge hammer and blow torch reducing it to rubble."

"Wow. What did you do that day?"

"I hid out in my room. Scared to death he was going to. . . .I don't know. Hurt himself?"

"Oh, sweetheart, you've been so brave."

"It doesn't feel that way."

"So, how does it feel?"

"Scary. You know? Really scary."

"The anger?"

"Yep." The sad, little-girl smile again.

"Carly, this was a huge, huge loss. Please know that I think you are doing great. You're making a future. That's amazing really, considering what a catastrophic loss you've endured, and that's where anger comes in as a gift."

"A gift?"

"Imagine what happened as a deep wound, okay? Well anger is a salve for survival no less than the clotting of blood. Imagine forgiveness as the scar that comes later, but anger comes first." She waited for some sign the young woman got what she was saying. Finally their eyes met. Carly nodded. "So Carly, have you found helpful ways to express your anger?"

"Besides crying forever? Besides screaming sessions in the backyard? I don't know. I think I'm fine and then I am so not."

"So. Carly, look at me." She reluctantly raised her head and met Sabine's eyes. "I know we've just met, and I am so very honored you have chosen me to trust with all this. But before you go I want to ask one more question, and I want you to know I wouldn't ask if I didn't think it was important, okay? "

Carly nodded, breaking eye contact, her shoulders falling, her whole body seeming to hunker down.

"So, if your mom was here right now what do you think she'd say?"

Carly took a few moments to think, gather herself. "She'd say she is so glad it was her and not me." Her voice broke.

"Good. Take your time. What else?"

"And that she just wants me to get over this, have peace in my heart again, be able to be open to new love again." Then Sabine just let her cry.

After a few minutes, she wiped and sniffed. Took a compact out of her purse and delicately begin to repair the damage. "Thank you. I'm going to share this stuff with my dad."

"Good."

"And do you think we can talk again soon?"

"Of course," Sabine said, smiling warmly

"I'm just waiting for the new college fieldwork calendar to come out. Then I can plan."

"Just call the office. My secretary keeps my schedule. What's your field work site?"

"Fidalgo Nursing Center."

"Really? We have several people from the church there."

"Yeah, I recognized a few from the church newsletter. Amy Spring, for one. I got to visit her a couple times before she passed, and I've also been seeing Mr. Parcher for about a month now."

"Really?"

"Tough old guy. Keeps up a good face, but he seems more frail every time I visit."

"Well, good. One of our male stewards brings him communion every week, and his younger brother Warren is very attentive. He keeps me informed."

"Oh, Warren! Sweet man. But Mr. Parcher? Well, this might sound terrible, unprofessional and all, but he kind of creeps me out some."

Sabine smiled. "Perfectly fine. Just be aware of those feelings and maybe something to talk about with your supervisor." And then she thought, *Considering I still feel nauseous at the mention of his name, maybe I too should bring him up with my spiritual director.*

* * *

A few days later, Carly had just finished reading aloud to Mr. Parcher, the second chapter of Charles Dickens' *Bleak House*, and was about to slip quietly from the room as he appeared to have fallen asleep in his hospital bed, when he whispered. "Will you hear an old man's confession?" He smiled weakly when he said it, as if making a small joke.

"I'll call Rev. De Luca for you, if you like, Mr. Parcher," she said, mirroring his enigmatic smile.

"Well, you see," he said, reaching out a gnarled, liver-spotted, quivering hand, "Not every pastor is the right fit for every parishioner."

"Ah."

"Sabine is a wonderful person. Heart for God, lovely, you'd agree and so gifted, but. . . ."

To his apologetic little shrug and sad smile, she reluctantly finished for him. "Not exactly the right fit."

"No, not now. Not so close to the end. Miss Soderholm. Carly, may I call you Carly? What my soul really needs is empathy, and I think you just might be the one for that." She slipped her hand across the crisp white sheet remembering a bullet point from class: *appropriate touch when used with careful discrimination can be a powerful therapeutic tool.*

An innocent enough request it seemed at first, and clever really when she looked back. The quiet old man, wasting away in the "Maple View" room with his windows looking out on the courtyard garden through the rose-tinted limbs of the mature Coral Bark Maple. The Japanese hybrid's delicate scaffolding fusing the sunlight with a lime green wash making it feel to Carly as if she was visiting a bedroom placed in a forest glade. Artful how this emaciated sketch of an old man with the hungry eyes appealed to her heart, choosing her for such sacred intimacy in his final days.

When their eyes met his were bright with tears. "It's impossible for you to see the man I was now buried in this ruin."

"Oh, Mr. Parcher---."

"No, no, please. I'm not fishing for compliments, child. Only time for the truth now. Could I have drink?" She brought the tall cup with a straw to his lips. Watched as he struggled to get a sip.

"Thank you." He sighed as she placed the cup back on the nightstand. "Could you hand me my Bible? I think it's under the newspaper." He waved toward the window ledge as if shooing a fly. She reached the newspaper from her seat and found the Bible underneath it as he had said, and placed it gently on his lap. His hands did a palsied dance as he struggled to open the onionskin pages.

"Maybe this should wait for another day?" she said. "Have you seen your brother today?"

"Come and gone. Come and gone, and I may not have another day. Just let me catch my breath." He closed his eyes and gulped air like it was something gelatinous. She anxiously waited. After a few moments, he patted the dark pebbled leather of the book cover and said, "I was a teacher, did you know that? Lay brother. Latin. All girls. First in Boston, St. Teresa's Academy, then Minneapolis, and finally here. Small schools. Just the nuns and me, usually. Oh, priests, yes, the priests. Doing all the sacramental stuff, but overburdened even then. In and out. In and out. Really no time to spend getting to know the girls. There were, in all those years, an exception or two, but not many. So, mostly I was the only man, you see. Great responsibility. All those girls, just coming into their bodies, legs going on forever. Flirting with promiscuity." He gave a laugh and she sensed a meanness in it. "The '60s, early '70s, flaunting the dress code. Rolling up the waists of their uniform skirts after the nuns had measured them. Sitting in the front seats, letting the skirts ride up. Not caring if I looked or not. Such a funny little man! Having a good laugh afterwards. Oh, I knew what they said." She felt the heat come into her face, began to rise. The Bible fluttered open. "Here they are. Here's the worst of the bunch, the ones I made look in their own mirror."

Carly felt faint. Her heart quaked in her chest. She sat back down and took the half page of yellowed notebook paper from him. There were four names and then the phrase, *Lord have mercy, Christ have mercy, Lord have mercy.* "Mr. Parcher, I---."

"Hear me out, please." He began to speak quickly now, afraid he'd lose her, not bothering to hide the pleading in his voice. "You see, I know about you. Because of what happened to you, to your mother, I know you, of all people, will understand."

"Understand what exactly?"

"Boys, young men. The danger. How if you don't handle them exactly right, if they think you are leading them on, if you aren't exceedingly careful---."

"Are you saying that what happened to my mother was my fault?" She remained very still, as her wounded mind offered her a saving gift: an image of that innocent young woman she had not been able to protect years ago, now rising up, leaning over this old man, and in a fury beginning to pummel him with her fists.

"No, no, I am asking you..." He stopped. Tried again. "Look child, this all seemed a sensible response back then, but even if we disagree about the ethics of what I did, first let me ask you this. Do you believe God's grace is freely given, can't be earned?" Her non-response gave him a glint of hope. "We are all made of darkness and light, but nothing can separate us from the love of God that waits for us, all contrite hearts welcomed home?"

"Mr. Parcher, what did you do?"

"I took pictures. That's all." Her brows knit in confusion. "I was kind of a camera bug. Had this little hidden camera."

Carly struggled to process what he was saying. She ran her finger down the list of names on the yellow pad. And then suddenly she thought she understood. "Showed them a mirror of themselves? What does that exactly mean, Mr. Parcher?"

"Well, I sent them pictures of themselves."

"Pictures of under their skirts?!"

"Yes, but just to show them, make them see."

"Really? Really, Mr. Parcher?"

His voice went high and harsh with accusation. "Their shameful behavior was a threat to their souls. I was just...." He was nearly spent.

"What happened to these girls?"

"I don't know."

"You don't know?"

"Please keep your voice down, young lady. I can't remember. It's been so long ago."

"Bullshit! Mr. Parcher. Bullshit!" Carly's head was full of white noise.

She had formed the words, *Goodbye Mr. Parcher,* in her mind, but before she could get them out he said, "Child, please! Wait! Will you fulfill my last wish? Will you carry the cross?"

When she looked up, his face fisted in a pleading anguish. "Do what?"

"In my final instructions I've asked that you be the cross bearer at my funeral." When she just kept looking at him without speaking, he added, "Help me go home."

Keeping her eyes down, she stood trembling, and as she walked past his bed whispered, "Goodbye, Mr. Parcher."

When she got home that night to their beach bungalow, she lay face up on her bed, closed her eyes and thought about those girls, girls like her, just beginning to get over the wildly embarrassing and exciting astonishment at their new bodies that seemed to arrive overnight--to begin to find the nerve among fast friends to innocently pose and flirt. Imagined what it might be like to open an envelope and see a photo of herself, secretly taken, shameful. Suddenly something gave way inside her. An outside door to the back garden was opposite her room in a hallway. She launched herself through it and lost the little she had eaten at dinner in the azaleas. Wiping at her mouth, she headed out onto the short pier her family shared with neighbors on either side. A cutting wind had picked up from shore. It bore to her an icy menthol amalgam of evergreen, wood smoke and tideline decay. Carly stood facing the murmuring sound and screamed her frustration and pain into the night until her voice was raw.

* * *

The next morning she was up and had the coffee going when her dad came into the kitchen. "Hey, Early Bird, what's the deal?"

"Just need to get to school to do some research and wondered if you could take me over to catch a town bus on your way to work?"

"Sure. Special project?"

"Several. But I need the fast network at the library."

"Ah, yes. No cable. A nearly unendurable liability of living in the country," he teased.

* * *

She was impressed at how easy it was. Nothing in Boston, but *Google* had an index for *The Minneapolis Star Tribune* and when she typed in "Teacher" and "Illegal Photos." The story was barely three column inches and spoke of a possible lawsuit concerning unverified charges being made against one of the school's, quote: "most talented male teachers." The diocese lawyer for the accused, a Mr. Parcher, made the usual denials, and assured the public that the matter was being taken very seriously by the Bishop. She downloaded the news sections of the *Star Tribune* for the next few days, but found nothing else.

* * *

She wasn't scheduled to go back to the nursing home until Wednesday, but she needed him to know what she knew, make sure he understood he'd have to find someone else to be his cross bearer, and if she waited until her next appointed time, it might just be too late.

As often the case, especially in mid-March, the weather in the Pacific Northwest could be wild and unpredictable because of the Cascade Mountains lying so close to the sea. This arrangement of irregular, high ranges and passes creates many microclimates, and in a hundred miles, you could go from spring to deep winter and back again. This morning she only needed a windbreaker, for the misting of rain, but while she was doing her research inside, the temperature dropped twenty degrees and the mist sealed everything in a coat of ice. Yet when she walked back to Fidalgo Nursing that afternoon the temperature had risen again, so while the roads and walkways were still treacherous, everything sparkled like crystal in the sunlight and began to shed a chrysalis of ice.

She signed herself in, and feeling nauseous, walked to Mr. Parcher's room, but when she knocked lightly on the half closed door, got no response. Gently pushing it open she saw the empty, unmade bed. *Too late!* Then a warm breeze reached her, and peering out the open French doors to the patio, she saw Mr. Parcher in his robe and slippers with his back to her, one hand on his walker and the other holding a lit cigarette to his lips. His face was turned up seeming to study the hard blue sky through the gleaming branches of a centenarian Large Leaf Maple at the boundary to the property.

Just as she got to the open patio doors she heard a loud report and looked up as an ice-encrusted branch the size of a big man's thigh fell. "Wow!" she said under her breath, stepping out onto the patio. Then with a sinking heart saw the tips of Mr. Parcher's slippers poking up out of a debris of smaller limbs and leaves the ice had brought down. As she was about to go to him and see if she could help, he rolled over and shakily got to his knees and with the walker for a brace, began to pull himself upright. Clearly the large branch had only come close enough to scare him and make him lose his balance. He looked up and their eyes met. Fear fled and the warm pleasure of welcome came to his face. "Carly, my angel," he said and before she could respond, the old man's face changed again, as pain bucked through him. He twisted and went down upon on the ice-crusted grass, clutching at his chest.

She was on her knees and upon him in a moment, reaching out to touch him. Then recoiled, but to her credit, only for a moment. "Hang in there, Mr. Parcher!" Then she leaped up, went back into the room, pushed the call button by his bed and announced a Code Blue. She stumbled back out just in time to watch Mr. Parcher gurgle and writhe on the ground a final moment as if a great hand was pressing him into the earth.

* * *

"So, will it be an open casket?"

"No. That will happen at the funeral home." Forty-eight hours had passed since Parcher's death. Carly had arrived at Tully's early and secured two overstuffed chairs next to the gas fire, and had a double, tall mocha waiting for Sabine when she arrived. "Visiting hours are two to five tomorrow. The service is at the church on Tuesday, three o'clock."

"So, have you ever *Googled* Clive Parcher?"

"No. Should I?"

"There was a case I found. I can show you sometime, but I couldn't find what happened. Charges. Some indiscretion. Then nothing."

"What kind of charges?"

Carly made a sour face. "Well, he secretly took pictures of girls who were flaunting the dress code. Then sent the pictures to them to shame them."

"Oh, my God! Well, I wish I was surprised, but I'm not. Sadly, most of these things were settled outside of court with cash. Especially if it was a Catholic school." They sat quietly together for a few moments. "So, you've changed your mind about carrying the cross? I'd surely understand. I'd be glad to speak to Warren."

"No, I'm fine. Dying man's request. I'm thinking it will be good for me. Can anyone come to the viewing? Do I need to call or sign up or something?"

"No, it's open to the public." Sabine gave Carly an inquiring look. "How exactly is it good for you?" This was met with a small, tight smile.

* * *

The Ross Mortuary was designed to exude comfort and calm. Everything tastefully conspired to reinforce the feeling that this would be a good place to take a nice, long nap. Plush carpets, comfortable antiques, muted color schemes, indirect lighting, a crackling fire in a large fireplace to welcome all visitors.

Parcher's open casket rested on a funeral trolley, below a large print of William Holman Hunt's, *Light of the World,* which depicts Jesus holding a lantern and about to knock on a door. What charmed mid-nineteenth century Christians and made the work so famous was that Hunt only painted a doorknob on the inside of the large wooden door. Jesus knocks and waits but the sinner must open to him. The small alcove was filled with floral tributes and candles. There was a red velvet prayer kneeler centered in front of the casket. At the other end, was a living room setting of sofas and comfortable chairs where the immediate family could greet guests and chat quietly. To Carly's relief, one could pay respects in relative privacy. She decided for her purposes to arrive close to the end of visiting hours. Sure enough, only a few friends lingered. Everyone looked weary and ready for this ordeal to be over. She quickly signed the guest book, had a few words with Warren and went and stood beside the casket. It took only a moment to slip the sheaf of papers detailing his crimes under Clive's suit coat jacket and smooth it back down.

* * *

The participants gathered in the library for final instructions. Sabine and Carly were the last to enter. Both wore white albs and identical crosses. Sabine's robe was distinguished by a black stole. Everyone stood.

"Please, everyone, sit down." Four older men took the long couch. The laywoman who would carry the Bible caught Carly's eye and patted the chair beside her. Sabine remained standing. "So, United Methodists aren't much for processionals, but Clive loved them, so here's how it will go. The Ross Funeral Home people just pulled up outside with the casket. They will meet us in the narthex. You won't need to carry the casket in or out of the church. It's on a dolly. They will only need your help sliding it from the trolley to the gravesite following the service, which you know is right here, on an adjacent piece of property. So, the cross in first, then Bible followed by the choir, and finally each of you gentlemen with a candle. Slow, dignified walking pace, please. If you think you might be going too fast, you probably are. The casket comes in right behind you, gentlemen. Wait for it at the chancel. Put your candles in their holders on either side of the casket. I will come in last. Carly, you simply hang onto the cross through the processional hymn. When I seat the community, slip it into its stand by the baptismal font. We recess out, just like we came in, so, Carly, you are first in and out, and lead us to the gravesite. Watch me and I'll give you a clear sign. The recessional hymn is *Joyful, Joyful, We Adore Thee*. The gravesite is fortunately only a hundred yards or so from the entrance, so the casket will stay on the trolley until placed on the grave. That's when we will need your muscle, gentlemen. Just do as the funeral director instructs and you'll be fine. Carly, the cross is quite heavy, but you should have no problem. Any other questions then?"

Carly shyly half-raised her hand. Her heart pounded in her ears. She felt light-headed. "Where should the cross be? I mean," she stammered, "where should it be in relation to how Mr. Parcher rests in his, uh, coffin?"

"Mr. Parcher will rest with his head closest to the font and table."

"So he comes in head first?"

"Yes, exactly." Carly lowered her eyes and tried to concentrate on her breathing. "Okay, we're close. Gentlemen, get your candles." She gestured to where four oaken poles with large candles attached were leaning. Mrs. Morley, our Bible-bearer, will light them for you."

Carly got up and went and removed the large cross from its stand by the library doors. She tested the timber and balance, moving it from hand to hand. *Sabine was right. This thing had some serious weight.* Sabine had stepped into the narthex to check on the choir, but was back in a moment. "Stand down everyone. The Parchers' aunt has just pulled in the lot and Warren has asked that we wait until she is seated."

"Do I have time then for a quick restroom trip?" Carly asked.

"Yes, but be quick."

She felt great relief that the handicapped powder room was empty. She locked the door behind her, and leaned against the sink to try to stop herself from trembling. She had been fighting tears all morning, and now let them flow for a few moments. Then took several deep breaths, and wiped her wet cheeks and dabbed at her eyes with Kleenex. Finding the little collapsible brush she had stowed in the alb's inside pocket, she combed her hair in a fury as she stared at herself in the mirror, welcoming the gathering storm within her breast.

* * *

The sanctuary was constructed of a warm, caramel colored cedar, with the apex of the ceiling at least thirty feet high and formed in the shape of the body of an overturned boat. Thick chunks of stained glass in abstract patterns ran down both sides of the long rectangular room, starting with midnight blue at the back and getting lighter as one came forward with the yellows and golds saved for the last few feet before the altar. From floor to ceiling, the entire outside wall of chancel area behind the altar was clear glass framing a rock-sheltered, mossy, evergreen garden and reflecting pool.

The pews were packed. Parcher's immediate family and honored friends took up the first two pews on the left side closest to the choir. The rest of the church was occupied by parish and community people. This capacity crowd was causing the room to become overly warm, the air thick with the smell of women's perfumes in competition with the bold attar of Easter lilies.

The congregants watched as an usher greeted the aunt and escorted her down to the family pews.

When the usher returned, Sabine said, "Okay, I think we're good," and gave the organist a wave.

In a moment, the prelude concluded. A subdued fanfare seemed to seep out of the very pores of the building, announcing the opening hymn. The people stood.

A bell began to dully toll, as Carly led the processional in to the hymn. She stopped before the altar, keeping her back to the community and intently listening for the casket trolley to still. When Mrs. Morley came past her with the Bible, Carly turned back to the community. She held the cross steady and watched as afternoon sunlight used the highly polished, silver surface to semaphore blinding swords of white light across the chancel, making the singers hesitate, and some stumble, as they processed past and up onto the choir risers. In that same moment, the anger that had been buried and smoldering in her for days, ignited.

Standing in the chancel, three steps above the casket resting below her in the middle of the aisle on the floor, Carly leaned the processional cross away from her body, feeling the brute load of oak, iron and silver plate. Then she took a last look at Parcher's coffin, recalculating the distance, and pitched herself forward, letting her whole dead weight guillotine the processional cross down upon the lid. There was a splintering, dull crack. The cross bounced off the split casket top and then fell like a battleax, taking out two candles on the left and guttering wax across the closest worshippers. Carly tumbled head first into the candles on the right. The room erupted with a horror house of sound: bark-like shouts, strangled cries and screams came from men and women alike.

Sabine reached Carly first, sliding to her knees beside the stricken girl, carefully turning her over and pulling apart the snaps on the front of her robe.

"Carly! Carly! Hey, hey now." She ran her hand gently over the angry place on her forehead where a knot was rising, but saw no blood. Carly opened her eyes and immediately began to sit up. "Whoa! Whoa girl! You just stay down."

Parcher's own physician, a Dr. Patrick, now retired, appeared on Carly's other side, and had two fingers pressing on the side of her neck and the other hand taking her pulse at her wrist. Two ushers had commanded everyone to stay seated and the organist fumbled through the hymnal until she found,

"Abide with Me," which she began to play quietly. The senior of the two ushers said, "Should we call 911?"

"Let's just wait a moment." Doctor Patrick spoke without taking his eyes from his patient. "If she just fainted and this knot on the head is the only damage we probably will be okay. Her name's Carly?"

Sabine nodded.

"Carly, open your eyes. Good. Now, I think you just fainted. Okay? But everything is all right. May have just bumped your head a little. Do you understand me? Can you say yes?" Carly nodded dumbly at Dr. Patrick. "You need to speak child. Use your voice."

"Yes," she whispered.

"Good, very good," Dr. Patrick mumbled, as he continued to run his hands along her shoulders, collarbone, down her torso and legs. "Anything hurt? Let me look into your eyes."

"So, I didn't eat much breakfast and it's close to my time of the month, I guess. Besides my head, I think I'm fine."

"Okay. Okay. Well, Pastor? How do you want to handle this?"

"Carly, the truth now. You okay?"

"Pretty embarrassed, but fine."

"Right, so how about if I get one of the reception ladies to help her get cleaned up and sit with her in the library a bit. Once we finish the Parcher service, could you come back and check on her?" Dr. Patrick asked Sabine.

"Be glad to, Doctor."

"Thank you. Carly, you okay with that?" Dr. Patrick asked.

She nodded gratefully. As Dr. Patrick got to his feet, Sabine moved close and gave Carly an assuring hug, and then with mischief in her voice whispered into her ear, "Goodness, Carly, were you trying to wake Mr. Parcher from the dead?"

Carly pulled away smiling. "Oh, no! Absolutely not! It's me."

"You?"

"Yes, Sabine, it's me. It's me who needs waking from the dead."

"Oh." Carly saw the dawn of understanding come across her face. Sabine reached out and laid her hand aside the young woman's flushed, lovely face. "Well, just between you and me," she said quietly, "a truly spectacular and courageous new beginning."

Rodolph (Rody) Rowe spent forty years as a United Methodist pastor, which involved doing a compelling fifteen-minute stand-up every week, always seeking to be both intellectually and emotionally satisfying. Turns out that was great prep to be a short story writer. His poetry has been published in The Potomac Review, The Lucid Stone, Interlace, and The Christian Century. *Short memoir pieces have won prizes with* Whatcom Writes *and three times in The Frederick Buechner Narrative Writing Project Contest sponsored by* The Christian Century. *He is currently in the process of finishing final drafts of a spiritual memoir and a first novel.*

Unsaid, Undone

By William Cass

(This story was originally published in the August 2018 issue of The MOON.)

Growing up, Pete was a Navy brat, and he basically followed in his father's career military footsteps afterward. His father had been a pediatrician, while Pete had become an internist. When his parents passed away, Pete inherited their house in Coronado, and he finished the last twenty-five years of that career across the bridge at Balboa Naval Hospital in San Diego after serving on several deployments early on. Now, he'd been retired for almost two decades, his wife had been dead nearly that long, and he'd been told he had only months to live himself.

His cardiologist, a longtime colleague at the hospital, confirmed the late stage status of his congenital heart disease and renal failure on a bright, fall morning full of white light. But, Pete already knew it was coming; he'd given similar prognoses to many patients of his own over the years. That was why he'd called his daughter, Nell, and she'd flown out from Topeka to be with him. She understood what was coming, too; they'd talked about it a number of times as his condition worsened.

Nell drove them home after the appointment, and they remained silent in the car until they got on the bridge. At that point, Pete said quietly, "I'd rather not go the hospice route. Unless it's absolutely necessary to manage things."

"Whatever you want, Dad," Nell said. "I can stay and be with you as long as needed."

Pete nodded and pushed his rimless glasses up on his nose. He shifted his long, thin body in the passenger seat and looked over at his daughter. As always, he was struck at how much she resembled his wife; Nell was almost the same age Gwen had been at the time of her death. They both were big-boned, hopeful, still and calm, and wore their salt-and-pepper hair like a cap.

"Thank you," he said.

She smiled, took a hand from the steering wheel and patted his, then replaced it. As they crested the bridge, they both looked out over the green island with its canopy of trees, the old, wooden, red-roofed hotel at one end, the city's skyline across the bay from the other, and the wide, shimmering ocean spread like an endless fan out to the cluster of islands along the horizon.

"Is there anything special you want to do before..." Nell's voice trailed off. "Well, you know, buddy-jump from an airplane, sail out to those islands, anything?"

Pete sat considering as they descended the final stretch to the island. Finally, he said, "Actually, there is one thing. And it's something I've never spoken of, but have carried around inside of me for many, many years."

His daughter frowned and looked over at him quickly. "What, Dad? What is it?"

"Let's make lunch when we get home," Pete said. "Then I'll tell you about it."

They had vegetable soup, crackers, and milk and sat at the small iron table on the back patio in the shade of the roll-out awning. As always, Pete tucked his napkin inside his shirt collar, peppered his soup liberally, broke crackers into it, and ate slowly and deliberately. The little fountain that his father and he had built together when he was young trickled nearby, and a few hummingbirds flitted at the feeder that hung from a rafter where the pavers met the lawn.

Nell waited until they'd finished to say, "So, what is it?"

Pete took a last sip of milk, wiped his lips with the napkin, set it in his lap, and looked out over the yard. Nell wasn't sure if the ache in her father's eyes was from his illness or something else. Finally, he said, "This happened a long time ago when I was just a boy, nine or ten years old."

He stopped. Nell watched him clear his throat and smooth the thin wisps of hair on top of his head. "All right," she said. "Go on."

Pete nodded, hesitated, then began. "Well, a friend and I were playing catch in an empty lot just up the street." He gestured with his hand. "I threw the ball too high, it flew over a hedge and broke a window at the back of a house. The old man who lived there stormed outside and shook his fist at us before we could move. Captain Henshaw. He'd been my father's commanding officer before he retired.

'Which one of you did this?' he shouted. 'Tell me!'

My friend looked sheepishly at me, and I shrugged my shoulders.

He barked, "You're Dr. Kelly's son, aren't you? Wait until I tell him about this."

'Please don't,' I muttered. 'I'll do anything.'

"Can you pay for this window? You have twenty dollars for that?"

I didn't. That was a lot of money in those days, especially for a little boy. I didn't have five dollars to my name, but I nodded and said, 'I can. I will.'

The old man regarded me, scowling, I remember, and it was silent for a long moment until he said, 'Under my front door mat by five o'clock, or else I tell your father.'"

Pete grew silent then, staring off across the lawn. At a back corner of it, birds twittered in a pepper tree.

"My," Nell said. "What happened next?"

Pete shook his head some more before resuming. "My parents had a man named Luis who came once a week to do yard work: mow, trim, weed, prune, things like that. He was a kind, gentle guy who always had a smile and brought Mexican candy in his pants pocket to give me. He worked all day long and then knocked at the door off the kitchen when he finished and let himself inside the back hall to get paid his twenty dollars. My mother would meet him there. You'll remember how organized she was. She kept an envelope in the drawer of a little table there that always held enough twenty-dollar bills for several months of Luis' pay. I often watched her take a bill out of the envelope, give it to Luis, and then he'd make a little bow, and say thank you. Next, she'd replace the envelope, close the drawer, shake Luis' hand, and he'd smile and leave."

Pete had been gazing again out over the backyard, but turned and looked at Nell. He pursed his lips, then said, "So, that's where I got the money for Captain Henshaw. I snuck it from that envelope. I don't know, maybe I planned to earn it back somehow and replace it. I hope I did, but I'm not sure. I was so young and just scared of what would happen if my dad found out."

"That's understandable." Nell leaned forward. "Any kid might have done the same."

Pete's eyes met hers, then lowered. "It gets worse," he said slowly. "Luis was working in the yard that afternoon when I got home from the field. I took the money from the envelope right away and brought it over to Captain

Henshaw's before Luis had finished. Then I stayed in my bedroom upstairs with the door closed feeling ashamed until dinner. As we were eating, my mother told my father that she'd found money missing from the envelope she used to pay Luis and was certain he'd taken it. She said that when she'd confronted him about it in the back hall, he'd denied it, but it had to be him, so she'd fired him on the spot. I remember my father's eyebrows knitting together and him replying that it didn't sound like Luis, but he guessed you could never really know what someone was capable of doing. He said when word got out about it in that small town, he doubted Luis would ever find work there again."

Nell had put her fingertips over her mouth. She shook her head herself, then said, "So what did you do, Dad?"

She watched her father seem to seek out something in the distance. He swallowed and said, "Nothing." It came out in hardly more than a whisper. "I did nothing. I excused myself from the table as soon as I could, went back up to my room, buried my face in my pillow, and cried. But, I said nothing, did nothing."

Pete was silent again then, staring off above the pepper tree with his narrow shoulders slumped. A dog barked nearby. A moment later, sprinklers hissed on in the yard next door. They spit dimly until Pete said, "And I've done nothing since for all these years. And it's haunted me all that time. So, I'd like to do something about it now. While I still can. I'd like to make amends somehow." He looked at his daughter. "That's what I'd like to do."

Nell nodded slowly. "Do you remember his last name?"

"No. I don't think I ever heard it. All I know is that he lived in National City."

Nell continued nodding, her forehead furrowed, then said, "Well, I suppose we could put an advertisement in the newspaper there. Summarize what you've said, print his first name, and see if anyone knows anything about him."

"He had a birthmark on the back of his left hand," Pete said, raising his own. "I remember that it was in the shape of a half-moon. You could include that."

"All right."

"I suppose he'd be almost a hundred years old now, so he's almost certainly dead. But, perhaps we could locate someone in his family."

Nell reached over and squeezed her father's knee. "All right," she said again. "It's worth a try, isn't it? I can go call the newspaper now, if you like."

When her father looked at her next, something had softened in his face. "I'd appreciate it," he said.

Nell gave his knee another squeeze, then left him alone on the patio and went inside to the den where the phone was kept.

* * *

After the ad was placed, they heard nothing for several days. Pete tended his roses, napped, and he and Nell did things together that they'd done when she was young: worked on a jigsaw puzzle, played cards, read side-by-side, took walks, watched television, made simple meals.

The next Monday, just as they'd finished breakfast, the phone rang, and Nell went into the den to answer it. Pete cleared the table and washed the dishes while she was gone. It was raining lightly outside, and he was aware of the patter of it on the patio awning. He was drying a plate when Nell returned to the kitchen. She stopped in the middle of the room with a small smile on her face. Pete stopped drying.

"Well," she said. "That was Luis' son. He recognized his father from our advertisement and said he was sure when he read about the birthmark."

Pete lowered the plate and dishtowel slowly onto the counter. He leaned back against it, blinking.

"And guess what, Dad," Nell continued. "Luis is still alive. He's in a nursing home in National City. He's had several strokes, so he can no longer talk, but his son offered to meet us there and bring us to his room. So, we're going to do that at ten o'clock."

Pete shook his head, but a hint of smile had also creased his lips. "I can hardly believe it," he whispered.

"It's true. So, go get yourself dressed and ready. We leave in a half-hour."

* * *

They drove in silence with the windshield wipers thumping softly against the rain. The nursing home was a worn one-story stucco building on a busy street in a rundown part of the city. Nell held an umbrella over them while they shuffled across the parking lot to the entrance. When they arrived there, an elderly man about Pete's age held the door open for them. Once they were inside, he asked, "Nell?"

"That's right. Miguel?"

He smiled, held out his hand, and she shook it. Then he turned and said, "So, you must be Pete. And you've come to see my father."

When Miguel extended his hand, Pete took it in both of his. "Thank you for arranging this, for meeting us here," he said. "I'm very grateful."

"You're welcome. Why don't you leave your umbrella and we'll go to my father's room? It's just down that hall there. I've already signed us in as visitors."

Nell folded up the umbrella, set it against the planter next to the door, and they followed Miguel down a narrow hallway crowded with staff in scrubs, patients with walkers and in wheelchairs, and filled with the faint odor of urine and disinfectant. They stopped at the doorway of a room midway down the hall.

Miguel said, "I haven't told him that you're coming or anything about you, so I'll just introduce you, and then you're on your own. You know that he can no longer speak, but his mind is still pretty sharp. Remarkably so, really."

Nell and Pete both nodded and then followed Miguel into a small, brightly lit room with two hospital beds. The one closest to the door was stripped and empty. The curtain between them was pulled back, and Luis lay sleeping under a sheet in the bed on the other side, inclined so that he was almost sitting. Even after so many years, Pete recognized him immediately, a shriveled, frail version of the man he knew as a child. His mouth was open, and he snored quietly with his hands folded on his chest; the one on top had the birthmark. There was a television mounted high on the wall opposite the foot of the bed that was on, but muted. Miguel switched it off as he crossed to the far side of his father's bed. Nell stayed back under the television, and Pete moved to the near side of the bed. Miguel shook Luis' arm. The old man opened his eyes wide and looked up at his son.

"Hi, Dad," Miguel said. "There's someone here to see you." He gestured across the bed. "He's someone you knew many years ago."

Luis turned his head slowly and regarded Pete with confusion. His mouth was still agape, his eyes frowning with concentration. The left side of his face drooped, and a little bubble of drool had formed at that corner of his lips.

Pete reached over and put his hand on the old man's shoulder. "I'm Dr. Kelly's son. You worked on our yard for us a long time ago in Coronado. Near the golf course. Almost seventy years ago. You gave me candy."

Recognition slowly crept into the old man's eyes. He gave a short nod.

"Well," Pete said. He paused and took a breath. "I've come to tell you something. I've come to apologize for something I did back then. I stole money from the envelope my mother used to pay you, and I let you take the blame and be fired for it. I'm so sorry for that. I've been sorry for it all my life."

Luis stared up at him, his mouth still open. Then he nodded again, put his hand on Pete's, and began to cry softly. Pete began weeping, too, but more loudly; his shoulders shook with it. The two old men looked at each other, crying, while the rain fell steadily outside the window behind Miguel and a cart rattled by in the hallway. Nell bit her lip watching them. Miguel shook his head. It was warm enough that a ring of condensation rimmed the window.

Several minutes passed before Pete regained himself enough to take his hand away and use it to wipe his eyes and nose. He swallowed hard, then reached in his jacket pocket and took out an unsealed envelope, fat and full of twenty-dollar bills. He closed Luis' hands around it.

"I can never repay you for what I did," Pete said. "But this is a gesture in that regard."

Miguel said, "That's not necessary."

"No." Pete shook his head. "It is. It really is."

Luis' crying had decreased but hadn't stopped completely. He looked from the envelope to Pete and mumbled something out of the good side of his mouth.

"He's trying to thank you," Miguel said.

Luis nodded. Pete looked down at him and nodded with him. They did that until Nell finally said, "Dad, we should go and let Luis rest."

Pete nodded once more. "You're right." He looked from his daughter to the old man in bed and said, "Be well, Luis."

Nell took him gently by the elbow, and he stepped away from the bedside. "We can find our way out," she said. "Thank you both."

She led her father out of the room and down the hall to the entrance. She held the umbrella over them against the rain across the parking lot and helped him into the passenger seat of the car. Before closing his door, she saw that his glasses were sprinkled with droplets, so she took them off and dried them with a tissue from her pocket. Before replacing them on his face, what she saw in his eyes was not just relief, but something akin to childlike wonder.

They drove without speaking until Nell started up the freeway onramp towards the bridge. Then Pete said, "He was nice, too…Miguel. Like his dad."

Nell glanced his way. She realized suddenly that she'd never heard him utter an unkind word about anyone, and she wondered how much of that was because of the boy he'd become when he stole that money and remained silent about it. "Yes," she said. "He was."

They merged onto the freeway and continued in silence for several more moments, the windshield wipers making their soft, regular arcs, until Pete said quietly, "This has been a special day. How'd I get so lucky?"

Nell's smile was brief. She glanced again at her father and thought of all the lives he'd helped and healed, and the one, his own, that he could no longer do anything to prolong or save. But, this old, heavy burden had been lifted; he'd done that. She turned the car onto the long incline that led to the bridge. The rain had lessened. They could go home now and pass the days he had left as fully and peacefully and well as possible.

—

William Cass has had more than 100 short stories accepted for publication in a variety of literary magazines and anthologies such as december, Briar Cliff Review, *and* Ruminate. *He recently was a finalist in short fiction and novella competitions at* Glimmer Train *and* Black Hill Press, *received a Pushcart nomination, and won writing contests at* Terrain.org *and* The Examined Life Journal. *His story,* Those Words, *was previously published in* The MOON. *He can be reached at william. cass@sbcglobal.net*

A Private Pain

By Alexander Kemp

(This story was originally published in the April 2019 issue of The MOON.)

February 8, 2018

Today was another bad day. My hand is hurting, so I'll stop writing.

* * *

February 22, 2018

Last night I dreamt Violet was next to me in bed. Her face was inches from mine. I could feel her breathing. She opened her mouth, releasing cold air. The bedroom door burst open and two masked men entered. As I was pinned to the floor, I tried to scream, but there was only silence. I awoke. Violet was 29 in bed. She's always 29.

Dr. Bali will ask me plenty of questions about this dream.

* * *

April 3, 2018

My anniversary with Violet, the consummate rich girl, was today. Her sister called. I said nothing.

I've been doing more poems. None are completed. I'm akin to a black hole.

In my drawer, underneath this journal, is my purchase from Holster Co. That's my secret.

* * *

Leave a message after the beep. BEEP!

Hey Mom, it's Christian. Just returning your call. I'll try to come by this weekend. I hope pop's recuperating. Things are getting better each day. The spring weather helps. I went walking. Work's okay. My caseload is growing. A father of two is freaking out about losing his food stamps. So you know, the usual thing. Anyway, I've just been working a lot. That's why you haven't heard from me. And I mean it, I'll really try to come by this weekend. Please don't worry about me so much.

* * *

Dallas: What up, Chris? How u been

Christian: Good! Just been working and running (Running emoji)

Christian: And U?

Dallas: I'm straight. My wife and I will be in town Sat. Want 2 get together?

Christian: Sure

Dallas: I meant to come down after everything happened with Violet last year. My bad about that. I kinda got worried when I didn't hear from you for some months. But we'll have fun Sat.

Christian: Don't worry about it.

Dallas: U good?

Christian: I'm seeing someone.

Dallas: WHAATT!! (Smiley emoji)

Christian: It's early. Her name is Janelle. We don't know what it is yet.

Dallas: Congrats! We'll talk all about it Sat. Wanna do usual spot?

Christian: (Thumbs up emoji)

* * *

May 1, 2018

I went to the gun range after work. I'm improving. My Glock 19 is always so cold in my hands. Even as my index finger grazed the black trigger, I struggled to believe destruction was right there. But it was. Janelle is coming over tomorrow. I'll make her spaghetti. And maybe stuffed mushrooms. I'll need to buy mushrooms.

She's starting to wonder why she still hasn't met my parents. Janelle almost never asks questions about Violet, and I'm grateful for that. Maybe she's not curious. It's been over a year now. I'm looking at the photo Janelle texted of herself. She never smiles with her teeth. She's self-conscious of the crookedness. Violet had impeccable teeth.

* * *

June 21, 2018

Margaret,

I've read the email you and Lauren sent a couple of times. It has taken me three days to respond because I want to give the most thoughtful and forthright answer I can to the concern you've raised. To put it simply, I'm fine. I completely understand why you, as an HR person, needed to do outreach, but I'm fine.

As you already know I've been serving as a case manager for the last six years and the incident from Thursday was the first of its kind. As I acknowledged to Lauren in the official report, I made a mistake in regards to the incident. The people we serve should be able to come here without fear for their safety, but as determined by the investigation, I was not the linchpin to the incident.

I'm declining the generous offer of a three-week sick leave. I feel fine. So unless you're planning on suspending me for some reason (which would obviously have to be substantiated) I'll continue showing up every day.

Thank you for checking in. I assure you last Thursday won't be repeated. I'd prefer not to discuss it again, if possible.

Regards,

Christian

* * *

The Gatsby Syndrome

The flash of the smile was the fall of my mind

Please know my passive ways were to escape your kind

Blasting into my heart and beyond, you smiled, knowing I was bound

Waiting for your words of approval had me worshiping a sound

Reflections of your rampant rancor infect and confound

August 5, 2018

Not until I opened this journal did I think of Violet. Maybe I am getting better. Pop's hip is still bothering him, but otherwise, he's happy. I'll try to see my folks next weekend. I should see them more. Janelle's birthday is soon. She'll be pleased with whatever I get her. I won't put too much thought into it. She has an overabundance of happiness. Her unrelentingly positive outlook is remarkable. It's her best quality. I loathe it.

* * *

Father, hallowed be your name. Your kingdom come. Give us each day our daily bread and forgive us our sins, for we ourselves forgive everyone who is indebted to us; and lead us not into temptation. Forgive me for the thoughts I've been having for so long now. The life you've given us is sacred; I do know that. Please help me with Janelle. I don't want to hurt anyone. I don't want to hurt anymore. Heal me, please. For thine is the kingdom, and the power, and the glory, for ever and ever. Amen.

* * *

Janelle,

You deserve all the happiness in the world and I hope on this day, your 27th Bday, you have everything you want. Enjoy the enclosed gift card for the spa. Eventually, every nurse needs someone to take care of them (this is my way of saying you need some R&RJ).

Happy Bday, beautiful! I'll give you a big kiss next time I see you.

Christian

* * *

Leave a message after the beep. BEEP!

This is Mom. I haven't heard from you in a couple weeks. Let me know you're okay.

* * *

Dallas: U didn't show for lunch. U good?

Dallas: I tried calling but U didn't pick up

* * *

September 24, 2018

I took out the Glock today. I cradled it in my lap. I cried. Funny part is I don't even remember the last time I shed tears. Not even Violet's death did that. I didn't go to work today. Maybe I won't go in tomorrow. Mostly I slept. My hand shook the first few times I held the Glock. Not anymore.

I'll pray and go back to sleep.

Saved Message—*Violet* [March 05, 2017]: I love you! Have a great trip. Can't wait to be together again, xoxo!

* * *

Incoming Call: Janelle

Call Declined

Janelle: I tried leaving a message but your voicemail is full. Pls call when you have a chance

Janelle: Baby, where are you?

* * *

Transcript: 11/5/2018

Dr. Bali: It must have been cold.

Christian: It was. And the wind kept blowing but Janelle said her legs weren't cold even though she was wearing a skirt. To invoke Violet's name had always been too difficult, but with her, I finally did it. Opening up was petrifying, but it felt good, at least after a while. I still had that nagging urge to claw at myself, to escape. But then we were both at the gravestone. Afterward, when we were at my place I locked myself in the bathroom. I still have the majority of my painkillers from the dental thing last year. So, I decided that way over the gun...I could at least let my mom do an open casket. I know you're wondering why I'm being so candid.

(Long pause)

The thing is my bathroom smelled of Spring Rain, Janelle's perfume. From one corner to the next, that aroma filled the room. Even though everything inside me was dormant, and the word "tomorrow" was agony, Janelle being there was soothing. I know you will diagnose my relationship with her as unhealthy, and I suppose that's an accurate analysis. Even so, I wanted there to be more time because the only thing coursing through my mind was a feeling, a hope of being found. I was hungry for one more hour, maybe two. So I opened the door. Janelle was there. She knew. We kissed. And kept kissing. When I woke, my arms were around her. My head on her bare stomach. Both her arms were around my naked shoulders. Her hand, the left one, massaged my scalp. It was morning.

(Brief pause)

Dr. Bali: Okay. If you had to take a guess, do you believe what you experienced was a saving grace or merely the eye of the storm?

Christian: Probably the latter, maybe not. I just know, with all due respect to your previous recommendation, I'm not going to be medicated up, comfortably numb. That's right for some people, just not me.

Dr. Bali: And yesterday?

Christian: However my depression ends, I'll be okay. You know, when you think back on me as a patient, remember this day. Recall the way I am right now. I actually said, "Good morning," back to your secretary without thinking, "fuck you." I've peaked.

(Brief laugh)

But to answer your question, yesterday was beautiful. Those moments still exist. Maybe they'll become more frequent. Remember I was capable of optimism. Anyway, yesterday was something...lovely, fulfilling. Magnificent.

—

Alexander Kemp received a BA from Aquinas College and recently graduated with an MPA from the University of Southern California. He currently lives in Kalamazoo, MI.

CJ the Prince

By Daniel Larson

(This story was published in the October 2013 issue of The MOON; originally published by The Sun magazine; used with permission.)

Conclusion

THERE ARE STILL candles on the sidewalk where they shot him in the head two months ago — the big frosted-glass kind with Jesus on the side that you can buy at the Mexican grocery for ninety-nine cents. The flowers are fresh. The giant photo of him is still visible as you pass by in the team van, but the laminate is peeling from the top right corner, the weather starting in.

Setting

The youth and community center in South Central Los Angeles, where you coach basketball, is a block-long, two-story concrete bunker funded by the Salvation Army. By day, two hundred kids attend day-care and after-school programs. By night, fifty high-schoolers and young adults lift weights, browse the Internet, take music lessons, and hang out in the social core of the whole neighborhood, the gymnasium. The center looks a little different from every other nonresidential building around here. It's the lack of graffiti that makes it stand out. No tagging on any of the outside walls, only a scrawl or two on the alley side.

Brothers

They're at the center all the time. You've really got to keep the two of them straight, but it's difficult. They've got the same face, down to the pimples along the jaw line. They're both taller than you, the older one by at least five inches. The younger's a bit quieter, but when he does speak, it's with the same inflection and rhythm. So you take a guess: "Hey, Rye-Rye, what's up?"

"I know how we all look the same to you, Tim-Tim, but you can call him 'Rye-Rye,' me 'CJ.' "

"You're kidding. Really?"

"We'd appreciate it."

"He means *I'd* appreciate it," says Rye-Rye. "He dreams he was me."

"With your chicken arms? I'm twice you already. Tell him, Coach. Tell him CJ's your starting center, long as someone helps you tell us apart."

Birds

No exaggeration: you fear helicopters. On a good day, driving south down the 110 to work, you don't see any over South Central. On a fair drive into work you don't see any to your left, the East Side. On a bad day there are three news teams and two police choppers in the air above Fremont High School (the building with metal detectors at the front entrance, steel grates on every window, and a fifteen-foot-high wrought-iron fence surrounding it) because a Mexican kid hit a black kid in the cafeteria, and the black kid's friends joined in, and then so did the Mexican kid's friends, and soon pretty much all the kids in the school were involved, and the 77th Station officers had to call the riot squad, with their helmets and shields, and now it's a lockdown, and there's no basketball practice at the center today, because no one's getting out of school until their guardian arrives, and, well, that's going to take a while, if.

Television

You can't pay attention to the actors on the screen. You should have been more patient at basketball practice today. You shouldn't have closed the weight room so dramatically. Was this the first water-bottle fight in the history of the world? What did those kids do after you booted them from the center? Tomorrow you'll have to start out right, maybe plan a three-point shootout or a barbecue or —

"Hey! Where'd you go?" your girlfriend asks, pulling you back into your apartment, back into Echo Park. "Be here," she says. "With me."

Gymnasium

The action on the court is lively. Santwaan's already dunked twice, Jeremy is reigning in the lane, and everyone's playing defense for once. But the real show's in the stands, where CJ is sitting this one out: CJ the sun. CJ, shit-talker extraordinaire, delivering a medley of boasts and taunts. Something for everybody:

"Tonio, you little bug-eyed fly child, look at you. Probably seeing two thousand of me — *watch out!*

"Rigo, Rigo, Rigo. Shit, Rigo, you white, man. Just face it. Tim-Tim more Mexican than you!

"Candy. Nice belt, Candy. And they was saying, *Who's gonna keep K-Mart in business?*

"Curtis! Curtis! Look at your grill, homeboy — like you *hate* toothpaste!

"Miles, oh, my, Miles. Got your shoelaces tied around your ankles? Reebok making skates now?

"Shari, Shari, it's ok. Don't nobody but us two know what happened last night. Don't you worry. . . . I'm just playing! Just playing!

"Tim-Tim. Look at those ears, people. How much your ears weigh, T.? Just think — lose them and you'd be dunking! No, really, my bad, my bad, T. We just playing — but, honestly, what they saying downtown right now? I bet you can hear the ocean."

Shoes

You can't decide: Nikes or New Balances. Back and forth you go, yea and nay, up and down the aisles. The real question is: Who do you want to take shit from — your friends in Echo Park, or the kids in South Central? You feel like you're in middle school again, when you'd be shopping for school clothes with your mom but hearing your classmates in your head. Would they mock you? Now you hear the gallery in the gym if you face down all the homeboys while rockin' the NBs. But if you choose Nikes, then, back in your Echo Park circle, you'll have to hear about the social consequences, Nikes being somewhere above feedlot beef but below offshore drilling on the scorn meter. So finally you just lay it out, ask your shopping companion. And CJ, shaking his head in an expression of pained disbelief, doesn't hold back: "Man, shouldn't no Chinese shoe-gluer stop *you* from looking fly."

Offense

"Man, why don't you go back to Beverly Hills?"

"Wearing those mirrored shades, look like the po-po."

"So smart, and here you are working in South Mental."

"Think you God, saying who can come and go. Shit. Try telling me again one time. Oh, I'd *love* you try that."

"We all know you rich — you white."

"Don't remember nobody asking you to be here anyway."

Research

Naturally you did a little before sending in your résumé. From Wikipedia: "South Central Los Angeles remains known for its notorious gangs. The tension between black and Latino gangs has led to increased racially motivated gang violence."

Initiation

CJ swears "Crip talk" is for real, but you can't believe it: "They don't really talk like that."

"You'll see in a minute, Tim-Tim. *Cror* is *for*; *croo* is *to*. You work at the 'Cralvation Crarmy.' "

"They have to do it for a whole year?"

"A whole year."

"Even *fuck*?"

"*Cruck*, man. *Cruck*."

"This already hurts my brain."

"Just wait."

Your journey is only four blocks, but everything changes after two: No more red graffiti. Almost entirely blue tagging once you reach Glade Street.

" 'Sup, homeboy?" CJ says to the teen who answers the door.

"CJ! Crup, crup, cramigo? Crelcome croo cry crasa!"

"Nah, man, we can't stay. Is Randy round?"

"Croo cris?"

"Just Tim-Tim, my basketball coach. He runs the center over on 76th and Central. What about Randy?"

"Crat crigga? Cree creft crith crat critch."

"Who, Shari? Shari ain't no bitch."

"Cratever crou cray."

"Later, homeboy."

"Crater."

On the walk back you notice the kids playing in the front yards are all wearing white, black, or gray — no colors in these neighborhoods.

"Unbelievable."

"Oh, come on, T. It's like, whaddya call that frat thing . . . rushing, right?"

"I wasn't a frat boy, CJ."

"No? But my cousin Amber told me that's how you white boys get laid!"

Sign

Across the street and half a block down from the center, right next to the car dealership with the Ford Explorer forty feet up in the air, its rims spinning in the wind, there's a little store with no name on the door or windows, just a yellow sandwich board out front with black hand-painted lettering: "GIFTS 4 Inmates. Bus Saturdays."

Smoke

CJ looked you straight in the eye as you spoke, didn't worm-hunt the linoleum like Rondale and Eddie did. He nodded as you explained how the center is a special place, worthy of respect. He kept nodding as you talked about home and public space, about wearing different coats, playing the game to get your goal. He smiled as you described how the last thing you ever feel like doing is suspending folks, how this is supposed to be *their* center, not yours. He elbowed both his sidekicks, one to each side, when you said you hoped they were listening, because that's the only way they'd be coming back here: by listening, displaying remorse, thinking of a way to make it up to you. He maintained rapt attention the whole way through, looking grave when you got more serious, smiling (but just slightly) when you tried to lighten your tone a touch. He shook your hand when you said you hoped they'd be back, that they only needed a little time off, some vay-cay from the center to learn to respect it and all. Then, right before he turned and left, he said with a wry smile: "Just one question, Tim-Tim: how you know the smell of weed so well, anyways?"

Ammunition

Ain't it funny that no one knows his real name? Just "CJ." But the truth is right there in the computer at the front desk, in the KidTrax attendance program, in the membership folder: Cornelius Moreland Junior. This is your eureka moment for the week — wait, the month, maybe the year. At last you've got something you can use against him when he starts in on you; you can fire back. Cornelius Junior? Yes! Nobody knows yet, but they will. Let CJ trot out his jokes about your ears tonight, 'cause you're loaded and ready.

Promotion

"Well, look at you now, Tim-Tim: shiny black FBI shoes, button-down Bachrach, matching silk tie — ladies and gentlemen, the new king of the Salvation Army South Central Youth and Commune Center is *styling*! Shit, you trying to make me look bad? It's not working, but nice try. Out with the old, in with the new, eh, T-dawg? No more Sketchers for you! No more value menu, that's for sure. Ah, Tim-Tim will have the supersize, please. Just look at my boy — blinding! They sure they got the right guy? Did they really mean to make the *basketball coach* the director around here? My, oh, my. Standards be slipping; things going to hell all over. And you know what I've been saying: I blame it on the youth. No, no, but seriously, Tim-Tim, you gonna remember us little folk now you way back there in that big office? Old CJ still needs you, you know. Don't be forgetting about me and Rye-Rye, now. Don't be forgetting how you was that first day down here when we found you in that old gym back of Fremont, ya hear? You looked at the two of us like we just escaped Chino. *Please* don't be forgetting about that. OK, white man?"

Higher Ups

The white-haired colonel and his silvery-blond wife, the new team running divisional headquarters downtown, arrive the morning that Marina and Miguel's mom gets beaten up outside the front gate, her left eye swollen shut and patches of hair missing. But they've worked in places like this before; their questions are so much better than ones from other suits; you can see the impact of this tour in their eyes. And you know not to get your hopes up, that these visits are about goodwill and optimism. Of course they're going to be touched and impressed — you engineered this, after all.

Despite all the history of neglect, the broken promises and bureaucratic incompetence, you're actually able to keep your eyes closed during the prayer circle, your mind focused on the blessing, not on the swirl of center activities around you — the little kiddies zipping out of the lobby, the teens sailing in — but on the kind, hopeful, soothing words that flow from somewhere above the soft, warm, pink hands that have actual authority, influence. So you hold on tight and keep your eyes closed and listen to their prayers and know they mean well, and you want to believe that they will do what they say they will do, and it feels good, holding these hands and closing your eyes and simply listening — for once not having to do anything else, for just this one moment — and trying to believe in the speaker's words and hoping, not completely, not foolishly, but in the simplest way, that maybe these people will act on what they're saying; that maybe together you can make a difference in this neighborhood; that maybe, just maybe, there's a bunny's chance in a lion's den that this simple wonderful feeling alone will actually matter. That someone is listening.

Pops

"He locked away, Tim-Tim. Feds, they say. I don't even really know him. He wrote us a letter, and we seen him like twice. Rye-Rye's never met him. Everybody says, 'Just look at us, and you know we brothers,' but he won't claim Rye-Rye. I mean, we brothers, just look. One thing for sure though: he is a big Blood, like way up from way back. I guess they take care of our moms because of that."

Friends

A bar in Echo Park. Tight, tapered, black jeans and ironic T-shirts everywhere you look. You realize how long you've been working south of the 10, how much your clothes are now sagging: jeans, shirts, baggy, baggy, baggy. You need a beer and some friendly ears. It's time to make a decision, see if you can stick it out at this job or move on.

Sometimes your friends don't immediately see you. Sometimes you're pinned behind them in a sea of unwashed hair and vintage blouses, and it's all you can do to strain and hear their drunken talk:

"Tim's probably late because he's carrying the center here again."

"Hey, our boy's an angel."

"Oh, I love him, but it's Friday night."

"I know, I know — it would be nice of him to keep it light for once."

You'll have to think on this some more, alone. You're pretty sure you can't deal with it and may leave town entirely, move up north and take classes or something.

Defense

"Don't you ever think of leaving us."

"You home down here, pale rider. Believe it!"

"We don't like being bullshitted. You're good like that. You say it straight."

"Fuck, before you came, wasn't nobody getting leagues going. Wasn't nowhere to play organized."

"Hell no, hell no — not a chance you're leaving!"

Moms

And when you and CJ stopped by to get the extra basketball uniform, because Rye-Rye was sick but the Sanchez twins could each play a half, CJ introduced you as his coach and picked up his littlest brother, who was fingering a bowl of cereal-stained milk, and then said, "Mama, look. He just eating sugar again." She replied, "Just leave him alone. Didn't nobody pick on you. He's just a little man. Let him some peace. Damn."

Dice

You've never been very good at the discipline side, but you do your best. You understand how every youth worker needs to run his own justice system. In each room you are 911-switchboard operator, first responder, detective, district attorney, judge, and probation officer. Do all these well, and your citizens might respect, obey, and trust your authority. Fail — underinvestigate, assume, punish too severely, forget to follow up with the parents — and you'll have little South Central up in here. The trick is to do each job evenly, skipping no steps, always being wary of rushed judgments. If, for instance, you do have to arrest, judge, and punish some teenagers for playing craps in the kids' restroom during a basketball tournament, try to make it reasonable. Make the punishment fit the crime, a "logical consequence" they called it in that seminar you went to in San Diego. Maybe make them clean the stalls. Maybe have them volunteer a couple of Saturdays. Definitely don't let the long day and the losses on the court and the lack of sleep again last night and the seeming lack of appreciation for your efforts lately cause you to forget almost five years of history with certain individuals and erupt and say something like: "GET THE FUCK OUT OF HERE! GET OUT! FUCK! ALL OF YOU! CJ, RONDALE, SERGIO, EDDIE — GET THE FUCK OUT OF MY CENTER! NOW! I DON'T EVEN KNOW WHEN! MAYBE NEVER! YOU'RE IN NO POSITION TO ASK QUESTIONS! GET! OUT!"

Shooting

However you expected to react, that's not how it is.

They got CJ.

OK.

Hang up the phone.

Sit.

You can't breathe, yes, but it's not because you feel punched in the gut. It's the cold. The cold that sunk in so fast and deep your insides are freezing. All ice. And the radio in your brain is playing Rigo's words from just a week ago: "CJ goes anywhere. It's like he got a pass. He'll hit the barbecue in the projects, hit another on Grape, stop and shoot dice with Swans on his way home. CJ's dad is like royalty, and CJ the prince, man. CJ one guy they just let be."

CJ one guy they just let be.

And, of course, the kernel of pain deep in your core — the last two words you remember saying to him: "Get out."

Records

What's the record for saying *fuck* in a week? How about for ignored voice mails in a week? For ignoring direct questions from the woman you live with? How about beers opened but abandoned? Hamburgers fried but not eaten? What's the record for pulling over during a single drive to work and trying to cry in your car but instead just pounding your steering wheel again and again on the side of the freeway?

Killer

They did it. *Them.*

Swans, Bloods, Crips.

Someone did it. A cold, hardened veteran in the wrong mood, probably twenty years old.

Or a new recruit, a rookie needing to prove himself, probably seventeen, sixteen, fifteen, we could be talking.

Fourteen.

"What's up, blood? Why you stepping?"

"Nobody doing shit, kid. Just minding my OB and walking home."

"'Kid,' motherfucker? Man, shoot his ass so he dies."

Young Men

This is a neighborhood full of young men. This is a neighborhood full of *un*men. Babies with guns, loaded ones, and everybody's a cowboy or an Indian. These are short-term survival strategies. This is extreme nearsightedness. Some days you're in the van on Central going north to the food bank, and you consider continuing onto the 10, driving straight out into the desert and just going. Some days you want to accelerate down the sidewalks and through the stoops on Glade Street and 74th and Jefferson and MLK, stack up piles of unmen on your front bumper until it meets a concrete wall. Some days you contemplate these options much more carefully than you do traffic lights and the recommended stopping distance for a twelve-passenger van loaded with expiring canned hams.

Survivors

"I'm fine. How about you, Rye-Rye?"

"Whew. Rough, T. It be all right during the day, though."

"I know it. I know that."

"You wanna go shoot some hoops?"

"Not really. . . . Actually I don't know what I want to do."

"Let's go play some twenty-one, T. I'll teach you a thing or two about ball-handling. Promise. You might as well learn something today. No charge for the first lesson, just for you, T."

Grace

You're raking through the utility drawer in the kitchen. You brought it up, but that doesn't mean you want to talk about it.

"Don't say that, honey," she says.

"What?" But you aren't really listening. You're still looking for batteries.

"I mean it, Tim. You can't hold on to this blame."

Now you're paying attention. But now it isn't you: it's someone who hears those words and mashes his hands together, trying to control them, but he can't, so he spins recklessly to the left and grabs the driver from the golf bag by the door and swings it back at the conversation with such violence that he doesn't even hear her scream until after the club head has disappeared into the drywall. Then the scream catches up to you, as you start turning back into you, and it sticks, rings, rocks between your ears for the next fifty minutes as you explode out of the house and drive reckless laps around Dodger Stadium.

The porch light is on when you return, the rest of the apartment dark. She's probably left. She probably should leave. No, wait. There's a light on in the bedroom upstairs. You don't know what this means. You almost don't expect your key to work as you enter. Inside the first thing you notice is how clean everything looks. The second is that there's no longer a golf club sticking from a hole in the wall. In fact, there isn't even a hole visible. There's a picture of Phil Mickelson scotch-taped over it. There's a pair of scissors on the dining room table, and your *Sports Illustrated* is on a chair. And there's a woman upstairs in bed, reading while she waits.

Field Trip

The boys are quiet on the hike to the huge canyon filled with giant boulders. You're dying to know their thoughts. Have they ever seen such raw beauty, six city rats who've never traveled past the Valley, Long Beach, or the 710? But there is zero talking the whole way, and it's torture.

Finally Rye-Rye starts giggling.

"Whatta you think, Rye-Rye?"

He laughs some more, then says: "I just realized what CJ would say if he were here."

This gets Antonio going.

"Oh, Christ," you say. "Let's have it."

"Hey, Tim-Tim," Rye-Rye says, pointing at a line of hikers on the canyon floor a mile below, "how about you angle them ears and tell us what they talking about down there?"

Introduction

Did your supervisor really only hand you that whistle and the ball bag and the blue T-shirt with the red shield and say, *Please be back by 5:30 and don't forget the sign-in sheets*, because clearly 97 percent of the kids in this gym have less respect for you than they do the custodian who's being heckled in the far corner, and just about 100 percent of these kids look like the picture you had in your head from TV and movies of what South Central gangbangers look like, especially the two approaching with the sly grins, like they know one heckuva lot more than you do (which, of course, couldn't be more true), wearing white T-shirts down below their knees. (Do they really make them that big? Heck, these guys are like six-one and six-four.) And what do you call those nylon head wraps NFL players wear all the time? Wave hats, that's it. You don't yet know if taking this job was the best or the stupidest decision you've ever made, and these two beanpoles, they must be brothers, because they have the same face, same acne. They get right up close, and the taller one extends a palm, leaves it out there for you to slap, and says, smiling: "Yo, so wassup, white man? You lost?"

Daniel Larson was a fisherman in Kasilof, Alaska, for three years and a youth worker in South Central Los Angeles for five. He now directs youth programs in the Mission District in San Francisco. Contact him at dperu@yahoo.com.

Made in the USA
San Bernardino,
CA